POWER PLAY

Charlotte Stein

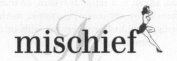

mischief

This novel is entirely a work of fiction.
The names, characters and incidents portrayed in it are
the work of the author's imagination. Any resemblance to
actual persons, living or dead, events or localities is
entirely coincidental.

Mischief
An imprint of HarperCollins*Publishers*
77–85 Fulham Palace Road,
Hammersmith, London W6 8JB

www.mischiefbooks.com

A Paperback Original 2013

First published in Great Britain in ebook format by
HarperCollins*Publishers* 2012

Copyright © Charlotte Stein 2013

Charlotte Stein asserts the moral right to
be identified as the author of this work

A catalogue record for this book is
available from the British Library

ISBN-13: 978 0 00 753328 2

Automatically produced by Atomik ePublisher from Easypress

All rights reserved. No part of this publication may be
reproduced, stored in a retrieval system, or transmitted,
in any form or by any means, electronic, mechanical,
photocopying, recording or otherwise, without the prior
permission of the publishers.

Chapter One

When he tells me to lift my skirt and bend over his desk, there's a moment where I hesitate. There's always a moment. It's like the feeling just before the lock springs under the pressure of the correct key you've somehow chosen. My body goes completely still and the word *no* makes a fist in my throat, and then I just do it.

I wriggle my tight skirt up over my thighs and expose my backside to his waiting gaze.

In fact, I do much more than that. Mainly because I've started anticipating these little trips up to the thirtieth floor, and this morning I went without knickers. Plus, when I bend over my legs somehow automatically spread, so he doesn't just get a view of the dark seam between the lush curves of my ass cheeks.

He gets to see the slippery pink flesh between, as flushed and swollen as ever I've felt it. Of course I like to pretend I hate these little excursions up to the thirtieth floor, and that what Mr Woods does to me is degrading and disgusting and oh, isn't it awful. But the fact remains that the moment he tells me to bend over in that silvery voice of his, my clit swells. My sex plumps. Wetness trickles from the clenching

1

hole between my legs, down over my quite possibly quivering thighs.

I quiver, for Mr Woods. I bend over, for Mr Woods. I forget that I was ever Ms Harding, Executive Editor of Barrett and Bates, and I become this other creature.

I don't even know her name, to be honest. She looks like me and talks like me and even acts like me in some respects – I still lay my hands on the desk so that they're apart but parallel to each other – but she can never have that little buzz of respect before her name the way I so often do: *Ms*.

And she could never let herself be used the way I'm going to let Mr Woods use me right now. I turn over in my mind each way he could possibly debase me as he stands behind me in his crisp grey suit with his crisp grey face and his mouth in that mean line it so often falls into.

He could push something into my cunt. He's never done it before, but that doesn't mean he couldn't do it now if he wanted to. I'm as slick as I've ever been, but more than that I feel greedy down there, as though I could take anything he wanted to offer. That award he got, for excellence in business or something like it? That big, thick, curved one, with the little nubs all around its length like a thing just made for stirring the nerves inside someone's body?

Yeah, he could fill me with that, if he so chose. In my normal life, the life outside the strange, still unspoken relationship we've struck up, I would never let someone choose something like that for me.

But here it's different. Here he doesn't have to say a word, and my mind floods with a million options, each more disgusting than the last. In fact, I suspect that my mind is actually far more disgusting than his. After all, he's never actually fucked me. Most of the time he doesn't touch me between my legs, and he hardly ever pushes me into touching him.

It's just this, it's just him behind me with the thought of what he *could* do buzzing through my body. He could order me to oil my own ass and let him slip his cock inside. He could cane me until my flesh sang red-hot songs, until I bled and wept and begged him not to.

And though I'm sure I've never wanted any of those things, there's something about him that makes me give in anyway. Something about his eyes, as calm and colourless as a midwinter day. And his tone, his perfect, metallic tone.

No order is ever barked; his voice is never raised. His orders don't seem like orders, to be honest. One day he just said to me, quite matter-of-factly: *I'd like to see your cunt now, Ms Harding.* In the same way one might ask to see the quarterly reports or the latest projections or something of that nature.

And then a sort of haze had descended over me, as though his words had thrown a veil over my head. The veil is with me right now as he murmurs that I should spread my legs wider, wider. He wants to see just how wet I am, just how bad I've been, before he progresses to anything further.

And oh God, how I'm longing for anything further. *Use the award*, I think at him frantically, while my cheeks turn crimson and my body shudders over the idea. *Force me to take your cock*, I think at him, though somehow I know he never will.

I'm not allowed.

'I see you're very wet, Ms Harding,' he says, then follows it with more disapproving words that I don't want to hear. 'Yes, very wet indeed. Would you care to explain to me how you got into such a disgusting state?'

No, I would not care to explain. My entire body sizzles

with embarrassment and I have to force my hands to remain flat. And yet I find my mouth opening and words that aren't my own come out, as though I have a talk-string on my back and he just pulled it.

'I've been thinking about fucking,' I say, which at least has the virtue of being honest, if not the virtue of being what I actually wanted to say.

'Fucking who?' he asks, just as I knew he would. Only this time I find the wherewithal to lie. I *have* to find the wherewithal to lie. He always asks me this and I always answer the same way – with something that affirms him as the one who controls me – but this time, it's not true.

And I can't possibly explain to him why it isn't. I can't. It's more embarrassing than the long, slow throb between my legs.

'You,' I say, and then I think of the new guy in the hallway, spilling his armful of papers everywhere. The way his shirt had been untucked at the back. The look on his face, like someone lost inside a maze created by a superior race that *hates* him.

'You thought about my cock inside you?' he asks, and oh that delicious deliberation in his voice still gets me. I have to rub my stiff and aching nipples against the desk just to take the edge off – though I know he will punish me for it soon.

Any transgression, he punishes me for it. Once, I rubbed the toe of my shoe over the back of my opposite ankle to scratch an itch there. And in return for this minor slip he had made me bend double and grasp that said same place while he paddled my ass with a ping-pong bat.

To this day I have no idea where the ping-pong bat came from.

'Yes.'

4

'You think about it often?'

'All the time.'

'Describe how you imagine it would feel, sliding in.'

God, why does he always have to make me describe? I'm terrible at it. I'm the worst.

'Mmmm, so good,' I say, limply, and for my crimes I get a hard slap to the ass. Of course I do. I should have said *solid* or *satisfying* or what I'm really thinking: *not as good as that new guy's cock*.

The one I could practically see through his pathetic trousers, as he bent and stretched and reached for all his fallen papers, face red, everything about him so awkward and appalling. He should be taken out of his misery, he really should. He should be planted over a desk and made to see the error of his ways, just as I am now.

And then maybe he'd beg like me too.

'Oh please, please just fill me with something. Please,' I blurt out, but it's the strangest thing. I don't know if I'm saying it for Mr Woods, or for the other thoughts that are pushing their way through my addled mind.

Thoughts such as: if it was the new guy behind me, would he fill me now? I don't think I'd have to beg with him, but somehow that doesn't seem like a negative. Instead, my body flushes with the thought of how eager he'd probably be – cock so stiff and swollen it's almost touching his belly, pre-come welling at the tip like a promise of all the copious slickness he's about to spill.

And he'd spill it inside me. Of course he would. Two thrusts and he'd be done, cock spurting thickly in my waiting cunt, hands all sweaty on my hips and oh God maybe he'd moan too. He wouldn't be like Mr Woods – silent, implacable, unmoveable. He'd actually say something as he touches me, and if he didn't want to, if he couldn't …

I'd *make* him.

The realisation shoves its way through me, as hard as those first words from Mr Woods did. *I'd like to see your cunt now, Ms Harding*, I think, and then hot on its heels: *I'd like to see your cock now, new guy.*

Benjamin, I think his name is. *Benjamin*, I think, as Mr Woods rubs something too cold and unyielding against the slippery lips of my cunt. And then when I moan to feel it, and squirm against it, he eases it down, down until the smooth tip is rubbing against my swollen clit.

I don't mind admitting that I forget about Benjamin then. Hell, I forget my own name. Pleasure whites out all of my higher thought processes and leaves behind this: this shame-riddled, wriggling mess. This thing, that can only plead:

'Uhhhh, yes – more. More.'

I try to angle my hips to catch whatever he's using – *the award*, my mind screams, *the award*, even though I know it's not – and get it inside me, but naturally he's too good for that. He just pulls back further, until the thing is barely touching me at all. In fact, I'm sure I can only feel it because my clit is so sensitive, so ready for any little touch that stirring the air over its surface makes me liquid between my legs.

Makes me moan, too loud and too long. Outside his doors, hundreds of people are working away, oblivious – but they won't be oblivious if I carry on like this. If I buck and pant and tell him to just fuck me with it, fuck my cunt with it.

'Such a filthy mouth, Ms Harding,' he says, and then he does something worse than all the rest of this nonsense combined.

He slides the tip of whatever this is up, up, past my ready and waiting pussy to a place I'm completely not prepared for.

I'm so not prepared for it that I lurch forward against the desk, and actually almost say something weak and pathetic, like: *Please don't. I've never had anything there before.*

Luckily, my perfectly perpendicular hands save me. The thought of that *Ms* at the start of my name saves me. The idea of Benjamin stumbling and fumbling and just being such a mess saves me.

And I don't break. I don't say anything at all as he offers me one tiny, amused sort of sound. He never laughs, Mr Woods – of course he doesn't – but sometimes I'm sure my struggles and my boundaries entertain him.

And this is such a petty boundary to have. Who hasn't had something in their ass? Yet the fact remains that I haven't, and the more he pushes and twists and makes that amused sound, the harder I clench and flame red with mortification.

I don't know what's worse, either – the fact that he's doing this with something impossibly thick and still achingly cold, or that I can feel how slick its surface is. As though he didn't just coat it in my liquid before he decided to rub it over my arse.

He oiled it in advance, for this specific purpose. He knew he was going to penetrate me there before I even walked into this office, and no amount of my squirming and whimpering is going to change that.

I just have to squeeze my eyes tight shut and let him ease it slowly in.

And oh God he does, he does. He braces one hand on my tense ass cheek, and then twists this thick and slippery thing until my body starts to yield to it. The tight ring of muscle there clenches and tries to deny the intrusion, but then everything just seems to give and I feel it slide all the way in to the hilt.

Worse than the hilt, in fact, because once the thing is lodged firmly inside me I can make out the press of his fingers where he's gripping it at the base. Somehow it's the most intimate touch he's offered me since this whole thing began.

'I think I would like you to rub your clit as I fuck you. What do you think, Ms Harding?'

I think nothing. I'm made of nothing. All I can feel or respond to is the slow slide of this fake cock as he pushes it in and out of my ass. As it stirs all of these little nerve-endings that I didn't know existed, everything so glossy and slick that the feeling is almost unbearable.

'I think you'd like that. Now reach between your legs and find your clit.'

I flop around for a moment, trying my best to do as I'm told. My arms feel rubbery and unresponsive, and with this fake cock working back and forth inside me it's hard to lift my body to get at what he's asking for.

And it doesn't get any easier when I finally reach my stiff little bud. Just skimming the pad of one finger over its tense surface is like a punch to the gut. It feels immense, and every touch of it burns too hotly, and then he actually makes a sound as he forces the thing into me and oh God I can't take it, I can't.

I can accept something fucking my ass. I can take being bent over his desk. I can't endure him grunting like that, as though maybe this whole thing affects him a little more than he usually lets on. Him grunting makes me imagine torrid, glorious things, like his cock all stiff and solid against the material of his impeccable trousers.

And though I daren't look to check, I can almost picture him stroking himself as he does this to me. One hand on his hard cock, one hand on the fake one he's pumping in

8

and out of my willing body, until finally he gives in and lets himself spurt all over –

'Oh fuck, Mr Woods,' I moan, because everything is just too much. The heated pulse between my finger and my clit, the feel of the fake cock fucking into me, raggedly, the idea of him coming on my upturned ass … I can't take it.

Instead, I press down hard on my clit and let the first trembling waves ebb through me, pushing back against the pounding he's now doling out until said waves become a great wash of pleasure.

'Yes, keep doing that, keep doing it, I'm coming – ohhhhh,' I tell him, because by this point I'm beyond all good sense. I don't know who I am or where I might be, and all I care about is the orgasm that's shoving rudely through my body.

And God, it goes on and on and on. By the time it's finished I'm a wet, trembling mess on the desk. Perpendicular hands forgotten. Perfect clothes sweated through. Ass so sore I'll barely be able to walk for the rest of the day.

Though that's not unusual, for our cold little relationship. At the very least I'm usually sitting on some red handprints in any afternoon meetings I then have – meetings that are actually going to start very soon.

In fact, they're going to start so soon that my real self comes back to me far quicker than usual, and I go to straighten before he's given me permission. I try to stand, but before I can get anywhere near said position that tented hand is back on my ass. His metallic voice is back in my ear.

'Stay still, Ms Harding,' he says, only he sounds different for just a second. That metallic tone peels away and reveals something rusted and old beneath, and then I actually feel it on my skin, just as I had imagined.

9

Charlotte Stein

A searing stripe of something slick. And then another. And another.

Though that's not the shocking thing. I mean, I've often imagined him losing some of his control. Sometimes I've hungered for it, with my hand between my legs and orgasm just one wretched inch away.

But in all of these fantasies of him breaking, I'll confess: I never imagined him moaning something heated. The Benjamins of this world moan heated things. They let themselves go and can't control themselves – not people like Mr Woods.

So why does he tell me: 'Oh yes that's so good' just as he's coming? Why?

And more than that: why does it make me feel so *low*?

Chapter Two

Of course I know something's wrong the minute I look up and see Benjamin stood there, framed in the meeting-room doorway. He never, ever, on pain of death interrupts the Monday morning break-downs. Never. I suspect he'd rather die than let every grey face in here see him up so close, with his shirt perpetually untucked on one side and his expression always so naked, so naked.

But he's here, and he's obviously waiting for me to say something. *Speak, boy*, I think, like some sort of ridiculous internal sneeze. Like a reflex I don't really want to have, but which comes anyway, unbidden.

Then I get a hold of myself, and straighten, and greet him more normally.

'Yes?' I ask, but it's the strangest thing. Somehow it comes out sounding like *speak, boy*, anyway. And even worse, I think he might know it. The faintest flush spreads over his face after I've spoken, and when he finally manages to explain he's all expansive and blunder-y about it.

'Ms Harding,' he says, and this time I really get a flash of something unwanted. That buzz, I think, that buzz at the start of my name, only different to the way I usually hear it. Usually I don't know what to do with it.

But I know right now.

I tell everyone to take five, and walk briskly to the door. All of these strange and new parts of me very aware of how fumbly Benjamin suddenly appears. How like he'd seemed in my head when I hadn't meant to think of him.

'Uh, yeah,' he says, the minute I've closed us into the narrow hallway.

I resist the urge to tell him that those words are decidedly *not* the ones to use. A man of his size and stature should be clear and precise; he should tell me directly what he means. He shouldn't be like this, all awkward and half-crouching down – though I don't know why it suddenly bothers me so.

It never bothered me before my last meeting with Mr Woods. Before that sense of strange *lowness*, of a sudden shift in the way things are between us.

'Go ahead, Benjamin,' I say, though again those aren't the words I want to use. The real ones are in the back of my mind somewhere, being ignored until I can think about all of this more clearly.

'I'm supposed to take you up to your office, Ms Harding,' he says, and that's when I know it. I'm not going to get the chance to think about this strange little buzz in the back of my mind at all.

And it's mainly because of this sudden and creeping sense of unease.

Of course, I felt that way the moment I walked in this morning. But it's far more obvious now, as I take in every little nervy tic of the strange man in front of me. He's not uptight exactly – it's not like that. He's not wound up inside himself, unable to escape. It's more like his insides have escaped far too much, and are currently spilling themselves all over me. The urge to brush bits of him off my vintage Yves Saint Laurent suit is strong, very strong.

'I see,' I say, though of course what I really want to do is ask him what all of this is about. He has a lot of papers in his hands – which had seemed perfectly right in my head. It's just that it doesn't seem perfectly right now. 'Lead the way, then.'

He does. He lollops on ahead of me, every stride so immense that after a moment I actually find myself almost trotting to keep up. Of course I don't let it show – he's so obvious in his movements that I anticipate his head turns, and always slow to a near halt – but even so. There's an element to it that's mildly disconcerting. Like something about him doesn't quite match up or work, and it's my job to figure it out. Though I'll be honest, I've no idea when the task fell to me.

'Here we are, Ms Harding,' he says, and I notice several things at once. I notice his voice first, despite the fact that doing so is the wrong thing to be picking up on. I shouldn't be thinking about his odd, slightly glassy and very American sort of accent, while stood outside Mr Woods' office.

And I definitely should have taken in the new brass plate on the door, before anything about Benjamin occurs to me.

But the truth is, I don't. For a long moment I simply stare at him, in a much meaner way than I intend. I watch him ruffle through his papers, most of them almost sliding out of his grasp as usual. That ridiculous, All-American-Boy hair of his falling into his eyes, as he attempts to function like a normal human being.

And then finally I ask, without letting any of my deep, deep concerns about this entire situation affect me. I don't let them show in my expression, I don't give them time in my tone. I already know what's happened here, but I keep it cold and below the surface.

'Perhaps you could tell me why my name is on the door, Benjamin.'

Of course, I half-know what his reaction is going to be. And I'm proved right when his mouth kind of flops open and his big eyes get bigger. The search for some unnamed thing amidst his pointless papers gets more frantic.

'Oh,' he says. 'Oh, I thought you knew, Ms Harding. Did no one tell you?'

I think of the people above Woods, from the board of directors. Julian Wentworth, with the little pointed beard and the fidgety hands. Derek Carruthers, who so rarely visits that I don't even have a few bullet points to pin to him. He could have three heads and one eye for all I know.

'No,' I say, and this time the expression on his face is so clear I could have read it from across a room. *It's you who were supposed to tell me*, I think, and then I watch with the strangest sort of detachment as he searches in vain for something amidst his papers.

'Ohh Geez, I've made *such* a mess,' he says, under his breath. He needn't have bothered. I can tell he's made a mess, with or without his help. He has mess written all over him, in bold black marker. 'I knew I'd forgotten something.'

'Did you forget to give me a letter, Benjamin?' I ask, because it's torture watching him do this. My hands itch to do God only knows what. I can feel terrible, terrible words clawing at the back of my throat – words like *we're going to have to do something about you, Benjamin*. Even though I know that's one of the first things Woods said to me.

'I think … yeah. Maybe … just hold on, Ms Harding.'

I don't want to hold on. I want to say it: *We're going to*

have to do something about you, Benjamin.

'Oh, man. Here it is. Here,' he says, and I have to wonder if I looked like that when I first stumbled into Mr Woods' office. Clothes barely fitting me, words all fumbling one after the other. Scorchingly sensible of a mistake I've just made.

Though when he speaks again, I'm almost relieved. There's at least one glaring difference between the way I was and the way he is – and it comes to me as he tells me he's always getting things wrong.

He's not ashamed like I was. He's almost bright and boyish about it instead, the expression on his face full of a kind of hope I don't know how to process.

'I'm so sorry, Ms Harding,' he says, as some of the papers spill out of his hands. And then I simply have to stand there, frozen, as he tries in vain to gather them up. Everything about him so big and clumsy and sweet somehow, in a way I know I never was. 'But I swear, it will never happen again. I swear to *God*.'

What a strange creature he is – though I confess, I'm grateful to him. For a long moment I'm so transfixed by his utter awkwardness and his ever-hovering grin that I can't focus on the true matter at hand.

Woods is gone.

And I am his replacement.

* * *

I have three contact numbers for Gregory Woods. One is for his office, which would now mean I'm ringing myself. The other is his mobile phone, which always goes directly to his curt little voicemail message: *Woods. Speak.* And the last is his home number, which I have never on pain of extreme torture rung.

I will never ring it, not now. He's done this thing, and that's all there is to it. It's the sort of person he is; it's the way he operates. He makes a decision as brisk as a knife coming down, and if you get one of your limbs chopped off in the process, well.

So be it.

Though I swear I don't feel that way. I feel calm and composed, all the way through the rest of the Monday morning break-down. I am like a summer breeze as I field questions from the head of the sales division about targets Woods has decidedly *not* set. I'm the very soul of inner peace, when I discover the other seventeen thousand problems no one ever thought to ask a man like Woods about, because Woods always looked like someone in control.

He treated me like someone in control.

But as I learn at one-thirty-five on Monday afternoon, his legend was definitely somewhat exaggerated. In fact, by the time Benjamin asks me if I'd like my midday Scotch, I'm convinced Gregory Woods was some sort of magician.

I knew him in so many appallingly intimate ways, but I didn't realise his level of incompetence. And judging by what Benjamin is now telling me – in all innocence – it wasn't *sober* incompetence.

I think I actually say to him: 'Are you serious?' though I swear I don't mean to.

It's Woods I'm angry at, of course it is – and yet I snap at Benjamin so hard his teeth practically rattle. His mouth comes open again, though this time it at least has the wherewithal to seem voluntary. He almost catches it before it's reached the halfway mark, but I still glimpse those odd teeth he has – so perfectly straight and white and gleaming, apart from the hint of point on the incisors. It's not a hint really. It's strong and obvious and like he should have a lisp, though I'm not sure how I come to that conclusion.

And I can still feel the words he wants to get out, pushing at the back of his throat.

'Uhhh … well …' he starts, and that urge to correct him beats on me so hard I'll be feeling it tomorrow. *Don't start your sentences like that. Don't, don't, don't oh God don't please I hardly know what's happening to me.* 'Mr Woods tended to like his Scotch with –'

'Benjamin, sit down,' I say to him, while my insides scream at me: *do not ask him to sit down.*

I should never have sat down when Woods asked me to, that first time.

'O – K,' he says.

I'm grateful that he looks so bemused, I really am. Though I'm less grateful when he seems to have the most appallingly difficult time picking a chair. At first, he actually seems to think I want him to sit next to the antique sideboard, on a leather wingback that has no real purpose being there. I mean, he does realise that thing is about twenty paces away from my desk, right?

'Sit *here*, Benjamin,' I say, but when I do I realise something even more horrifying than all of the rest of the weird urges bubbling up inside of me. His name … the way it sounds …

It's better than the way Woods used to say *Ms Harding*. The whole thing just rolls right off my tongue, with emphasis I don't intend on syllables that shouldn't have it. And when he takes the chair opposite my desk – all of his big body folding down into it as though he's half the size he actually is – I'm almost certain he knows it.

17

He knows how I'm saying it. Those guileless blue eyes and that almost-smile on the faint imprint of his mouth ... they tell me what I need to know.

'Are you OK, Ms Harding?' he asks, as I sit behind the vast safety of the desk that once belonged to *him*. Unfortunately, doing so just makes me wonder if he ever needed to hang on to it the way I'm doing right now.

I'm like the survivor of a shipwreck. Barrett and Bates is going down in flames, and I'm thinking about some awkward creature's secret face signals.

'I'm perfectly fine, Benja–' I catch myself this time, though I'm sure he notices. Something flickers across his otherwise completely innocent gaze, something I recognise without even trying to. And then I get control of myself and start again. 'I'm fine, Ben. I just want to get across a few things to you, before we go any further.'

He nods, eagerly. I wish to God I didn't have to add that 'eagerly' onto that description.

'Of course, Ms Harding. I mean – I guess I'm *your* assistant now. And to be honest, that suits me a lot better. You're so *direct*, you know? So –'

'Stop!'

I don't mean to shout it, I swear. It just happens. A lot of things seem to be just happening, and I don't know if I can cope with them all.

'Sorry. You go ahead, Ms Harding. I'm listening. I'm really doing my best to be all ears.'

Lord, he punches the air a little, after that last statement, the way a cartoon character from the fifties might have done. *Gee willikers, Ms Harding! I sure am glad I'm working for you, gosh yes!*

'You're doing fine, Ben. But what I really wanted to stress

18

to you is this: you're not my assistant. You weren't really Mr Woods' assistant. You –'

'Oh my God, am I fired? Oh man, I –'

'*Benjamin*,' I say, and am deeply disheartened to find that his full name has the exact effect on him I expect. It freezes him in place, big hands clutching the chair arms. Those soft eyes caught somewhere between wounded and a promise that he can do better. I wish he wouldn't want to do better for me quite so badly.

'You're not fired. I'm simply trying to tell you that you're a *clerical* assistant. That's what you were hired for – to help with general office paperwork, mail and filing. You're not here to bring me a Scotch.'

He isn't really anything of the sort – he was always Woods' PA. It's just that I can't have him being something like that right now. I need him to be away, writing letters for other people who don't need a letter writer at all.

'Oh,' he says, but he doesn't look as embarrassed as I'd feared he would. There's a hint of sheepishness there, true, but then I imagine that's his default state. Whereas the other emotion on his face – disappointment – probably isn't.

He looks like the kind of guy who takes most things in his stride. Unless it's his brand-new boss telling him she can't possibly spend her time ordering him to do humiliating menial tasks on her behalf. Then he just seems as though his entire world is falling apart, right before his eyes.

And oh, I don't like what that completely naked expression on his face is making me want to do.

'I don't need you to caddy for me at the golf course.'

I really, really don't like what it's making me want to do.

'I don't require you to dry my hands for me after I've been to the ladies' room.'

19

God, I know it's going to make me do it.

'But if you want, you can ... compose letters for me. And compile some reports.'

Damn it.

'Really?' he says, and oh Jesus he just looks so hopeful. No one should ever look that hopeful over the prospect of writing to the head of the board to ask what the fuck is going on. I mean, a phone call might have been nice, you know? Promotion would have gone down a lot easier if it hadn't been phrased thusly, in a letter:

You're now the managing director of Barrett and Bates, effective immediately. If you have any concerns, contact several people who don't give a shit.

'I hardly see why not,' I say, though I know it's a mistake. And I know it more strongly when I ask Benjamin to leave, and on his way out of the door he says:

'Thank you, sir.'

Of course, he realises his error almost immediately. He's that sort of person, I think – the kind that makes many goofy blunders, but is intelligent enough to know he's made them only a second later.

Though it doesn't make it any easier, I know. It still makes his mouth open and close, that sweetly curving upper lip of his compressing as he searches for a way to rectify what he's done. He called me sir, even though I'm a woman. He called me sir, and for reasons we won't go into it's making him all flustered.

'Sorry – I meant –' he starts off, but I cut him down dead. 'Sir is fine,' I say, as I wave him out the door.

* * *

Of course, sir is *not* fine. And after he's gone I sit at my new desk and consider all the ways in which it isn't fine at all. It's what I used to call Woods, for a start. It's meant for a man, for afters. And then there's the fact that it makes my body flush from the tips of my toes to the roots of my hair.

Yeah, there's that.

I close my eyes and try to think of something else. There are a million things *for* me to think about, after all. Woods had apparently allowed a whole department to keep operating unnecessarily, for reasons left unclear in the paperwork he never actually did. Tomorrow I'm going to have to fire every one of them, while he most likely suns himself in Barbados.

And yet my mind returns to that one word over and over, so casually said. *Sir*, I think. *I am somebody's sir*, and then I have to count all the things about him that aren't right, just to keep myself on an even keel.

His mouth is strange. It's like it has no corners or definition around it, no real shape to keep it in place. Of course, occasionally when he talks it's given a proper outline, but then, it's not really the outline I want it to have. Movement just makes those lips plumper, more obviously sensuous, and then when he stops talking all I can see is how smooth and soft that mouth is. If he didn't have that heavy jaw and all of that overflowing size, he'd *look* like a cute cartoon character, and nobody wants that. They want men with intense, cold, manly gazes. Not that warm, soft-focus eagerness. Not those sooty lashes that probably look beautiful spread over his cheeks – when he closes his eyes in ecstasy, maybe.

God. *God*. How did the word 'beautiful' get into that sentence? How did 'ecstasy'? I have absolutely no clue, and yet for a long moment it's all I can think about. All of the things that are exactly right about him crowd out the things

21

that probably aren't wrong at all, and I'm left helpless on the burning ship again.

Though I don't clutch at my desk this time. I turn to my computer – the ridiculous wood-backed thing my former paramour ordered from Japan, and that I've already searched for any evidence of his impenetrable motivations – and do what I'd wanted to the moment I knew he was gone.

Hell, I wanted to do it the moment I knew he was different, on Friday afternoon.

I go online, and start looking for someone who can give me the things he no longer knew how to. The things I'm no longer getting, and apparently need so desperately that I'm willing to actually venture onto Craigslist and read insane ads like:

I want to piss on your head. Call 1-800-asshole, if you're into that.

No, 1-800-asshole. I'm *not* into that. But of course the problem is I don't know what I *am* into. It was just easy to do the things Woods wanted me to do. It was calming and pleasurable and a distraction, from Anderson in sales being a doucheknuckle. From Patterson in marketing smacking my ass as I pass by his department – then acting like *I'm* the sourpuss when I tell him he'll lose a finger the next time he pulls that shit with me.

It meant I didn't have to go home and stare at the walls of my pathetic apartment, with my pathetically neat little dinner for one in front of me, and know that *this* is my life. I am the managing director of a mid-sized but well thought of publishing house, operating out of the tiny city of York.

And that is the most of it.

Even if it's not, exactly. After all, I am here in this plush little office, in my prim little suit with the perfect cuffs, looking at images of women who've been doing some very dirty things. And though that's not quite on the level of what my predecessor was getting up to between these classy-painting covered walls, there's a certain frisson to it, I have to say.

I can understand its allure exactly, and not just because I want something to replace whatever Woods was providing. It's the look of things, I think. It's the smell in here, of varnish and too-thick carpets, as I bring up a picture of a woman facing away from camera.

Though I confess: it's not her face I'm interested in. It's her back, her naked back, and the pattern of stripes working its way down over that flesh. Red on white, red on white, from the slim span of her shoulders to the curve of her ass, everything so perfectly uniform that it's almost not a line of cane marks at all. It's like a dress she's wearing, made of a million crimson stripes. And if I could just find the right person, if I could meet someone who understood the insides of me, he could give me a garment just like it.

Or I could give the garment to him.

Of course I try to shake it off the moment the idea occurs to me, but the trouble is, it doesn't want to go. It's there right behind my eyes, along with the image of Benjamin's ever-shifting gaze, and his strange mouth, and his big hands. What would hands such as those look like dressed in red? Do people even do that – do they crack something down on their palms, in the same way someone has done it to her back?

I've got to imagine they do, because the thought holds a sweetness for me that the idea of being caned across my back doesn't. When I think of the palms of my hands, I think about holding a pen and suddenly getting an echo of that sting. I think about sitting in a meeting, and just squeezing my hands into fists until the pain blazes out and reminds me of who I really am.

I am a person who thinks about being bent over a desk, so that someone faceless and nameless can cover my ass with a million red lines. In fact I'm thinking about it right now, while I'm supposed to be composing an email to one of the senior editors about a promotion he's suddenly going to have.

And it feels like a long, cool relief after everything that's happened today. I can see it so clearly in my head – knickers around my ankles, legs just ever so slightly spread. The glistening slickness of my cunt in between, so like the girl I'm looking at right now. The one called Veronica, who likes to expose herself in public.

I know how Veronica feels. I'm in that same mind-set currently, as I almost but don't quite press the heel of my palm over my suddenly tender mound. It's close enough to my clit that I get a little jolt of pleasure, but not so close that anyone could stroll in and know what I was doing, and that's the line I want to walk right now.

I want to be on the edge again, so close to being caught doing something very bad indeed. I'm not the prim and proper correct choice for this job. I'm a dirty girl who likes looking at filthy websites during office hours, nipples stiff beneath my immaculate shirt and jacket. Clit suddenly swollen, and just begging to be stroked.

Though of course I don't do it. I just flick through the images on the screen, restlessly, stopping when I find something that sparks my interest. A woman with a cock in her mouth and another in her pussy, struggling against intricate bonds that I follow eagerly with my gaze. More red stripes on flesh, some so bright and brilliant they hurt my eyes.

But I go in close just the same. In fact, I'm leaning so close

24

to the screen that it's almost like I've got my nose pressed to the glass – like I'm a child craving sweets that I'm not allowed to have – and that's how I'm poised when someone knocks on the door. Hunched over my desk as though I've turned into some sort of lust-crazed animal, hand almost over the sensitive swell of my pussy through my skirt. My arousal so sharp and keen, suddenly, it's like slicing myself open on a knife's edge when said someone doesn't wait for me to invite them in. They just barge right on through as I jerk back in my chair, hand fumbling for the mouse, everything about me so red and raw. I know it must look obvious. Woods would have seen it immediately, and demanded I pay the price. *Show me how wet you've gotten yourself, Ms Harding*, he would have said, whereas Benjamin just seems trapped somehow in my doorway. It's that thing again, I think, of blundering and yet knowing he's made the blunder a moment later.

He shouldn't have come in, and he understands that perfectly. I can see it on his face, but he still doesn't move away. He doesn't leave and close the door behind him, then knock again a moment later.

And there's something about that fact that I can't shake. I want to, I desperately want to, but I can't. He's saying something to me without words and, though I don't want to hear, I'm listening anyway. Like I did with Woods.

'Sorry, sir,' he says, and my entire body melts and slides right off my chair. Whatever I was feeling before – a kind of weak and watery horniness over some paltry little pictures – folds in and doubles back on itself until I'm left like this. Stunned by arousal for something I barely understand.

'You should probably go back to your cubicle, Benjamin,' I say, and though it holds a hint of whatever frisson I'm feeling, it's not what I want to say. Instead, once he's left me to my own devices, I imagine telling him something very different.

I think you'd better come inside, I near-murmur, and in my head he does. He comes inside and sits down on the chair across from my desk, hands clutching the arms in exactly the way they had before. That little pink tongue of his peeking out, to wet his plump lower lip.

And then I tell him, just as Woods told me.

We're going to have to do something about you, Benjamin.

Of course he asks what, in reply. He looks at me all wide-eyed and half-unsure, as I stand up and cross to where he's sitting. I remember Woods leaning against the edge of his desk, one leg over the other, everything about his pose suggesting casual, but not quite reaching it.

And in my head I mimic that stance almost perfectly, the whole scene a carbon copy of the one that came before. Only instead of saying *cunt* I say *cock*, obviously. I tell him clear: *I think I'd like to see your cock now, Benjamin,* and though I know in reality he'd probably refuse, in my head he barely puts up a fight.

In my head he laughs at first, but then lets said laugh trail down to nothing. Realisation dawning all over his face, so bright and clear and sweet somehow, and when it happens something happens to me, too. I stop thinking about Woods, or the computer screen, or the stripes on her back.

And I think about making that expression happen all over his face instead.

I can't do that, Ms Harding, he tells me, but that one word – *can't* – just sizzles straight through me. It punches down hard on a button I didn't know I had, and I give the person I am in my head permission to run with it. To say to him: *Really? I would have thought a little slut like you couldn't wait to get their clothes off*, while my heart pounds hard and heavy in my chest. It's the *little slut*, I think, that does it. Even though none of this is real and I'm sure I'd never say it to him, those two things together get to me. *He's a slut*, I think, *a greedy, lustful little trollop*, and then I watch as my mind provides the visual for this.

He puts a sudden and shocking hand between his legs, and rubs at the stiff shape he finds there.

Of course I know why I'm doing this. It's so I can be like Woods, and tell him off for being so inescapably horny. But the thing is, it's different this way around. It's crazier somehow, more perverse, and when the head-me gets a hold of him by the hair and slaps his too smooth, too perfect face, I actually have to dig my nails into my thighs.

The urge to masturbate is so strong it's more a physical pain than that sensation is, but it's still only five-fifteen. I can't just slip my hand under the waistband of my skirt with the door unlocked. Though if I go ahead and lock it, what then?

Then I'm just going to fuck myself in my office, while my suddenly backwards mind imagines pinning Benjamin to my desk so that I can do something Woods never did to me. The furthest he got was masturbating on my ass, and even that made me feel as though he'd lost some of his allure. That he'd given up control for one second, and left me stranded.

And yet somehow in my head I'm grinding my slippery pussy all over this fumbly, awkward guy's face, without a hint of that strange lowness going through me. I don't feel low at all. I feel packed tight with unspilled pleasure, clit as stiff and swollen as the cock I'm imagining. Liquid soaking through my panties already.

The heel of my palm really pressing into the curve of my sex now.

I think of his hands, blindly searching over my body to

make up for the things my thighs are blocking out. I think of rewinding the tape, to see him peel out of his clothes in fits and starts. And finally I think of him shoved down over my desk, cheek pressed to the wood. My hand somewhere very bad, like the back of his head. Fingers tight in all of that thick, messy hair, exerting just enough pressure to keep him there.

And then the thin metal ruler I have on my desk in my other hand, to make him wear the garment I only half-heartedly wanted to. Because that's the thing, you see. All of these replacements I think of, for Woods … they're half-hearted.

But the thought of striping Benjamin …

The thought …

It's enough to make me come harder than I ever have in my life, with just a hand in my lap, over clothes. It's enough to make me say those three over-emphasised syllables into my fist, as pleasure gushes direct to my clenching sex.

I don't know when it happened. I don't know why. But it's there now, inside me, no matter how hard I try to deny it.

Chapter Three

I decide it, before I've walked into the building and said hello to Kelly on reception. Today, I am going to be normal. Perfectly, respectably normal. I'm not going to practically masturbate at my desk to fill the void Woods has left. I'm not going to think mad thoughts about the people under me in an illegal and inappropriate way.

No. Today, I'm going to do ordinary things. Like speak to Aidan Harcroft about his promotion, for example. And then maybe speak to Anderson the doucheknuckle about his lack of one.

All of which will go something like this, I believe:

Anderson, I know it's a terrible tragedy that I got the managing director position ahead of you. But if you just remember what an absolute toilet of a person you are, I'm sure you'll understand why.

And as for my conversation with Aidan Harcroft ... well. That can't possibly be predicted. Nothing about Aidan can be predicted, because he's the human equivalent of quicksilver. Fantastic eye, of course, but the problem comes when you're trying to imagine what's behind said eye.

Mercurial thoughts, I believe. Mercurial thoughts about

not taking the bullshit job I had. I mean, in all fairness, no one wants to babysit people like Derek Hannerty. He's tried to get that book about the guy who likes enemas past me so many times ... and he's going to ride Aidan just as hard.

'You've got to be kidding, Harding.'

Or maybe he's not going to get the chance to ride him at all.

'You think there's someone better for the job?' I ask, as he presses the phone to his chest. He's talking to some author, I believe – though the author isn't going to mind in the slightest that he or she has been put on hold. I've known newbies faint during a conversation with Aidan.

Not that I blame them. He talks so fast and so smoothly, it's like having a discussion with the magical emperor of a world that doesn't exist.

'Janet,' he says, but I can tell he's just throwing it out there. He doesn't really mean it at all, because Janet Everly regularly falls asleep at her desk in the middle of the day. I could pretend to overlook it, back when I was just the gatekeeper.

But now I'm the actual fucking gate.

'You may as well have pulled a name out of your ass. Come on, Aidan. Even you can do better than that.'

He sighs, and swivels his chair around – but him doing so only gives the game away. He's not annoyed at all. That shark's grin is cutting its way across his sharp-boned face, and when he answers there isn't a hint of weariness anywhere in his words.

'I'm not going to have long discussions with Derek about *Endless Enemas*,' he tells me, while doing something that seems to have an ever so slight hint of lewd – like maybe rocking in his chair a little until I can't help flicking my gaze down to his groin.

It doesn't disconcert me, however. It's just the way Aidan is – louche, I would call it, and the rather unsubtle hints he gives about his sex life only back this one word up. There are rumours he fucked James Wentworth in the men's room, rumours that he had a threesome with the two girls from marketing, rumours that he banged our receptionist in the underpass down by Collingham Street.

And I know at least one of them is true, because last Christmas said receptionist poured an entire bowl of punch right over his head.

'Fine. He bothers you, send him to me. I'll fire him.'

That grin gets broader, as does the faint lilt of his half-Irish accent.

'So that's the kind of boss you're going to be, huh?' he says, and for just the briefest moment I go cold, before he quite suddenly follows his question up with: 'Knew you were on the cusp of some epic ball-breaking. Don't go easy, OK? I won't respect you if you go easy.'

Of course he uses the jolting pause I then descend into to return to his phone conversation. But unfortunately, I can't do the same. I don't have a phone conversation to return to, and if I did I'm not sure I'd make it. Instead I go hot and cold thinking of how close he's just come to a slightly more personal issue I seem to be going through.

I'm on the cusp, I think, and then I walk over to his desk on new feet, and push the hold button on his phone.

'I'm not asking,' I say, and that shark on his face tries to *eat* me, I swear.

'Good,' he tells me, as I stride back out of his office.

* * *

My second conversation of the day goes even better than the first one. I tell Anderson that I really do not give a shit if my promotion has bent him out of shape, and he doesn't lose it. He doesn't threaten to murder me, or the board of directors, or all of us in one big clock tower massacre.

No – he just has a nervous breakdown instead. He actually cries in front of me, which is so completely the opposite of what I was expecting that I leave his office wondering if I've stepped into an alternate universe. One where Woods is gone and I'm in charge, and Anderson the douUcheknuckle is actually a guy who's just had someone he's never been respectful to promoted over him.

I can see why he'd think it doesn't bode well for his future.

Though naturally, I reassure him. Sales are up by two per cent since we went digital, and a lot of that is his work. Despite his bullish attitude and his hideous two-tone shirts, he's a reliable member of the team.

And I'm going to need reliable, if I've got a prayer of getting through this month. This week.

Today.

Aidan might have faith in me, but I don't. I feel suddenly small inside the grey pinstripe I picked out this morning, these dagger heels making me less sure instead of how they usually make me feel. Strong, I think, strong, as I stride down the hall between sales and marketing, back to where I'm safest.

The mess that is editing.

It's not an open-plan office really. It's just a big jumble of egg-carton cubicles, most of which have been knocked through into three or four massive spaces as the editing staff declined and the mad grab for power rose.

You get a couple of egg cartons knocked together and you're practically a junior no longer. You're a senior, just waiting for Aidan or Janet to die so you can take their place and publish eight hundred undiscovered masterpieces.

All written by you, most likely.

'Harding!' somebody hollers as I pass by – though they quickly seem to gather themselves. 'I mean, uh …' *Sir*, I think, but of course silly little Terry Samson doesn't go with that. He goes with something more normal, like this is high school and I'm now his teacher. '*Miss* Harding, is there any word on whether we're getting a little extra to the autumn budget?'

I answer without looking. I have to, because Benjamin is coming from the opposite direction and by God I need to build up a head of steam. His trousers are too short for his massive legs today, and when he sees someone he knows in editing he waves at them. He actually *waves*.

I can't let him get his mad, awkward hooks into me.

'No chance,' I say, as I barrel on by.

Or at least, I *try* to barrel on by. I really do. I get as far as my office door, breathless and flushed with victory.

Only to find that Benjamin has actually *followed* me, as though my single-minded expression said *yes, come right up and bother me. I cannot wait to relive every moment of the fantasy I had about you directly to your face.*

'Um, Ms Harding?' he starts, which is promising. At least he doesn't lead off with *sir*, though the question he packs in there is a bit much. It's so tentative, I think. So lacking in confidence. And then of course there's the *um* at the front of it all, like a big red sign:

This is the way I am. You know what way I mean, don't you? It starts with a sub and ends with a missive.

God, I wish I hadn't spent all that time looking at those websites.

'Yes, Benjamin?' I say, without turning fully. It's best not

33

to, all things considered. Showing him my front might inadvertently be a sign, of things I know almost nothing about. Like some sort of D/S mating signal, maybe.

'I have those letters you wanted drafting.'

Is that all? And if so, what more was I expecting, exactly?

'Good,' I say, then think of a way of putting even more distance between us. Why, by the end of the week I might never have to see him at all. 'But in the future, you can just leave things of that nature on my desk.'

'Oh,' he says, and nods. Though I swear, a hint of disappointment flickers across his always obvious face when he does so. 'Well, OK. Sure thing. Hope you like them.'

He hands me two slim, perfectly folded pieces of paper. Fingers almost brushing mine as he does so. Eyes fixed on that near-meeting, before drifting ever so slowly back up to my face.

Of course, it's then that I realise something appalling. Something I've been veering away from, with lots of talk of pointed teeth and lineless mouths – though I swear, I'm not going to let myself think it until I'm safely inside my office. I can't, because it's not like Aidan's handsomeness, that just *exists*.

This is something else altogether. It's heated and too intense and it squeezes a little fist somewhere, deep down inside me. It pushes a very particular sort of thought on me, before I can scramble and urge it away again.

He's lovely, I think, and then hate myself.

'Did you know that you're kind of staring at me, sir?' he asks, and I'm not sure what's worse. That he's noticed; that he's almost sort of smiling around his own incredulity; or that he uses that dreaded word on the end of it.

All three make me want to do something very bad indeed.

'I think you need to go back to your desk, Benjamin,' I say, in my lowest and most deadly voice. However, instead of sending the fear of God through him – as I'm hoping – it does something I did not intend.

Something that doesn't so much as sock me in the gut as punch a hole right through my body.

A flash of heat blazes across his gaze, so obvious that for a moment I'm trapped between two versions of myself. One who's still the blundering girl I was, shocked by the things Woods wanted her to do. And the other who sees with Woods' eyes, and knows a million intimate things about a person before they know it themselves.

'Of course,' he says, once he's reined that little response back in. 'All you have to do is say the word, and I'm totally your man.'

He can't *possibly* be saying what I think he's saying. He can't be. It's all just my sex-fevered imagination; it's my body missing Woods and wanting something to fill the void. There's no heat in his gaze, no slow sensuality in his otherwise breezy voice. And by *totally your man*, he means: *I love writing letters for you, Ms Harding*.

Not anything sexual or suggestive at all. In truth I think he's too boyish for those sorts of kinky games, too gauche. He doesn't realise the double meaning of the words he's saying.

Or at least I think so, until I open the letters.

* * *

I try to be calm about it at first. Any normal person would be calm and rational about the whole thing, I'm certain. Aidan, for example, would most likely give him a gentle dressing-down before offering him a biscuit.

35

And that's what I need to do. I need to find some biscuits to offer him, after I've tried to strangle him with two bits of paper.

Because that's what I *want* to do, of course.

I don't know what he thinks he's playing at by writing the letters in this way. But he's playing just the same, and I know it. I can't deny it. No one could write this way for their boss and fail to understand that they've made a complete mess out of it.

Most of what's in the two letters isn't identifiable as something a human being would do. There are sentences without endings, words misspelled so badly they're not really words any more. Blotches on parts of the paper, as though maybe he drank a gallon of strawberry-flavoured liquor while writing them and some of it spilled out of his mouth – and the truth is, I can really imagine him doing just that. He's so excessive somehow, so full of extra gestures and obvious greed. It's like he's just finished cramming a box of cakes into his mouth a second before you see him.

And the only thing he could find to clean his hands and his mouth were these letters, apparently.

I mean, they're just an unmitigated disaster. But worse than that: he's clearly done it on purpose. He wants me to tell him off, *he actually wants me to* – though if he thinks it's going to be that easy he's mistaken.

I'm a professional person, for fuck's sake. I can't be goaded into the kind of thing Woods did, by a misspelling of the word 'potato'. Even if there's no godly reason why the word 'potato' is there in the first place. Even if I can see his face behind my eyes when I close them, all heavy-jawed and somehow much more perfect than I'd ever allowed myself to think he was.

It's the hair, I think; that thick maze of toffee-coloured hair, as though someone dipped him in something sticky and delicious only a moment before. Or maybe it's the tender shape of his mouth, caught between the heaviness of the rest of his face – that near sullen jawline, that broad, clear brow.

Those eyes of his, all hazy with longing as though he's been left out too long on a summer's day. They say things he doesn't want to or can't quite make himself, those eyes, and they're the first thing I think of when I picture myself going to tell him off.

Even though I'm absolutely not going to do that. I'm not. I'm just going to spend the rest of the day as I had planned – calm and collected. If he wants to do things like this, he's entitled to. But he's not getting a rise out of me in return.

He's just going to get me walking to the cubicle he occupies at five p.m. Everything about me glacial somehow, in a way that should be comforting. It should, but it's the strangest thing. By the time I turn the corner into his little nook – almost an office, if it were not for the lack of a door on one end – I'm not comforted by the coolness I've descended into at all.

It's *too* cool. It's almost as though I've coated myself in a pane of glass, and I can watch all of the things I'm doing and understand them. But I can't control them. When I try to, my fingers butt up against that sheet of something see-through.

And this feeling gets a hundred times worse when I see him.

'Hey, Ms Harding,' he says, all innocence. That big body of his folded into his tiny little swivel chair, one side of his collar sticking up ridiculously. A hint of bemusement touching those soft, entirely fuckable lips.

Which is never a good thought to start things off with.

And then there's the fact that he licks a stamp the moment

37

I'm focused on him, in a very deliberate sort of way. His tongue curls out to cover the little scrap of nothing completely. Those completely innocent eyes intent on me the whole way through it.

Everything slow, so slow, and so ... *slick*, somehow. Does he *know* how slick that looks, how lewd? He has to know, and yet sometimes when I look into his eyes I can't be sure. It's like there's a veil over his gaze, and the second something dirty happens he just draws it all the way down, over that sweet boyishness.

Then waits, to see what I will do. He's struck the match. Do I want to put the fuse to that little flickering flame?

'Can I help you with something?' he asks, and then he *licks the damned thing again.*

Would it be so bad if I just got a fistful of his hair and shoved his face into the carpet? He doesn't look as though it would be a bad thing. He looks as though he wants me to grab a fistful of hair and shove his face *between my legs*.

'I really hope I don't have to tell you these letters are unacceptable,' I start. It comes out much better than I thought it would. More like a boss and less like a sex maniac.

'Really?' he asks, and it's then that I start to hate him. It's not even a start, in truth. I loathe him already. I despise his fake innocence and his stupid handsome face and these letters, covered in stuff that most likely fell out of his gorgeous mouth. And unfortunately, all of these things make me ball them up and throw them at him before I speak.

'I'm not sure how you could fail to realise. You've misspelled the word *and.*'

He blurts out a little *oops*, which seems to send me into some sort of tailspin of indecision. On the one hand, the word sounds genuine. The breath he puffs out sounds real, and his big eyes go bigger. In fact, by this point they're so big that they're starting to swallow me whole.

But on the other hand … he misspelled the word *and*. Twice. I'm not sure how that's possible.

'Do you have some sort of issue I'm not aware of, Benjamin?'

He shrugs. He actually *shrugs*.

'Nope,' he says, and I don't know what I despise most. His sloppy, ridiculous approach to things, or his utter American-ness. Both just sing out of that *nope*, so blatant and too much for me to handle. 'I guess I just made a mess of things, huh?'

'You *made a mess* of things?'

'Yeah. I probably wasn't thinking.'

'You *weren't thinking*?'

I have no idea why I keep repeating what he's saying back to him. But I at least know this: if I don't get a handle on myself soon, I'm going to do worse than getting a fistful of his hair. I'm going to put the heel of my shoe into his back, and dig in hard enough to make him scream.

'But I swear to God, I'll do better next time.'

'You keep swearing to God. Is he likely to make you better at your job?'

'Oh, well –'

'The job that you failed to do on Monday morning, when you gave me a vital letter of great importance about four days too late. The job that a chimpanzee could do, if you gave him enough paper and his own desk.'

His face actually flushes red at that. It's satisfying, in a way I don't want to acknowledge.

'I'm so –' he starts again, but I cut him off. I'm on some sort of roll now, and the longer I let it go on the worse it gets.

'Perhaps the responsibility of a desk is a little too much

for you. If so I could hire this theoretical primate to take your place, and you could come and work in my office. I have an absolutely wonderful spot on my floor somewhere for you to play with some coloured blocks.'

I notice, absently, that his mouth is hanging open. It looks like the expression someone would make if they'd just recently been stabbed in the gut. Sound seems to want to come out of him, but all he can manage is a strangled gasp.

'Are those words you're trying to form, Benjamin? Because if they are, allow me to fill in the only ones you should be using: *yes* and *sir*.'

I pretend I don't see his eyes drift closed, briefly.

'Rewrite these letters, without a mistake in them. Do so, and I might let you keep your job. Fail, and ... well. I don't think you want to know what will happen if you fail.'

'Yes, sir,' he says, and my mind immediately goes back to the last time I heard two words spoken like that. When Tim Lockley was underneath me, body almost completely out of control. Hips jerking upwards, cock fucking into me hard.

Voice breathless, as he told me *yes, now*.

That's how Benjamin sounds, I think. Like he's shaky with lust and ready to come at any moment – though naturally I try to evade the obvious. I turn around and stride right out of his cubicle, the second the thought occurs to me. And if my legs feel like water as I do so, well, what am I supposed to do about it?

I can't keep reprimanding him like that, I can't. I went harder than I'd ever intended to, but it hadn't seemed to put him off. He'd still looked heavy-eyed and weird once I'd done it and even now, as I stand shaking in the sanctity of my office, I can recall the softness of his parted lips. His breathlessness.

The way he'd seemed to tremble minutely the second I left that little suggestion in the air. *If you fail*, I think, and then can't ignore the pulse of pleasure that goes through my sex. I'm aroused because I told someone beneath me off. I'm aroused because I abused my power, and probably upset someone who only maybe sort of deserved it.

And for a moment I'm so ashamed of that fact I can't speak. I can't do anything. I just stand there, thinking about that incredulous look on his face as I suggested a *monkey* would do a better job than him.

It's just unforgivable. Woods might have done more to me and worse, but that doesn't give me the right to do the same to someone else. I *liked* what Woods did to me. How do I know for sure that Benjamin does – because he sounded aroused?

That's crazy. It's insane. I have to go back and apologise, I have to.

Though by God I wish I hadn't, the minute I get to that partition around his little non-office and take in the long, lovely slope of his body.

Of course, there are many, many things he could be doing. He could be crying. He's leaning against the wall of his cubicle, back to the entrance. Shoulders shaking as though with emotion, everything about his gait somehow sloppy and like he's lost control of himself.

And yet I know without a shadow of a doubt that he isn't upset. It's like the strange understanding I have of his facial expressions. I can tell just from looking at his hunched shoulders and the way his arm is twisted around his body …

He's masturbating. He is absolutely, one-hundred-per-cent masturbating.

I can see his hips rocking forward into what is almost

certainly the press of his hand, and when I make myself as quiet as I can, the sounds he's making become obvious. Little breathless sighs and moans that would probably escape anyone else – they'd just think he was distressed in some way, and get his attention, at which he could turn and straighten himself and pretend to have been blubbering into a hanky.

Or in this case: the piece of paper he's got crumpled in his hand.

I can see it the second he lets himself get completely out of control – the letter I balled up and threw at him. But he hasn't just got it crushed in his fist, as he pushes all of those sounds against the back of his hand. No no no.

He's got the *paper* pressed against his mouth. He's got the paper *in* his mouth practically, as he shudders and bucks into his own grip. And now I can hear it too – the slick slide of a hand over a very slippery cock. All of it just a little muted, because of course he's doing this under the cover of his trousers. He's just kind of slipped one hand inside, to work himself all quick and frantic like this.

And though I wouldn't admit it before, I'll admit it now: the idea is thrilling. The whole of it – him purposefully making a mess of those letters, the things I said and his reaction, and now this – it's just horrendously exciting. My cunt clenches around nothing, in some kind of bizarre sympathy for his predicament. My clit swells, ready to be touched or rubbed or … God …, if he would only lick it the way he'd licked that scrap of paper. If I could just make my legs move and go to him right now, he'd do it, I know he would.

But knowing is somehow worse than not. Now it's real. Now it's true. Being belittled and told off excites him, in the same way it excited me – more so, in fact. I never masturbated at my desk, thinking of Mr Woods telling me to be better, do more, stop making a mess.

But God, Ben is. He's really going at it now, as though he's barely aware of the people who could be in the office at this time. Aidan usually stays late, for example. I always do, and he had to know that it was possible I'd return to apologise.

Though somehow, I don't think he does. I don't think he cares about anything but the feeling of his fingers wrapped around his cock and that paper crushed into his mouth, everything about his body language so intent on the task at hand. From where I'm standing I can make out a million arousing little details – like the clench of his ass cheeks beneath those thin trousers, and the shuddering he does every time he hits it just right – but even then I'm not prepared for his orgasm.

It seems to lurch through him, and when it does he makes a sound. More than a sound really – even with the paper in his mouth I can tell he says my name. He just blurts it out, full of a kind of reaching desire that I've never heard from another person. Voice shaky and torn, hips bucking towards the circle of his own grip, body shuddering under the stress of such impossible pleasure.

He just gives himself over to it, and I realise something in that moment. I realise it amongst the ruins of my own arousal, clit still pulsing slow and steady. Wetness now making its way down my inner thigh, the whole of my lower body so thick and heavy with sensation.

Even with Woods, I was never like that. I never gave my all the way he is doing.

I'm not sure if I know how.

Chapter Four

He knocks this time. And after I've taken a deep breath and told him to come in, I notice something different about him. Something I probably shouldn't notice, as a person who's definitely not obsessed.

I'm not. I'm not.

In fact, I almost let him leave the second he's put the letters on my desk – tentatively, but in that same almost clumsy way he has. Eyes on me, as he just kind of nudges them over the wood.

But then he turns to go and that different thing impresses itself on me immediately. His shirt is tucked in at the back. He's tucked it in, and pulled the ridiculous stripy cardigan he has on over it right down, so that it covers the waistband of his trousers.

I suppose it's the small details that mean the most.

'Benjamin,' I say, though I've no idea what's going to follow it. I just want him to stop for a second, and be easy in my presence. Hell, I want to be easy in his.

Though that seems unlikely to happen when he turns back to me and I have to take in a million things about him. His face, those eyes, how broad his shoulders are. How big his hands look, even though he's kind of clasping them one over the other. It looks for all the world like he wants to crack his knuckles, desperately, but is resisting.

And I guess I'm resisting too, because Lord the sight is arresting. I don't know what's arresting about it. The length of his fingers? The way they kind of jab out at me like that, all awkward and not like fingers at all?

I don't know. I don't know what to say next. What did Woods do, after our first encounter? After he first knew I was raring to go? Because it's inescapable now – I know Ben is. There's not a small series of clues, like the flush I got whenever I was around Woods, or how eager I was to do his every bidding.

He masturbated while stuffing a remnant of my reprimand into his mouth. A blind buffoon would know what that meant.

'Yes?' he asks, so full of hope it's unbearable.

'Thank you,' I try, but I know before I've said it that it's wrong. It leaves an opening, and he takes it effortlessly.

'Oh, no problem. I think you'll find them more to your liking this time.'

Why? Is his cock in there somewhere?

'I'm sure I will.'

I turn away then, and look at my computer screen. Of course there's nothing on it – but he can't see that. Hopefully I look like I'm all business, and not poised on the edge of insanity.

'Well, if there's anything else I can do for you, Ms Harding …' he says, and so I can't be blamed. It's the fault of that little ellipsis he leaves on the end of his sentence, that little trail off into nothing.

Anyone would want to fill that nothing up, immediately. Anyone.

But still I wait, until he's backing towards the door. Until he's waving at me, casually, in lieu of a goodbye he doesn't know how to give. *See you later* sounds too informal, I suppose. *Until next time* is almost a threat.

Like the thing I then give him.

'You could possibly not masturbate in your cubicle.'

I see him freeze in position without turning my head, those soft-focus eyes of his bright and wide, on the periphery of my vision. Everything about him clearly stunned, even without the benefit of the sound he then produces.

It's almost a croak, I think, and it makes me snap my gaze to him. I want to see, I realise. I want to see how open and soft his mouth looks, how wide his eyes are, how rigid his body has gone. And once I've taken in all of these things undercover of a steely stare, my sex clenches, just once.

'That is what you did, isn't it?' I ask, though of course we both know I'm not really asking. Or at least, *I* know. Because after a second, he answers.

'I have literally no idea what you're talking about.'

'Don't lie.'

'I'm not – I –'

'I would certainly advise that you not continue lying.'

He spreads his hands out, as though they're going to find the correct answers for him.

'Just let me explain –'

'Stop talking.'

'Please, I –'

'Just stop talking. Stop talking.'

He's breathing very hard, I notice – but he does what I've told him to. He even compresses his mouth into that oddly mean line, as though he needs a little extra barrier to hold his frantic words in. And when I just keep right on eyeing him, he actually wipes his clearly sweaty hands on the front of his trousers.

I'll confess: the gesture tweaks something inside me that I don't want it to tweak.

'Now. Answer honestly. Did you masturbate in your cubicle, Benjamin?'

He doesn't hesitate this time, despite the perspiring and the wide-eyed terror.

'It's … a possibility.'

'Just a possibility?'

'Well, yeah. OK. I kind of did it.'

He laughs nervously, and that same thing inside me twangs. It makes me wonder if this would be easier if he weren't so adorable … or would it be harder? If he was sure of himself, confident – a real Aidan Harcroft – would I be able to do this?

And more to the point: does he *know* that I keep asking myself that question?

'And what might *it* be?'

Ohhh, this time he hesitates. I see his tongue touch the roof of his mouth, and those hands toy with the bottom of his cardigan. Of course I notice then that the thing isn't buttoned there – in truth, I'm not sure if it really fits him, because it seems to splay out over his hips like a half-forgotten striptease – but that's all right.

What fun would it be if he improved all at once, in a single shot?

'Come on,' he laughs. 'You know what *it* is. You just said it to me half a second ago.'

God, he makes it so easy. I don't have to try for the irritated look that comes to my face.

'Remind me,' I say, while his eyes search my room for inspiration. He looks cornered, I think, and for a second the idea makes me hesitate. It makes me want to back out, quickly – give him an exit sign, if he so sorely wants one.

But then he says: 'What exactly do you want me to do?' And he puts far too much emphasis on all the wrong things. His *want* is hoarse and husky, his question mark like a hook curling around my waist. I'm tugged into this before I'm sure I want to be, and that's prior to his gaze jerking its way back to my face.

His eyelids are heavy, now, I notice. His mouth looks … tender. Though really I'm only using the word 'tender' there because my mind wants me to say *like the spread split of a woman's sex* instead.

'Say the words,' I tell him, softly, so softly. And though he tells me: 'I can't,' I can hear something else below the refusal. Something that's not quite as unsure as he claims he is. For example, I'm not certain an unsure person would go from toying with the edge of their cardigan to kind of … sliding his hand underneath it. You know … just to maybe rub over his own belly through his shirt, with the softly stroking tips of his fingers. … 'If you can do it in your cubicle, you can say it,' I say, but now *my* voice is hoarse. And I've crossed my legs beneath my desk, though not because I want to. Because I *have* to. It's the same thing as his pressed-together lips.

I need something to keep the feelings in.

'I was masturbating,' he replies, and then unfortunately said feelings just gush their way out. Not even the leg-crossing can stop them. In fact, I think the leg-crossing makes it worse. A low pulse has started up right at the heart of my sex, and it gets stronger the longer I let this go on.

'I see. And why exactly were you doing a filthy thing like that in such plain view?'

Filthy thing, I think, and that pulse becomes a throb. I

can feel the exact shape of my clit, without so much as a
finger on myself.

'I don't know.'

'I think you *do* know.'

He swallows thickly. Tosses that thick hank of glossy
hair out of his eyes even though it's too buoyant to ever
actually get close, then has to stroke through it nervously when it won't stay exactly where he wants it to.
The gesture is incredibly boyish and should be incredibly
annoying, I know.

But somehow it's something else instead. It's not childish or
silly. It's just him, it's the way he is. He can't help being this
open and ready and kind of like he wants his face fucking.

'I guess …' he starts, and I can hardly believe I actually
hold my breath, waiting. But by God, I do. Which of course
makes it a hideous disappointment when he just finishes with:
'I guess I just did it because I wanted to.'

In fact, it's so much of a disappointment that I actually
almost do turn back to my work for real. I finger some of
the contracts waiting for approval on my desk. I think about
calling Anderson in here, to go over some of his slightly
skewed projections.

There's a full day ahead of me, and I don't have to be
like this.

Until he *rolls his eyes* at himself.

After which, I don't know *how* I need to be. I mean, I
actually see him do it. I know that's what it is. All of his
expressions are so big he could star in a silent movie about
himself: *Benjamin Tate Can't Control His Cock.*

But somehow, the way he looks doesn't quite compute
in the manner it should. Instead, it just makes me realise
something: I've never met a man as handsome as him who

behaves the way he does. Who wears all of his expressions on his sleeve and puts a hand up his own cardigan and doesn't seem aware that he's utterly, utterly lovely.

Because he is. I don't see how I could reasonably deny or push that fact away now. He hides it well beneath the goofiness and the too-big grins, but the lust haze he's descended into makes it almost unbearably clear. His lower lip almost sulks all on its own. His eyes are like an early-morning mist over something heated and heavy.

God. *God*. What's happening to me?

'I mean … it's more than wanting to.' He pauses, considering. 'It's more like … I *need* to. Man, I always need to soooo badly.'

I know what's happening to me. He says all the things I most want to hear in a tone like melting butter, and then I turn into a sexual psychopath. Observe:

'So you masturbate often?'

I mean, why am I asking him this? Why? And why is it that the shakier I get, the more confident he becomes? When he answers his voice seems almost … dry. Just hinting at a bank of sardonicism under the clean-cut exterior.

'Not in public places, no.'

'But generally speaking.'

He straightens.

'Yes,' he tells me, and I can't help it then. I have to hear the rest.

'How often would you say you need to do it?'

'I don't know.'

'You're going to wear those words out, Benjamin.'

He takes a breath, but it's different to the ones he needed earlier. More restless, I think, as though he's just as frustrated as I am at his sudden inability to express himself properly. I mean, usually he's almost crazy with words – he's a goddamn word volcano. I've seen him terrify Kelly with his need to share a hundred details about his childhood in Hawaii, and all at a thousand words a minute.

But now he's stuttery. He doubles back on himself, as though he's on trial and has to get everything just right.

'Sorry. Sorry. OK – I guess maybe once or twice a day.'

And when he does finally get words out, they're not the correct ones.

'You know it's very easy to tell when you're lying. You get this little awkward crinkle above your nose,' I say, though I've no idea that I'd figured out such a thing until the words emerge. It's like what Woods used to say about the subconscious clues, I suppose – that people do things without knowing it.

I can't be sure, however, if this applies to him, or to me.

'I do?'

'Yes. And you look sort of ... stunned by your own capacity for falsehoods.'

He squirms for that one. But shamefully, this only seems to create further problems between my legs. When I shift, I can feel the slickness coating my slit. Can feel it easing over things both delightful and torturous.

'OK. OK,' he says, and then he does something that makes me want to do more than cross my legs. It makes me want to shove my skirt up and fuck myself right there in front of him, though I've no idea why.

He just counts on his fingers. That's all. And if he's counting how many times he masturbated yesterday on said fingers, well ... what does that matter? How is that an arousing thing to witness?

'I'd say I maybe do it ... three times a day.' He checks

his fingers and nods, then seems to change his mind when he finally looks up at me. Like he knows. Like he can feel me unravelling the lie before I've said a word. 'Sometimes more, depending on what's happened.'

I can't describe the heady rush that goes through me, to know that my expression alone forced him to make that correction. All I understand clearly is that it puts a quiver in my voice, when I finally get words out.

'And what has to happen to make you so desperate to come?'

Not that it matters. He has his own quiver to deal with, and oh Lord it's *big*. It seems to affect his entire body, from sudden slump of his shoulders to the slow drift of his eyelids over those foggy eyes.

It's like all his self-control slides right out of him. And I know it does for sure, when he quite abruptly pants out: 'Oh, that sounds so dirty when you say that word. I think I felt it go right through me.'

But the words aren't the worst part about it. No – the worst part is when he just kind of rubs his hand all over his chest and then up to his neck, after he's spoken. And though I try to deny it, what I'm left thinking of is a stripper, doing her best to be as blatant and sexual as she can.

You know. To lure people in.

'Say it again,' he says, and then I have to cut him off. Have to. Of course I do it with words that have absolutely nothing to do with how I feel, but in truth I'm just glad I manage to speak at all.

'I think you have the wrong idea, Benjamin,' I say, while molten lava makes its way down my body to settle in the pit of my stomach. Strange, really, that my voice comes out quite steely. 'You don't tell me what to do, I tell you. Of course, you can decide not to do it. But here's the thing: I rather think you won't.'

His eyes flash in a way I can't quite reach with the outer edges of my imagination.

'You're right,' he tells me, all low and steady. 'I won't.'

I don't know what happens inside my body after that. If I tried to stand, I'm fairly certain I wouldn't make it. My sex is so swollen, so full of that sweet ache, that the idea of moving so much just makes me want to pass out at my desk.

And he's definitely starting to know it now. He takes a step forward without my say-so, that wicked tongue of his just ever so slightly flickering out to wet his bottom lip. Gaze now as bright as it is heavy, eager and mischievous in a way I don't want to quite face.

So instead, I say the first *put him off* kind of thing I can think of.

'So if, for example, I told you to lick my arsehole – you would?'

It's like I'm suddenly playing chicken, I think, and this is my first daring play. The lewdest thing I can think of on such short notice, and one that's bound to put a man off. Bound to.

'Do you want me to do that? I could, if you wanted me to.'

Or you know. Maybe it only puts men who aren't Benjamin Tate off. Because Lord, I swear, I've never heard anyone sound so eager to do anything. I've told children they can have ice cream, and not had them respond with such breathless anticipation.

He starts unbuttoning that grotesque cardigan, as though a prerequisite for an ass-licking is nakedness from both parties – though naturally I stop him. I mean, I can't actually have him lick between the cheeks of my arse, in my open office in the middle of the day. That would be ridiculous.

Even if he doesn't seem to think so in the slightest.

'I mean, I've thought about doing it,' he says, before I've got past the hand I've held up to halt him in his immense, ridiculous tracks.

And then said hand is the thing that feels ridiculous, in all honesty. He's actually thinking about ass-licking while I'm the goddamn lollipop lady stood in the middle of our road.

'I see,' I say, because it's just noncommittal enough. It's just enough without going all the way into yes, go ahead, do whatever the fuck you like. Instead it hovers on the edges of *explain yourself to me*, as cool and detached as my face nearly feels.

'Though obviously, you know. Not in a lot of detail.'

'You haven't thought about licking my ass in a lot of detail? Well, how comforting.'

'No – I mean … I mean I try not to think about you that way. Most of the time.'

'And the rest of the time you're spreading my arse cheeks and going to town, in your head?'

One of his hands pauses, mid-gesture. Finger half-uncurled from the loose fist he's made, as though he was just about to make an absolutely fascinating point, and now has no idea what it was. Even his mouth seems caught in this feedback loop, that soft shape suddenly tense around words he's now failing to get out.

'You need to answer me, Benjamin – and quickly. I really don't have a lot of time to watch you standing in front of me unable to speak.'

He wets his lips. Closes his eyes, briefly, before continuing.

'Pretty much.'

'Describe it to me, then.'

'Wait – what? What do you want me –'

'Describe what you do to me, in all of these fevered imaginings,' I say, though I don't do it because I really want to. I do it because I can't *not*.

And apparently, he feels exactly the same. It's like he wants to stop, really he does. He wants to have control over himself, and maybe laugh all of this off. But instead he just takes a big breath, and goes right ahead with it all.

'Sometimes … sometimes you tell me to do it. Like this – only fiercer. But other times I'm in the hallway or your office and I drop something, the way I always do when you pass by. And while I'm down there, on my knees, I just kind of … get my face between your legs.'

He doesn't look away as he tells me this, which I think is to his credit. After all, I have to look away the second he's said it. I simply can't keep staring at him, with all of these newly framed thoughts about his clumsiness rattling around inside my head.

He doesn't drop everything because he's just like that. He drops everything because of *me*. I mean, that's what he's saying, right? And if I ask, will that startling and too foggy fact become clearer? Will I be able to look at it head on?

'So you drop the papers on purpose?'

He shakes his head, wrinkles his brow. Glances sideways, as though he's trying to map out his fantasy exactly for me but is struggling to do so.

'No, no. I just do it because I can't help myself. And then I can't help pushing my face between your legs.'

'And after that …?'

'After that I lick you until you let me do it. Until you're all wet there and turned on, you know, and I guess sometimes other stuff happens – like you rub your clit while I lick

56

between your ass cheeks. Or maybe the other way around.'

I'm loath to interrupt him, because I can see he's getting to that place. The one where he'll say just about anything and doesn't really seem sensible of it – though of course this is somewhat more revealing than 'and one time a shark almost ate me while I was surfing'.

And if he doesn't seem to see the difference, well. That's fine. He can carry on not seeing the difference all the way into the most arousing tale I've ever heard anybody tell.

'The other way around?' I ask, and sure enough, he just slides on into the rest of it.

'With me licking your clit and you ...' he says, and for a second I'm sure he's just going to leave that last part trailing. I mean, it's obvious what he's suggesting. He's already labelled the two body parts, and it's not as though we're talking about hands and feet here. He doesn't need to go into detail.

Even if he just takes a second to wind himself up to it – one hand actually twirling in front of him, like a goad to his confidence – and then absolutely says the real live words.

'... fingering your ass. Or maybe just rubbing over it, I don't know. I guess I just understand that you're doing something there, while I lick your clit and stroke your pussy.'

'And that's all you do?' I ask, as though none of that's enough on its own. He has fantasies about eating my cunt in office hallways, for God's sake. How did I ever think I would shame him by bringing up a little light masturbation? 'You just stroke me?'

He lets out a little flustered breath.

'Well, no. Obviously not.'

'Do I actually have to prompt you, Benjamin?'

He spreads his hands again, but this time it's like he's

trying to hit a reset button. It's like he's trying to rewind everything and go back and be better.

'No, no – I … I fuck you. With my fingers.'

'I see.'

'And … uh … sometimes you're so wet, and so turned on, that I don't just use one or two. I get three of my fingers into your pussy, and when I do you twist your hands in my hair. You make me do it harder, faster, until I can just about feel you coming.'

I'd call his fantasy very unrealistic, if I didn't suspect that he could feel me coming from all the way over there, if he so chose. In fact, I think he's going to do just that really soon. The pulse in my clit feels immense, all-consuming, and whenever I let my eyes wander down over his solid body, said pulse gets worse.

He's hard, and very obviously so. It looks like a great thick fist beneath the material of those crappy trousers, so swollen that I can just about make out things I probably shouldn't be able to. Like the fact that he isn't circumcised, despite being as American as an over-sweet slice of apple pie.

'I see. And if I said to you that your babbling mouth really needs a ball gag … would you wear one around the office for me?' I ask, because really I'm going to need a lot more than a bit of mild ass-licking to jolt him. Or at least, I think so until he actually replies.

And then I'm just not sure where his boundaries lie at all.

'Oh my God. You wouldn't really ask me to do that, would you?'

'Whether I would or not is hardly the question. Read it back to me, Benjamin – what was I asking, exactly?'

He strains, briefly, to remember – then seems almost overjoyed when it finally occurs to him. He snaps his fingers at me, which only suggests how much trouble I'm in. Even so silly a gesture gets me going.

'You asked whether I'd do it.'

'And would you?'

His eyes drift closed again, but that's not what I notice. It's his hand I see, as it slides down over the jutting shape in the front of his trousers. And I don't mind admitting the sight jolts me, like a little electric shock applied to the base of my spine.

He's touching himself. He's touching his obviously hard cock right in front of me, without a hint of shame or restraint. In truth, I'm not sure if he knows what shame or restraint are. His prick is stiff, and he wants to touch it.

So he just does.

'Yes,' he says, almost too faint for me to hear. It's like he's lost inside himself, suddenly – but that's fine. I'm more than willing to drag him back out again.

'And just me looking at you a certain way makes you this … sluttish?'

He squeezes himself through his trousers on that last word, in a way that exposes most of the shape to my greedy gaze. And it is greedy by this point. My mouth practically floods with saliva to see that solid, lengthy outline through his crappy trousers.

'Is that how I seem?' he asks, breathless and just ever so slightly incredulous. I don't know why the latter's there, however. He's playing with himself in my office, for God's sake. He's got a hand under his shirt now, and I can actually see the pale, flat expanse of his belly.

He's the epitome of a slut, and I tell him so.

'I don't see how you could fail to realise,' I say, but here's the thing – he doesn't then get a hold of himself. He doesn't stop groping his cock or the skin underneath his shirt.

On the contrary.

He goes at both things more lewdly. That hand disappears all the way up inside his clothes until I'm fairly certain he really, really wants to touch one of his own nipples. Maybe pinch it a little in a way I'm imagining doing to him, right now.

'I'm sorry,' he says, but he isn't. He isn't at all. He's biting his lip and getting very close to just out and out masturbation, right in front of me.

And ohhh, it's almost desperately arousing. If I had half of his abandon, I'd put my hand inside my own shirt right now. My nipples feel almost sore beneath the crinkly press of my too-lacy bra, and every time I move it's a kind of agony.

One that he doesn't seem to be labouring under.

'Don't be sorry. Just answer my original question: does me looking at you a certain way arouse you?'

'Yes.'

'And what way would that be exactly?'

'The way you're looking at me now.'

I almost put my hand to my face, just to check whatever's actually on there. Am I stern right now, am I a mask? Does he look at me and see the grey implacability of Woods written all over my features?

'You like it?' I ask, and have to work to keep my own hint of incredulity out of there. He doesn't hesitate, however.

'Yes.'

'You like me telling you off?'

'Yes.'

Of course, I knew what the answer would be. It's obvious by this point – and yet the admission still makes me jerk, in the same way the word *sluttish* had made him jerk. I feel my clit swell between already swollen lips, and I have to do something crazy – like maybe pinching myself somewhere horrible – just to keep my manner as cool and collected as he seems to think it is.

'I see. Well. That does leave me in a rather difficult position, Benjamin.'

My God, is *that* the understatement of the year. I can almost feel my sanity sliding away from me as we speak, but somehow I manage to cling onto the reins. I focus on the matter at hand:

He likes to be told what to do.

And I definitely have something I'd like him to participate in.

'I mean, how am I supposed to successfully reprimand you for doing something so disgusting?'

His breath hitches in his chest, and those maddening fingers just sort of slowly, slowly slide over the now thrillingly clear shape of his cock. It's so clear, in fact, that I can make out the ridge around the head. I can make out the suggestion of his balls below. And I can definitely make out that thing I thought I saw a few moments earlier.

Though of course I pretend I'm not looking at all.

'The second I do, you're just going to get yourself into this state again.'

His gaze slides sideways the second I use the word *state*, in a manner I'm now starting to find familiar. He did the same thing when I suggested he sit on my floor and play with coloured blocks, and somehow I don't think the expression means *I'm so ashamed of myself*.

Or maybe it does, but it's almost certainly followed by *and it feels soooo good*.

'I mean, you're so hard I can just about make out the fact that you're not circumcised.'

Of course, I expect him to flush when I say it. But though he looks awkward and fumbly and faintly embarrassed by my confession, he doesn't go red. He half-laughs instead, and says, 'You can really see that?'

Swiftly followed by yet more completely irrelevant chatter. 'It's 'cause my parents were kind of hippies, and they –'

And I know I keep doing it, but I have to cut him off again. I can't possibly let him see how intriguing I find his frankness. How odd it is to me, to discover someone who will just go into a mess of detail on the strangest and most private topics.

'I didn't ask you to tell me your life story,' I say, and feel mean about it. But here's the thing – he just keeps right on *talking*.

'Is it a problem? I thought most English guys –'

I shake my head, far more abruptly than I'm actually feeling. Inside I've turned to some sort of inescapable mush. It's like having sinking sand in the place where my heart used to be, and I'm slowly getting sucked into it.

'It's not a problem. The fact that you're masturbating in my office is more of one, in truth.'

'Sorry, sorry,' he says, and again I notice that odd mouth. Sometimes it hardly seems to open at all, when he talks. 'I'm just so … God. I don't think I've ever been this excited in my life.'

Though I pay less attention to said mouth when he's finished with those particular words. Instead, two sides of myself war. One is almost as thrilled as he seems to be, just at the sound of him saying something like that.

The other tells him: 'I doubt that's true. You seem pretty excitable to me.'

He shrugs one big shoulder, like the non-verbal equivalent of the word helpless.

'I guess I am. A strong wind can make me hard.'

'I see,' I say, while the heart I don't have in my chest beats and beats, between my legs. God, he *is* a slut. 'Well, that is an interesting fact.'

He squinches his face up, as though sensible of a mistake he's just made.

'Yeah, I know it's not interesting at all. I realise how it makes me seem – my last girlfriend said I was like a big puppy dog.'

The description is so apt I almost laugh, but manage to rein it in at the last moment. I have to, after all. The one in charge of proceedings isn't permitted a giggle.

'Your last girlfriend was very bright, if a little remiss in the doing something about it department.'

'Really? What do you think she should have done?'

He's practically on tiptoes now. Body leaning forward in lieu of those last few steps towards the desk he can't quite make.

That's fine, however. My legs are feeling just as wobbly as they were before, but I think I can manage to stand. I *want* to stand, and cross the beautiful cream carpet to him – though of course the moment I do his breathing quickens. His eyes get bigger.

'Taken the matter in hand,' I murmur, when I'm close enough to do so. From where I'm stood – not two inches from his shivering body – I can smell his cologne. It's Davidoff Cool Water, I think, which is just so very *him*. Sort of clumsy, with a side order of handsome, clean-cut American-ness about it, the scent easily conjuring up images of wholesome types diving off cliffs in their underwear.

Preferably right into my vagina.

'Really?' he asks, but he's surer now. I can see it, in the way he leans down just a little. That foggy gaze of his stroking all over my face as he does so, lips parted to let his warm breath ghost over my skin.

He thinks he's going to get something now, clearly. And I don't mind admitting that I want to give it, Lord how I want to. I have to make a little circle around him, just to keep everything inside myself straight and true.

'Of course,' I say, each firm step making me steelier, stronger. *I'm on the cusp*, I think, and then I just let my fingertips trail over something innocuous, like the solid black line of his belt, just above his ass. 'A man like you needs a firm hand, don't you think?'

This time when I stand before him he doesn't *suggest* he's leaning down. He just does it, that full, soft mouth of his searching for mine. Eyes near closed, everything about the moment so sweet and delicious in a way that makes my heart ache.

Yet just as I'm about to finally feel his lips against mine, just as I'm opening to him, I realise something. It's not just about me being in charge of *him*. It's about me being in charge of *myself*.

And then I turn my head to whisper in his ear: 'You're forbidden to touch yourself for the next three days.'

Chapter Five

I know he's obeyed me, the next time I see him. Truth is, I don't have to try very hard to come to that conclusion. He looks like the before picture on an advert for something that stops you starving yourself. He looks like he's sort of gone mad overnight, and now his big stare-y eyes are darting around the insides of this tiny elevator, checking for the people who are almost definitely coming to take him away.

And if all of that wasn't enough, he has hair on his face. Actual hair, all grey and bristly and rough over places I hadn't expected it to be, like his neck. Like his heavy-boned cheeks, as though he could grow a full beard if he so chose.

Of course, the sight immediately makes me wonder something completely irrelevant, like: *how old is he, exactly*?

But I can't blame myself for that. It's been on my mind ever since I creamed my panties over him. Prior to this moment I'd thought he was maybe twenty-seven, twenty-eight, but just the thought of that number makes me clench all over. Five years younger than me isn't much, by most people's standards.

But it's too much for me. I can't be a cougar at the age of thirty-two.

And judging by that stubble, I might not have to be.

'Good morning, Benjamin,' I say, as I take my place next to him, against one of the mirrored walls. In return, he tries to say something back. Something faint that's not really a word, followed by the kind of silent tension I've never experienced in my entire life.

Not even with Woods. We used to ride up together in this elevator like we didn't know each other, but the problem is, Benjamin's not closed down enough for that. And even if he was, I seem to be doing a piss-poor job of that very thing.

The moment I'm certain he's not looking, I glance up and sideways.

Only to find he *is* looking. He's looking so hard I feel sure he wants to kill me with his eyes.

'Did you have a good weekend?' I ask, because he's not talking. In fact he's sort of tilting towards me, in a way that reminds me of things it definitely shouldn't. *Like an animal*, I think, unbidden. *Like an animal, seeking out the warmth and heat and scent of another body*.

And the awful thing is, it doesn't get any better when someone else enters the elevator on floor seven. Instead, that strange sort of tension between us seems to get worse and worse, culminating in the strangest little details – like his grey jumper-covered arm brushing faintly against mine.

Or the feel of his overheated breath on the side of my face.

Of course I don't dare turn now. If he's actually managing to breathe on me, he must be leaning really far down. He's about six foot seven hundred, and I'm five-five in heels. And though that thought is strangely exciting – his closeness, his size – I can feel a calm settling over me. I can feel it in the same way I can feel my own arousal, the two things now somehow inextricably linked.

I have to be in charge of myself, I think, and then when

Henry Breckenmeyer's back is to us, I just reach one slow hand up and find the side of Benjamin's face. I don't look at him, I don't outwardly react, I don't give any indication of what I'm doing. I just ever so calmly push his face back into the position it's supposed to be. But here's the kicker: he makes a sound when I do it. And by God, it's not an innocent little noise of complaint. It's this big, blurty, rude-sounding motherfucker, so loud that he has to smuggle it into a cough a tuberculosis sufferer would be proud of, while I fight to keep the weird, trembling smile off my face. I don't know why a smile wants to come, to be honest. Woods never smiled. So why is this urge bubbling up inside me? 'My office,' I say to Benjamin, the second the doors slide open on the fifteenth floor. And he not only understands exactly what I mean, he follows me through the still carpet-quiet corridors, like someone who's about to faint.

No, really. He looks like someone who's about to faint. I see it all over him when I sit myself in my big leather chair, to watch him attempting to do something as simple as close a door. And then once he's done it, he practically staggers to my desk.

Though unfortunately for Benjamin, he doesn't stop where he should.

There's a line, you see. I've drawn it in my mind, right where my desk ends and the rest of the office begins. It's perfectly clear and straight, starting on the sharp edge of that wood and continuing cleanly on, invisible, to the bookcase on the left and the sideboard on the right. And Benjamin crosses it, without so much as a by your leave. He puts his big, clumsy hands all over the polished wood as he staggers around my desk to get at me. Because that's definitely what he's doing. He's actually trying to *get at me*, in a way I've never seen a man do before. He looks almost greedy – no, in fact he looks crazy – and I have to say … the sight of such a thing almost overrides the line. For one delirious second I imagine just spreading my legs and hiking up my skirt.

Come on and give it to me, I could say, and for once in my paltry little life I know someone actually would. He's hard already, before I've done anything, and every step he takes seems to shoot a sort of agony across his features, as though he's carrying something far too hot and far too heavy between his legs.

'Where exactly do you think you're going, Benjamin?' I ask, but I do something far worse than that as I speak those clear, cold words.

The second he gets close enough to actually reach out and touch me, I just unfold one leg from its position, crossed neatly over my knee. And then I plant my heeled foot right in the centre of his broad chest.

I'm really not certain which startles him more – the words, or the feel of my near-stiletto suddenly pressed against his firm flesh. But either way, he jerks to a halt. He has to. I'm holding him there with one braced leg, and I'm not certain I mind that his eyes dart directly down to the dark place the move has revealed.

It's sort of hitched my skirt all on its own, and I'm sure if he squints hard he'll be able to see the panties I'm not wearing. Or smell the slickness that's already all over my bare cunt.

'I just thought …' he starts, but of course he has no idea how to end that sentence. I think it's pretty clear to him, by this point, that he can't go with *that I'd get to fuck you now*.

'Go stand back over there, on your spot,' I say, and for one glorious moment he actually *sags* against the shoe I've still got pressed to his chest. Words spill out of him, as his weary eyes close – words like 'oh, you've got to be kidding, I'm dying here'.

But even sweeter is the fact that he actually goes.

'That's better, Benjamin,' I say once he's stood there, just behind the chair on the other side of my desk. Of course the minute he does so, I notice something very obvious and very thrilling.

He's hard, as I figured out a moment earlier. He's painfully and obviously hard.

But he doesn't go to touch himself. In fact, he very pointedly puts his hands behind his back, and when he does it I can almost see how he's got them there. One set of fingers braceleting around the other wrist, to keep him from doing something he was told not to.

I told him not to, and he's obeyed me *to the letter*.

In that moment I fully appreciate how far he'd let me go. And it's about a million miles from where we're now stood.

'In the elevator you didn't answer me,' I say, as I fuss over things on my desk. Red pens lined up in a neat row, fresh pad of paper on my lovely felt blotter. 'How was your weekend?'

'Fine,' he tells me, but the word comes out so tight I practically hear it squeak – not to mention the way his eyes follow my every move. All I do is sit back in my chair, legs neatly crossed again, and he devours me as though I'm a stripper divesting herself of that last item of clothing.

'Well, that's good,' I say, though he doesn't break the way I expect him to. I feel sure he's going to blurt something out again, or maybe try to take a step forward. Suggest something, anything.

But he doesn't.

'How …' he says faintly, then has to start again. His words

seem to be dying in his throat. 'How was your weekend?'

It makes me ache again, to see his attempt at casual breeziness.

'Very pleasant,' I say, though of course I'm underselling it somewhat. And after this pause I'm dragging out, I'm going to let him know why. Just another second now ... another moment of his heated gaze all over me ...

'I spent most of it masturbating.'

His face goes almost completely blank, which I have to say is not what I was expecting. I'm still not quite sure what I *am* expecting, but it's there all the same. A little frisson of disappointment.

Followed by an almost inescapable urge to push him beyond that nothingness.

'For some reason, I found myself almost unendurably aroused. Isn't that odd? But I have this toy ... and when I put its slippery tip to my stiff little clit I can come in under two minutes.'

Even I'm impressed by how far I go. When I flick back through the empty pages of my life, there are almost no chapters called *and then I told someone about my masturbatory habits*. In fact, I'm not certain if I've ever revealed anything like that to longtime lovers or trusted confidants, which only serves to circle Benjamin in an even deeper shade of red.

He stands out, I think, in the Book of Me. He's different in some way, though I can't quite say how. All I know is that I tell him this thing, and after I've done it his expression kind of seems to slide sideways.

'Of course, that's not half as satisfying as drawing it out – don't you find, Benjamin? So on Sunday, I filled both my holes with my favourite vibrators, and just sort of let them ... hum me to orgasm.'

And then it just falls off his face altogether. I'm left to discern his feelings from his body language and the sound he makes, both of which resemble something large and wounded slowly dying. The words he next manages to squeeze out are just overkill, in all honesty.

'Ms *Harding*,' he says, in a manner I would call disapproving, if I didn't almost know him by now. At the back of his throat, I can just hear it – that hint of thrill.

'Did you masturbate this weekend, Benjamin?' I ask, as casual as you please. I pick a piece of lint off my skirt while speaking.

'You –' he blurts out, clearly aiming for outrage or indignation, before wrestling himself back under control. I see him do it – those shoulders of his going back as he takes a series of slow, deep breaths. '*You told me not to.*'

'And you obeyed?' I ask, though I don't have to. After all, it's like he then says:

'Isn't it obvious? I must look like an insane person. In fact, I *know* I look like an insane person. I couldn't shave this morning, my hand was shaking too badly. I can't remember if I washed my hair, because being in the shower was like having sex *rain on me*. My body feels like a giant nuclear power plant, and to top it all off – I'm pretty sure I just saw your business.'

Now it's *my* turn to be stunned. Though I confess, I'm more stunned by the urge to giggle than anything else. I've never seen anyone do mock-outrage and incredulity as well he does it, though I think it's really just a symptom. It's a side-effect of the wider problem he has – that inability to keep any of his emotions off his face.

He's worse than a silent movie. He's like a pornographic pantomime.

'My *business*?' I ask, because really. On Friday he called it my pussy, and talked about fingering it. But now he can't get the correct terminology out? Now he's shy all of a sudden?

Oh no nono.

'Yeah. You just … flashed me,' he replies, and for the hundredth time I honestly suspect he knows exactly what he's doing. I mean, he sounds innocent when he says those words. But he's definitely smart enough to know that's not what I was asking.

'And the thing I flashed you is called a "business"?'

His eyes roll up and to the left.

'No. No. I meant … your pussy. You just flashed your pussy at me.'

'I see. And do you really think it was appropriate of you to stare at my cunt?'

'I didn't say the c-word,' he breathes out, and I swear it takes everything I have to not fuck him right there on my office floor. I swear it does. He called it the *c-word*. He couldn't bring himself to actually say the word, as though the word is in some place far, far beyond the pale.

'No. *I* said it. Really, Benjamin, keep up.'

'Sorry, sorry,' he fumbles out, clearly searching in vain for the right thing to say.

'You're apologising for that, but not anything else?'

He searches harder.

'And for the … for staring at your pussy. And coming behind your desk.'

'That's two out of three.'

'There's another thing I did wrong? Oh Geez, I don't know it. Um … oh! The other week, with Hendricks, in the meeting. He wanted black coffee, two sugars. I brought him two coffees, no sugar.'

It's true. He had. But I've got no idea what that has to do with this.

'Do you really think I care about Hendricks? Tell me, Benjamin, why would I be interested in the coffee of someone I have no consideration for?'

He shrugs with just his upper lip. It's one of the weirdest and most obvious facial expressions I've ever seen, and just this side of absolutely adorable.

'I honestly have no idea. I'm shooting in the dark here.'

'Is that what I asked you to do? Shoot in the dark?'

'You kind of asked me to do the opposite,' he says, and then, you know, he's all the way into absolutely adorable and out the other side.

'Very amusing. But unfortunately, amusement gets you no points here.'

I take out a little bound notebook from my top desk drawer. Of course, it isn't for anything other than vague notes about things I'm never going to do, but he doesn't know that. All he sees is his insane boss putting pen to paper, somewhere around the middle of what could well be 'The Book Of Employee Transgressions: Kinky Edition'.

'I'm afraid I'm going to have to add another day to your punishment,' I say, as I put a little blue and meaningless tick on a blank page.

Funny, really, how something so ridiculous has such an *effect*.

'*What*?' he says, and then once he's barked out the word he actually cranes, to try and see what I'm writing. 'No, *no*. You can't – please. I'm going out of my goddamn mind.'

'You can go now, Benjamin.'

'Oh God, I can't. I can't. People are gonna notice,' he moans, one hand suddenly in his impossibly thick and

73

far-too-long hair. 'Look, you don't have to do anything. I could just –'

'Come on me? Rub your dick on my tits? Fuck my face?'

'Oh Jesus, please don't talk like that. Why do you keep talking like that?'

'I don't know, Benjamin. How does it make you feel when I do?'

'Like I just want to come, and come, and come until I pass out.'

I give him a quarter of a smile. Just with the very corner of my mouth, but I think he catches it. He catches it, and that shaky mess he's descended into stills itself somewhat.

'OK,' he says, and takes one long, shuddery breath. 'OK, I can do this. I'll just go back to my desk and start on that presentation you wanted putting together.'

I turn to my computer. Switch it on.

'I appreciate that, Benjamin,' I say, so bright and breezy that for a moment I'm staggered by myself. It's like I've found a well in the bottom of me, and it lets me draw all the strength I need direct from its depths.

And if it's because of Ben that I've unearthed said strength, well. I just won't mention that to myself, as I use it to navigate the rest of my morning.

* * *

I have a perfect plan for the remainder of the day. It's called *pretend I never said any of those things to Benjamin Tate*. In fact, it goes one worse than that. When I pass him at the water cooler and he opens his mouth as though he's going to talk to me, *I pretend he doesn't actually exist*.

And I do it well, too. I know I do, because it stings hard

74

enough to make me wince, once I'm safe back in my office. I have to lean against the door and close my eyes against the little flash I get of his suddenly stormy gaze.

Of course I'm better at this than I thought I would be. But even so, I can't quite manage the glacial indifference of Woods, no matter how much like a game this all seems. Or how hard Benjamin wants to play it.

Because he does, he clearly does. I know it automatically, the second he walks into my office just as I'm having a one-to-one with Aidan about scheduling. And I do so because of several very obvious things.

Firstly, he doesn't knock. He just blunders right on in, as though he's already forgotten how aware he'd seemed of intruding before.

Secondly, he makes *pistol fingers* at Aidan as he passes by the raised eyebrows and comes up to my desk.

And thirdly ... oh dear God, thirdly ...

He's wearing an *untucked T-shirt*, with a *coffee stain on it*.

Of course, I get the immediate urge to ask him where his grey jumper went, where the red collar went, where his *tie* went, for fuck's sake. But then the moment I do so a lot of things flood into my already overheated mind. Like the image of him carelessly tossing aside various items of clothing with a look on his face that's akin to the one he seems to be wearing now.

I'd call it insouciance, if insouciance was an actual thing people did outside of nineteen-fifty-five. Hell, I'd call it insouciance if I was actually able to speak, but for the longest moment I can't say anything at all. Neither can Aidan, as it turns out, though I feel this works out best for everyone.

And most especially for Benjamin, who apparently has

quite a few things he wants to say. Though of course, none of them are even remotely acceptable.

'Oh hey, Eleanor,' he says, which is more than enough on its own to make Aidan let out an incredulous breath. God only knows what it does to me. *No one* calls me Eleanor. I'm not even sure if Aidan knows it *is* Eleanor.

He probably thinks my name is Frank.

'I was thinking ... maybe I could make that presentation up for you tomorrow. I spilled coffee on myself and I'm sort of tired. Really not up to, you know. Doing stuff.'

By God, I didn't know he had it in him. I thought he was boyish, maybe a little silly. Capable of writing the odd misspelled letter to provoke me, and not much more. Certainly nothing of this size and scope.

He's practically outgunned me. I'm not sure I understand what kind of dirty punishment fits this, though one thing makes itself abundantly clear. That's what he's pushing for. *Dirty*.

He didn't appreciate me ignoring him, and now he's rolled himself in shit and pranced around in front of me, like he knows. He knows I can't just add another day for this.

But good goddamn I do it anyway. I reach into my drawer and get out my little notebook, right there in front of Aidan. Benjamin's eyes following my every movement, naturally, as greedy as a starving man watching a waiter take his food order.

Though of course there are no rare steaks coming for him.

'Tomorrow, did you say?' I ask, as I scan the blank page in front of me – like maybe I'm looking for a date, a time, a thing that doesn't exist. 'So that will be ... another twenty-four hours.'

I have the gratification of seeing his eyes flash big, just

before he yanks himself back under control. No other
outward signs to say he's suffering – apart from the impossibly tight tone he then uses to tell me that's perfectly fine.

'Right. Thank you,' he says, and then I wait. I wait until
he's just at the door before calling out:

'Oh, and Ben ... find a shirt from somewhere, would you?
Otherwise I might have to postpone the presentation for ...,
say ..., a week.'

It's almost terrifying to see his face go as slack with lust
as it then does. But not half as terrifying as Aidan saying,
once Benjamin's gone:

'What the fuck was all that about?'

* * *

The problem is, I suppose, that I don't really know what
this is all about. After every little step I take – and every
little blundering push forward he goes after – I'm just left
floundering, unsure. A million little warnings flash up in my
head, each more severe than the last. *You could be fired*,
these warnings say, and then of course I have to wonder if
that's what happened to Woods.

Someone caught him in the office with Ms Harding and a
dildo. Like a game of Cluedo, only impossibly filthy.

Is that what I want to be? A person who plays filthy Cluedo
with Benjamin Tate, just because Benjamin Tate deliberately
spills coffee on himself and then tries to provoke me into it?

Because that's obviously what he did. He doesn't even drink
coffee, for God's sake. And, worse, I suspect Aidan knows
all of the above. I didn't appreciate that hint of amusement
in his usually so cool and unsettling gaze. And in all honesty,
I didn't appreciate my own answer to his question either.

He's having trouble with his girlfriend, I'd said, but of course that one word had struck far too close to bones I don't want to have. *Girlfriend*, I think, even now, and then a parade of Benjamin's possible conquests march through my head, each more lissom and lovely than the last.

Or worse: I parade through my own head, with that word stamped on my chest like a scarlet A. As though I could ever be something like that. As though this thing between us is actually just hearts and flowers *disguised* as kinky perversions, and really we're going to end up on a date next Friday night, like normal people.

We're not normal people. I know we're not, because when I go the stationery cupboard to get something perfectly acceptable, like a fresh new ream of paper, he's in there too. And after I realise this fact, I don't quite know what I should do.

Go back out again? I can't go back out again. It will look obvious and weird and like he's won, somehow, though I've no idea when I started keeping score. And I can't stay, either, because in here there's no desk between us. There's nothing in the way, and no time limit like there was in the elevator, and even after I've told him that I just need something from the shelf behind him nothing gets better.

The space we're in is just too small for things to get better. He seems like a giant, stood amongst the Tippex and the Post-It pads, and when he turns every part of his body brushes every part of my body. I don't have to step away from the door to have it happen. He's just so immense that it occurs all on its own – or at least I think so, until he quite abruptly bends down to get the paper.

And then I stop thinking all together, about anything that even loosely resembles logic.

It's the way he does it, that's the thing. He doesn't bend

down the way normal men bend down when they need to get something. He bends down as though the only working joints in his body are in his hips, and everything else just has to stay exactly where it is. Even if this means that he has to take up a *lot* of space when he does it. And by a lot of space, I mean he bends over and then quite suddenly my back is against the door, while his absolutely gorgeous and frankly scantily clad ass almost pushes right into me.

Of course, rationally I know that his ass isn't really scantily clad. He's wearing perfectly acceptable trousers, truly he is. I keep calling them thin and crappy, but that's probably just because of the enormous erection he keeps sporting. I'm sure such a thing would make corduroy seem flimsy.

No, no. The trousers are fine. It's just my dirty mind. It's just this urge I suddenly have to reach one hand out and run it over the perfect curve of his tight little ass. Or maybe … maybe do more than that. Because I'm pretty sure that's what he's suggesting, as he takes an absolute age to find something that's *right fucking there*.

I can see it from where I'm standing, so God knows he should be able to. In fact I think he's got his hand on it right now, as he takes a step back and that solid curve gets much, much too close to me. So close that I almost say something, so close that I nearly break the game and tell him don't. Stop.

I can't take this much pressure, I really can't. His ass is in my lap, for God's sake, and after another second of this unbearably tense and completely ridiculous stand-off, it *is* in my lap. I can feel him just sort of … urging himself back against me, as though he wants me to fuck him with the cock I don't have. As though he's some heated, delirious animal, just waiting to be mounted.

And ohhh, that thought. I don't know why it does the

things it does to me. All I know is that I have to touch him, I have to. I don't care about the line or the notebook with the little mark in it or anything, anything at all. I just want to touch him in some unfathomably rude way, and dear God I do.

I don't stick with something safe and obvious, like maybe a little love tap on his upturned ass. I grasp him, hard, like I'm getting a fistful of him. Fingers curling just under the left cheek of his perfect ass, palm flat and firm to the meat of him. And when he gasps I squeeze so fiercely, like a man groping some sweet little secretary against her will.

Though even that isn't enough. Once I've done it I can feel something incendiary, something that explains why his trousers seem so thin. He isn't wearing any underwear – just as I had suspected the other day – and the knowledge makes me slide my hand down, down until I'm almost between his legs.

In fact, if he was a woman I'd be able to feel his cunt now through that material. But as it is I make do with the hint of his tightly clenched arsehole and that soft strip of skin just before his balls, as I grope him with something like greed running through me – as I lose my mind entirely, and press my thumb right between the cheeks of his arse.

'You like that, slut?' I say to him, but he doesn't answer in words. He ruts right back against my squirming, pressing hand, a long, low groan spilling out of him as he does so. And when I rub more firmly, right over that sensitive place, his groan gets louder. More desperate, I think, and naturally I know why.

If I keep doing this, eventually he'll come. I'm not sure if the right word is *eventually*, in truth, because the second I press down his entire body jerks forward.

'No, not like that,' he tells me, but how many times

did I say the same to Woods? Even if I didn't have that memory in me I'd know what he really means, and said knowledge just makes me work him harder. It makes me stroke closer to his balls, which feel tense and tight and too drawn up.

And when I do he tells me what I already understand.

'Please – I can't hold off. I'm too close,' he says, and I think of all the times those words have left me so disappointed. All the frantic bouts of sex, ended minutes too early with that exact phrase on someone else's lips.

I can't hold off, I think, and then something strange and new surges through me. My clit swells between the slippery lips of my sex, and that urge to push him unbearably close to the brink gets stronger, brighter. I *want* him to come all over himself, I realise. I want him to grunt and be unable to control his own reactions.

And I want him to do it right now, as I stroke some little near-innocuous part of him in a stationery cupboard.

'You remember I told you that you weren't allowed to come, don't you, Benjamin?' I ask, while this wonderful sense of duality slips over me. My body wants him to do just that more than anything, and yet the words that are coming out of me …

Is this how Woods felt? Was he filled with this need to make me give in, even as he told me not to?

'No, no,' he pants, suddenly lucid in the middle of it all. And I see why, a second later: 'You said I couldn't touch myself. You didn't say I couldn't come.'

He's right, of course. Even when he's close to spurting in his pants and so on edge his teeth are practically rattling, he's a better rule follower than I ever was. However, something does occur to me, the moment he's gotten the words out.

'So you've been cheating, then. You've been rubbing yourself off on things all this time?'

Another groan of despair comes out of him – longer, and higher on the end of it. Those hips of his roll, though he's clearly not trying to get some extra pressure now. He's trying to get away, I can tell, and him doing so just makes me want to be meaner.

So I slide my hand all the way between his legs and get a hold of the thickly pulsing length I find there.

'Fuuuuck no, no – I haven't. I haven't cheated. I swear, I haven't consciously made myself come in fucking days and days and –'

'Consciously?'

I can't help asking it. The word just jumps out at me before he's finished babbling, like a little blue tick in the middle of a blank-paged notebook. He made his words specific, though they didn't need to be.

And now he has to answer for them.

'Ummm,' he says, like he really is thinking. He's thinking long and hard about what he could have possibly meant by that, despite the fact that it's glaringly obvious. 'I guess I uh … maybe …'

'You use far too many uhs and ums, Benjamin.'

'OK, OK,' he says, and I can almost *hear* his face scrunching up with embarrassment. 'I woke up the other night and I'd … you know. Done it all over myself.'

'Done what all over yourself?' I ask, but I'm crueller than that. I don't just force him to say the proper words, I rub the tip of my finger over the ridge around the head of his cock, as I do.

'Ohhh-ohhfuck, fuck. Uh, OK – I came on myself. I woke up and I'd had an orgasm in my sleep.'

I think he's actually trying to climb the shelving by this point. If there was a hole in the cupboard he could crawl into and through the other side to safety, I think he'd do it.

'And do you remember what you dreamt about, to make you do such a filthy thing?'

'I don't – uhhhh, Jesus, don't do that. No don't, don't – I'm really going to come.'

'If you tell me, I might stop,' I say, though of course I'm lying. His cock feels like a red-hot brand through his trousers, so heavy and swollen it'd practically be a crime not to fondle it. It's making me breathless and near to orgasm myself, just feeling him like this and hearing him stumble towards that place he got to before.

That place I like to call Extreme Frankness.

'I dreamt about your pussy, Ms Harding. I dreamt about licking your clit.'

Ohhh yes, there it is. There, there. God, I can't get enough of the way he says that last word – like it somehow has seventeen syllables, and each of them sound more filthy than the one before it.

'Is that all?' I ask, so cool and calm and collected. As though him dreaming about licking me there doesn't send a fresh burst of pleasure direct to that said same place.

'No.'

'Then tell me the rest,' I say, and when I do I pinch the head of his cock. Just to give him a little extra incentive.

'I dreamt I spurted all over my own belly and thighs, and after I'd done it you made me walk around the office, naked, with it all over me. All my own come, glistening on my bare skin.'

Jesus fucking Christ. I'm not even sure how I'm still standing, or what force is keeping my tone this steady and calm. He's close, he's really and unbelievably close – so much so that I can almost feel his orgasm rolling through the length of his heavy cock – but I'm in far more trouble than he is.

I think I'm having an orgasm already.

'And that idea excites you, does it? The idea of me forcing you to shame yourself that badly?'

'God, yeah. One orgasm wasn't enough. I wanted more as soon as I woke up.'

'You wanted to touch yourself?'

'I wanted to hump the fucking mattress.'

'Like you want to hump my hand, right now?'

'Ohhhh yeah, fuck yeah I want to do that. Are you saying I can do that?'

I haven't the faintest clue why he's asking. He's practically doing just that anyway, right now. Every time his body shifts I feel his cock stroking over my open palm, as though he's kind of pretending that what he really wants to do is get comfortable. When in actual fact he's almost jerking off into my hand.

'Do you recall what I said about restraint, Benjamin?' I ask, and he near moans some words in response

'That I have none.'

'That's right. And what happens to people who have none?'

He already knows, I can tell. I can feel it in the way he suddenly presses right into my hand, to get at those few little extra strokes that would push him over the edge. Hell, I think one stroke of my fingertip over the swollen head of his cock would do the trick, but I'm not going to give it. I can't give it yet, no matter how much I want to.

The game would be over if I did – and what then?

Does worse come, then?

'Do they get what they're wanting?' I ask, and he takes a

series of shallow, panting breaths. Tries to wrestle back some control, even as I take a step away from him.

'No.'

'So what happens to them?'

'They get punished,' he tells me, only that last word comes out thick with something it shouldn't. 'Punished' should never sound so full of desperate longing, with that little gasp right on the end of it.

But apparently when Benjamin Tate says it, it does.

'And how do you think I should punish you, Ben?' I ask, but of course I'm already doing just that. I'm fairly certain he can hear, as I ease my too-tight skirt over my stocking-clad thighs. And the second I slip a hand between my legs – the very second that I do it – his whole body jerks.

As though I touched him, instead of me.

'Oh God, are you masturbating?' he asks, but here's the delicious part: he doesn't turn around to check. He just carries right on clinging to that shelving, hips bumping forward like he's pushing into a cunt that isn't there. Body trembling minutely all over as he listens and listens and listens to the lewd sounds I'm making.

And by God, are they ever lewd. It's just such a small space, that's the problem. The moment I do the tiniest, most innocuous of things – like, say, circling my pouty swollen sex-lips with the very tip of my finger – he can hear it. I can hear it. It sounds like someone slicking themselves all over with a quart of baby oil.

And it gets worse, the longer I do this. The more I work my finger through my slippery folds, until I'm almost but not quite rubbing my stiff little clit.

'Ohhh you're definitely masturbating. Can I ... can I watch?' he asks, as though I'm not being cruel at all. I'm not withholding something from him by taking this step back and putting a hand between my legs. I'm giving him something instead, something I can barely fathom until I let him turn around. After which it's obvious – it's all over his face.

I'm giving him the sight of my fingers working under the almost cover of my skirt. And despite the fact that he can barely see anything at all, his eyes never leave that moving shape. He just keeps watching as I furtively touch myself, that gaze of his like a second hand between my legs.

Though I can hardly blame him for it. I do exactly the same thing when he's finally stood before me, face so flushed it's almost burgundy, that thick shape making a fist in his trousers.

And all of this is before I get to the best part – the one I could just about feel through that material. He's made a little shadow of wetness, just to the left of his zipper. He's actually leaked through the material to the point where I can see it, even in the dim light of the stationery cupboard.

'Oh that's so …' he says, but of course he can't finish. If he found the word that went on the end of that sentence – lewd or wicked or something sweeter, like inviting – I think he'd have to give in. I don't think he could stop himself touching me, and Lord knows I wouldn't be able to do the honours in his absence.

If he reached out, right now, I wouldn't be able to be the Boss I'm turning into. I'd just let him slip his fingers through my soaked folds to find that oh so empty place and sink inside. And once he'd done it, once I'd let him take that step … there'd be no going back. I can almost feel the chain reaction that would happen because of it: his mouth suddenly on mine, frantic and sloppy. Those big, strong fingers of his pumping in and out of my greedy cunt.

And then his cock to finish with. That thick, heavy shape just ever so slowly easing into me – or maybe it wouldn't be slow at all. Maybe he'd just push and tug all his clothes aside then fuck into me without a hint of preamble. Hands on my ass, my legs around his waist … ohhhh.

'God, yes, I'm coming,' I tell him, though naturally I don't mean to. I wanted to be still and silent, as emotionless as Woods – but apparently I'm not any of those things when orgasm overtakes me. I'm just this flushed, frantic mess, fingers busy on my swelling clit, chasing and chasing after those waves of pleasure.

Though of course once I'm done I'm embarrassed. It's not embarrassment, really – it's like the low feeling instead, only in reverse. I'm just stood against the door, hand all sticky and face as hot as ever I've felt it, waiting for him to tell me something awkward. He'll say what I said to Woods: *well, I'd better get back to work.*

And when he doesn't, I'll be honest. I don't know whether that's better or worse. I only know this: that I *want* to be better. I want to be smoother, calmer, more in control, no matter how bright his eyes are when he looks at me.

In fact, those bright eyes are the very thing that makes me turn and walk right out of the cupboard, without a single word offered in his direction.

Chapter Six

He doesn't look at me when I walk into the room, which I should really take as a bad sign. He always looks at me when I walk into rooms, even if I'm doing my best not to look at him. In the elevator this morning he'd practically pressed his gaze right up against the side of my face again, but somehow here, now, he's not?

Of course, it could be that he's finally getting some control of himself. Maybe he understands now that there are lines and boundaries and things he's forbidden, and is going to behave accordingly. He's going to be the way I was whenever I saw Woods in a professional capacity. I used to simply sit in these meetings and focus on something ever so slightly to the left of his head, as though he didn't exist.

And for a long moment I'm sure that's what Benjamin's doing. He has found a spot he can safely stare at, without getting stiff or needing to squirm or beg. He's a model student already, before we've done anything at all.

I mean, what's a little masturbation in a stationery cupboard, really? It's not much, is it? And if part of me kind of believes it is and doesn't really want to stop thinking about it, well … that's fine. I can cope. As long as it doesn't show on my face as I give this presentation, I can cope.

Though naturally I can hardly keep it off my face, the second I get to page two on the PowerPoint project Benjamin has so diligently put together. Diligent isn't the wrong word, exactly, because I can tell without any sort of close examination that a lot of effort has gone into this.

It's practically a work of art. Every inch of it carefully planned – the first page clean and crisp and concise, so that I wouldn't stop when I first brought it up on the laptop and tell everyone something blustery and casual like 'It looks like the presentation has a fault. Let's just sit around and have a chat instead.'

And then the second page … oh, the second page. I didn't even know you could get a sparkly pink font to headline your neat little PowerPoint page. I had no idea there was an option to insert rows of dancing teddy bears around the text.

But apparently Benjamin Tate did.

'Cute, Harding,' Anderson laughs, only I don't hear him. I should, I really should, but the trouble is, it's hard to listen to anything beyond the sound of that veil falling over me. The one that used to signify all the things I was going to let Woods do to me, but now means something else instead.

It means everyone has to leave, now, and if I say something strange to make that happen, well, what does that matter? He's done more than write me a terrible letter or wear a T-shirt with a stain on it now.

He's given me the green light to be very, very bad indeed.

'Well, it seems I'm going to have to re-schedule the meeting for tomorrow,' I tell them all, and though they grumble and some of them are still laughing about the teddies and so forth, they go. Of course they do.

I'm in charge. I'm so in charge that I've reached a higher

plane of being-in-charged-ness, in which my body does things independently of me, like locking the meeting room door behind the last person. And once I've made that move, once I've gone that far, it doesn't seem like anything to take another step after it.

'Do you see where I was just standing, Benjamin?' I ask, in a voice that is not my own. It's this other person's voice, the one who locked the door a second ago and is now closing all of the blinds on the glass wall beside it.

'Uh … yeah. I think I can figure that one out,' he says, so big and bright and gauche, despite the thing he's just done. Though of course I realise now that it's partly a role he's playing – it's partly a game.

He's my big, dumb tons of fun. And I am his corrections officer.

'Go stand there,' I say, and though I don't turn from the window I'm not looking through, I know he obeys. I can hear his big feet on the carpet, can feel the shift in the room. He's not quite being coy any more – his breathing has changed. Now it's tense, anticipatory. Like my own.

'Okaaaay,' he says, in a way that suggests I've gone just a little bit mad. But somehow, him behaving like that just makes it sweeter. It makes it better than it was in the stationery cupboard, better than it was when I put my heel to his chest.

That note of confusion sends a lick of pleasure direct to my sex.

'Now bend over the table.'

'Sir, I –'

'Bend over the table, Benjamin. I don't know why you need me to tell you twice, I really don't. It's tiresome.'

It isn't tiresome at all, in truth. But if I said it was all of the things it really feels like – thrilling, arousing, intense – it would almost certainly lose some of those words. I'd be just as giddy as he seems when I glance at him over my shoulder, instead of how I know I must appear.

Bored, I think. Near indifferent. Not in the least bit thrilled to see him considering the table in front of him.

'Go on,' I say, and then I have the privilege of watching all the air rush right out of his body. I get to see his eyes drifting closed in that heavy, syrupy way they so often do, just before he actually obeys me.

He bends over the table like he's got no choice at all about it, those big hands sweeping over the varnished wood as he does so. Of course the movement makes me think of my own hands, and the way I liked to place them – but Benjamin is different. He doesn't keep some kind of order, or make a pattern on the table with them.

He strokes whatever he finds instead. He rubs it, as though just bending over isn't enough on its own. Savouring every ounce of the experience ... that's what he wants and needs.

And I can't fault him for that. I want to remember everything about right now, too – for later, when I'm alone and closed in by the cool walls of my pristine apartment. I want to be able to picture the way his shirt is untucked at the back, and how he has to sort of bend his legs just a little, to make his body fit into the position I'm clearly asking for.

He's too big for the table, I think. He's so big that he seems to almost swallow the wood whole, those broad shoulders nearly touching the oval edges. Hands like dinner plates, the firm arch of his perfect ass just *begging* me to do something bad, before I've even considered it.

Though I consider it now all right.

'Did I tell you to bend over with your trousers on, Benjamin?' I ask, and I know it's unkind of me. I mean, as

92

good as he is he can't be expected to mind-read my demands – and yet somehow I'm still suggesting as much. And when he just groans and shifts on the table, mouth almost parted against the wood as though he desperately wants to do something insane, like kiss it, I clarify for him. 'Take them off.'

'No nono. I can't do that. I can't do that – what if someone walks in?'

Of course, I know he heard me lock the door. But that's what makes him amazing, isn't it? That's what makes me weak from the waist down.

'Well, I suppose you'll just have to lie there like a whore if they do. Maybe I'll let them have a go at your ass, if you're really so eager for some punishment.'

'Ohhhh God, don't say that, don't say that, Ms Harding.'

'Why not? You did make a mess of this presentation on purpose, didn't you? You've done all of this so I'll do more than just briefly fondle you in the stationery cupboard, correct?'

He grits his teeth.

'Yes.'

'So what did you expect exactly? That I'd chastise you with a nice, friendly blowjob?'

'Please don't let anyone fuck my ass,' he says, which is startling for two reasons. One: it doesn't sound as though he's begging me not to at all. In fact, it almost comes out like a parody of a plea, all too breathy and kind of giddy. And two …

'I didn't say fuck, Benjamin. Read it back to me: what did I say?'

'Ohhhh Geez, I don't know. I can barely remember my own name right now. My cock's so hard I think I could get myself off on the edge of the table.'

93

'That's very, very dirty, Ben. And completely not what I asked for.'

'OK ... uh ... you said ... you said something like 'have at it' or 'do something to it' or fuck, *fuck*.'

He squirms harder against the varnished wood, but he's not doing the thing he suggested he could, I know. His back has this delightful curve to it and his ass is almost entirely in the air, and it's obvious why. He wants to keep his cock away from temptation – or in this case, the edge of the table.

'I said I would let someone have a go at your ass, but that could mean just about anything really. Don't you think?'

'Yeah, yeah,' he pants, and then I don't have to do what I was intending next. I don't have to demand he lists the possibilities, because before I've gotten the words out he just goes right ahead and does it for me. 'You could do that thing we talked about – you could lick me there. Or you could fuck me with your fingers or use something on me, something stiff and hard, like –'

'Like a cock?'

'Uhhh yeah. God, yeah. Just do whatever to me. Just do it, I don't care.'

'I will, the moment you do as you're told,' I say, and this time he obeys. He gets his hands beneath himself, starts unbuckling and unzipping in a manner I can only label *desperate*. Strips down to the smooth and completely bare curve of his perfect ass, without the smallest hint of complaint.

Though I think he might feel differently in a second.

'No underwear, Benjamin?' I ask, despite the fact that I've known this all along. How could anyone *fail* to know it? Even when he's soft you can see a shadow of his cock through those flimsy trousers – like he's just waiting for someone to reach out and grab it.

'Sorry. Do you want me to? In the future, I mean?'

I think about him parading around for me in some split-fronted scrap of silk. Everything lewd and on display, though that's exactly the way he is all the time. I've already got him like that, walking around the office with that big dick swinging around inside his trousers.

So what do I want now?

'No,' I say, as I ready the thin strip of metal that's somehow found its way into my hand. 'I want you to *behave*.'

And then I just bring it down in one quick motion, right across the smooth, honeyed expanse of his upturned ass.

Of course, I've no idea if that's how you're supposed to do it. I don't know if a strike like that will prove itself too much the second it's connected with his suddenly very tender-looking flesh. But once I've done it, and the mark is there like those stripes on that girl's back, I can't feel bad.

He doesn't want me to feel bad, apparently. He just wants to make a sound – hard and gasping and near breathless – before following it with such sweet, sweet words.

'Oh, *Ms Harding*,' he says, like his voice is melting. Like I just licked the tip of his cock instead of what I actually did: gave him a mark he'll probably have for the rest of the week. And when I do it again … oh Lord.

He'll definitely have that one for the rest of the week. He might even have it for the rest of the month, because the second it stripes him he makes a sound somewhere beyond a shaky moan of my name. This time he hisses in a breath over his teeth, and for a moment I'm sure I've gone too far. I'm sure I have.

Until he tells me otherwise, of course.

'Ohhhhh God. Oh God yeah, show me, show me.'

'What do you want me to show you, Benjamin?' I ask,

but I don't wait for an answer. I bring the metal down again, right in the middle of the words he's trying to get out.

'Sho-how me I'm bad. Show me I'm … oh Christ.'

'And what did you do that was so bad?' I ask.

'I made you –' he starts, then finishes just as I give him another stripe '– a really bad presentation.'

'And why did you do that?' I ask, only this time I keep going through all of it. I keep up the pace, stroking fast and hard over his now glowing skin. And when he responds, he's different too. His voice is more than up and down now – it's practically syrup, flowing drunkenly out of vocal cords that clearly don't want to work.

While his big, gorgeous body squirms around on the table. He's almost got his fingers in his mouth, I notice, though I don't think he's doing it to keep his own noise to a minimum. He's doing it for the feel, that slick feel of saliva on the sensitive webbing between each one, that feel of his slippery tongue working and working over something.

As the metal comes down for the tenth time.

'Because … because I want you … I want you …' he murmurs, and I'm sure he's trying to put something else on the end of it. I'm sure he is, something like *I want you to hit me so hard I scream*. But the thing is, as it stands … it sounds like something else altogether.

And that thought forces me to do it harder. Be meaner. Crack the metal down on the backs of his thighs until he jerks forward and tells me no. He actually tells me no, in the exact way I'd imagined him doing in all of my worst nightmares of this going badly.

Only with a different ending.

'Ohhhh my God I think I'm gonna come,' he tells me, and then I'm the one who's left with a pulsing ache between their legs. I'm the one who has to control their breathing and their utter eagerness to lash someone with a little metal pointer until they actually climax all over themselves.

I'll be honest: I hadn't realised that was a possibility. I mean, he looks that way. He's writhing and squirming around in a manner I've never quite seen another man do, and every now and then he seems to sort of ... surge forward. As though he's thinking of that imaginary woman again, and of fucking right into her tight, wet pussy.

But none of it really computes, until he says. And after he has, I'm just left thinking about the things he's doing. About the pussy that isn't there, and how it could well be *my* pussy he's thinking about. He wouldn't have to strain very hard to imagine it, in truth, because unless he's dead inside he has to know how aroused I am.

I'm shaking. I'm shaking and I can't bring the pointer down on his now viciously red ass, because if I do he might come. He keeps promising me he will and every time he does I feel the same way: like it's some piece of punctuation at the end of our sentence, and once it's there we can't go back.

There's no going back from someone doing it all over themselves because you spanked them.

'You're going to come just because I'm branding your ass?' I say, and I'm impressed with myself, really I am. I sound so disgusted, so incredulous, but here's the problem – he doesn't feel any of it. He's not in the least bit ashamed.

'If you keep doing it, yeah. I will.'

'So if I just tap you like this ...'

I do so, soft as a whisper. Almost like a little stroke over the practically humming marks all over his ass.

'No – like before. If you do it like before,' he says, but I have to note that he still jerks forward when I trail the tip of the pointer over the meanest mark. The one that looks almost like a lash or a burn, faint and white in the centre and then ebbing out to a beautiful dark pink.

'Like this?' I ask, and this time I give him a little sting. A little flick on the end of it, that I didn't really know I was capable of until it happens. Until he hisses over his teeth again, and tells me, 'No, no, don't do it like that' in such a frantic, desperate way that I can't fail to know what he really means.

He really means, *yeah, do it exactly like that and you'll make me come*. It's almost a question, I feel, and one that I hover on the edge of answering. I hover, with that pointer poised in my hand and my body humming through and through with arousal, and ohhh God, what am I waiting for? What am I holding back for?

'Are you telling me what to do, Benjamin?' I ask, and then I just crack that metal down so *hard*. Hard enough to send the strike all the way into him and back into me, every vibration running all over erogenous zones I didn't even know I had. They're in these weird places like the backs of my knees and the soft hollows beneath my arms, and when I strike him, when he grunts and gasps and writhes for me, they all wake up and take notice.

'No, no – God, I swear, I just … oh God, it doesn't feel anything like I thought it would.'

'And how does it feel?'

'Amazing. Amazing. My cock's so hard, seriously – can I just … I just need to …' he says, but he doesn't wait for an answer. He doesn't wait for permission. He just slides his hand under his body and though I can barely see a thing I know what he's doing.

I know as though we're still connected, through the marks I've made all over him.

He's trying to hold off his orgasm. He's trying to get a good, tight grip on himself, so that when I crack the metal down again he doesn't go off like a rocket – I'm certain of it. But of course, I don't *act* like I'm certain of it.

'Get your hand away from yourself, you filthy little slut,' I tell him. And then I crack the metal down again, just for good measure. I do it, and I do it hard, but I suppose the problem is that it's not really a punishment at all. It can't be a punishment when someone seems to enjoy it so much.

'Oh yeah, just like that. Make it sting like that – fuck that's good. I can't tell if it's pleasure or pain any more.'

'Because you're a slut?' I ask, though I swear I only do it for want of something to say. I'm adrift again, lost on a tide of him and his craziness, and he doesn't make it any easier the longer this goes on. In fact, he seems to get surer in it. More wanton.

'Yeah, yeah. I'm such a slut – seriously, you wouldn't believe how hard my cock is. Ohhh and it's all slippery, too … I've made such a mess …'

I'm going to make a mess soon. I'm only surprised there isn't a puddle on the floor already.

'What a dirty mouth you have,' I tell him, but it's me who keeps striping him with this metal. I'm the one who keeps winding him up until he's telling me things that shouldn't be exciting – because really, they aren't. It's not exciting when someone makes a mess or can't control themselves.

Even if it absolutely is.

'Stop me,' he says. 'Stop me.'

Which could mean just about anything. It could mean he wants me to cease this little production and let him stand up and be respectable and put all of his clothes back on. It could. But somehow I know it doesn't.

He means: *Stop me from masturbating.*

And ohh Lord that's exactly what he's started doing. I don't have to see it. I can hear it, because apparently he's as slippery and messy as he claimed only a moment ago. And though I don't think he's going at it hard exactly – his arm isn't moving in that familiar rhythm, and he's not quite going crazy with it, not yet – it's having the desired effect.

'I'm so close. Just a couple more strokes and I'm going to do it,' he warns me, in a way that suggests he knows I'll have to do something about it. He's my plaything. I'm his Boss.

'Put your hand on the table, Benjamin,' I tell him, but this time I don't punctuate it with a crack from the pointer. I go one worse than that – or at least, I go one worse for me. He seems to enjoy it thoroughly, as my stomach churns and the feel of him shoots up through my body like an electric charge.

It's not the same to spank someone with a piece of metal as it is to spank them with your hand. Too many things get in the way – the heat of his body sizzling into my palm. The brief feel of those strange ridges I've made all over his skin.

And finally him asking, all lust-shocked and frantic.

'Are you touching me, Ms Harding?' he asks, as though he'd somehow never imagined that could be a possibility. Through material, yes. With metal, yes. But never skin to skin like this, and so visceral that for a second I just want to spread my entire body over his.

Instead I dig my nails into his firm, glorious flesh, hard, and then I watch as he slaps that one filthy hand back onto the table, just like I told him to. And though I know that should be confusing – why obey for this, and not the metal? – I understand the reason for it.

If he does what I've demanded, maybe I'll continue.

'You like that, huh?' I ask, but again I don't wait for an answer. I just dig my nails in harder until he turns his face on the table. Presses his cheek to the wood, those gorgeous eyes of his almost closed, almost.

But not quite. I can see him sort of looking at me through the slits those sooty eyelashes have made. And I can see a lot of other arousing things, too, like that close-to-orgasm flush that's all over his lovely face, and right down over his throat. Like the way his mouth looks near-fucked, as though there's some invisible person in here with us and a moment ago he had his cock stuffed down Benjamin's throat.

And of course all of this gets hotter and sweeter the harder I dig my nails in. He rocks his hips to feel it, near rubbing his ass against the press of my fingers. And when he catches it just right, when those burning hot ridges run beneath the scrape of my nails, he tells me almost matter-of-factly:

'I'm really going to come now – I can't help it. I've been on the edge too long.'

Though it doesn't really happen as calmly as those words suggest. His eyes squeeze tight shut after one more long-drawn-out scratch down over the marks on his ass, and his body jerks forward hard enough to jam him up against the edge of the table.

But it's his hands I notice the most. One almost claws at the table as the sensation pours through him, and the other goes beneath his body, to stroke and jerk his cock through what seems to be a gloriously protracted orgasm. I'm not sure how long it goes on for to be honest, because after what seems like an hour he makes the first sound he's made since it started – a guttural gasp that almost forces me to put a hand over my swollen mound.

Almost, I think, *almost*, as he grunts again and rubs at himself frantically, body bowing under the pressure. Those sounds turning to words, as whatever this is proves too much.

'Hurt me again,' he groans. 'Make me feel it.'

But I don't know what he means. Is it the pain he wants to feel, or the pleasure surrounding it? Is that how it works? If I dig my nails in again, will it force his orgasm into some kind of stark relief?

I think of the way it had felt for me, to have someone strike me right in the middle of something so sweet – and then I just do it. I bring my hand down again, sharp and firm, and he rewards me with more words half-groaned with pleasure.

'Oh, Ms Harding, you're so good to me,' he says, as those slick sounds between his legs get louder, ruder, and I'm forced to imagine how it all looks. Disgusting, I think, all thick and sticky all over his hand.

And all over other places, too, apparently.

'Fuck. Fuck. I'm getting it on the carpet.'

I honestly don't know if he says these things in all innocence to himself, or if he's actually saying them for my insane benefit. I really don't, at this point. Because although I know it shouldn't arouse me, to think of him spurting so copiously that it's making a mess all over things, I can't seem to help it.

I put words in there like *disgusting* and *filthy animal*, but they just seem to make things worse. My clit actually jerks and swells when he tells me that it's running down his arm and making a stain on his shirt cuff.

If there is one, I'm going to make him leave it there.

'Are you done?' I ask, but really I don't have to. It's obvious he's done. His legs aren't holding him up any more – he's practically lying on the table, like a wet dishrag – and the desperate expression on his face has folded down into nothing. Now it's just this lax, near-exhausted sort of thing, that faint little smile the only suggestion he's still conscious.

And if all of that makes me want to do something very stupid, like stroke his hair and pet him softly, well. We just won't go into that.

'Stand up, Benjamin,' I say, though it makes no sense that I do. If he stands up, I'm going to see everything, aren't I? I'll see his fat and probably still pretty hard cock, come glistening at the tip. I'll see how dishevelled he looks, right up close and in my face.

I don't know how I'm going to get through it, I really don't. And yet I still whip him with the tip of the pointer, when he moans that he's trying, he's trying, and how bad would it be if he just went to sleep right now?

Bad, I think. As bad as spanking someone until they climax in the middle of a work day.

'Oh God, don't do – OK. OK, sorry. Sorry, I'm getting up,' he says, but I can't be thankful for the way he keeps his body faced away from me as he wrestles with his clothes and gets everything fastened up before turning.

Instead I'm just filled with a kind of disappointment I shouldn't be feeling. I mean, it's not like I *wanted* to make things worse. It's not like I *wanted* to see how he looks after he's just been fucked.

Right?

'You ... uh ... don't have a tissue do you?' he asks, while I absolutely refuse to look at his flushed, pleasure-stuffed expression. Even if that means I end up staring at the glossy mess all over his right hand instead.

You know. The one he practically shoves right in my face.

I eye it with something like disdain, though of course disdain isn't exactly what I'm feeling. I'm feeling something that makes me flick my gaze back up to him, as dark and deadly as ever I've felt it. And then once I've got it there, levelled on him, my mouth moves around words I didn't know I was capable of saying.

I'm *not* capable of saying them. It's this arousal thrumming through me. It's built a whole new person inside my body, one who speaks with my voice and looks with my eyes, but isn't me at all.

'Lick it off,' I tell him, and then I just let the words hang there as they dawn over his oh so open face.

'What? You can't be serious. You want me to …' he says, but once he's left it trailing, I don't feel any need to respond. I just stand there, staring at him, fuelled by the almost vicious ache that's swallowing my sex whole.

Until he does what I've told him to.

Slow, he does it, slow, and like he's still completely unsure about doing something as lewd as tasting his own come. But then after a moment something shifts, and those foggy eyes of his hold mine as he strokes his tongue over his fingers. As he licks, long and wet and rude, between each one.

Before finally doing the thing I realise I'm wanting most of all.

I want him to suck one of those long, thick fingers into his mouth, and when he actually does it I waver. I know I do. I can feel the longing on my own face, and that pulse beating so hard between my own legs I can practically hear it in my head.

'You dirty boy,' I tell him, but that's not what I mean. More than anything I want to give him the truth: that this is the sexiest, weirdest, most terrifying thing I've ever been a part of.

And that his mouth is so perfect I want to fuck it 'til he cries.

But instead I just watch as he practically rubs the palm of his hand with his tongue.

'You can go, Benjamin,' I say, but I think he knows now what I really mean. After he's dropped that hand down by his side he says, as though somehow he's sort of – ... I don't know – worried about me:

'Don't you want me to do something to you?'

Oh God, I wish I didn't want him to do something to me.

'You're shaking.'

I also wish he wasn't aware of facts like that.

'Just let me do something ... let me lick your clit. I swear, I'm good at it.'

'You can go, Benjamin,' I say again, because I'm really not capable of more. If I go for more I'm going to break down, and that's not the way this is supposed to go. I'm not supposed to lose control the way I did in the stationery cupboard.

The way Woods did.

'Well, OK,' he says, in the exact manner that people use when talking about a crisis the other person doesn't want to talk about. *If you're sure* ... I think, but unfortunately I do it just before he leans down towards me.

And then the question is left hanging in my head as his perfect, soft mouth presses with exquisite gentleness against mine.

I taste his come. Of course I do. He kisses me when my lips are parted, and even if he hadn't timed it right I feel his tongue, flickering just ever so slightly between. Like he wants me to know what he's just been licking off his own fingers, and once I do ... once I do I'll grab him. I'll fuck him, right here on this table.

So I suppose it's a surprise to both of us when I clasp

his chin in my hand instead. Hold him there, like that, as I murmur against his delicious mouth:

'If you don't go now, I'll never do this again.'

And then of course he obeys. Of course he does. But that's not really the problem, is it? The problem is that I said those threatening things, and they made him fearful and had the right effect and so on and so forth.

But they also included the word *again*.

Chapter Seven

I intend to be normal, I think, when he walks into my office. But of course the issue is: I'm only *imagining* that's what I'm intending. I can't say for sure, and I definitely can't say for sure when he goes to sit down in the chair I'm indicating.

I told him I wanted something innocuous from him, like a bit of simple dictation. He has the pen and paper in his hands ready to do it. But the second he goes to take his seat something happens, and then we're just right back to where we were in the meeting room two days ago.

He can't sit down. He tries, God knows he does. I see him sort of turn sideways a little, as though maybe he can avoid the feel of the chair against his obviously sore ass if he just gets his body into the right position.

None of it works, however. He gets about halfway into the chair before letting a little wince out, because apparently even the feel of his trousers pulling against his marked flesh is too much.

Hell, it's too much for me and I'm all the way over here.

'Is there something wrong, Benjamin?' I ask, and I can see it on his face. He has absolutely no clue how to answer. He isn't even sure if we're talking about this thing between us, I know, but that's OK. I don't know what I'm talking about either.

I'm too busy hearing the word *again* running through my head over and over, as though I've suddenly become an impatient child, demanding their favourite ride.

'No, I'm fine,' he says, but it's really unfortunate that as he does so, he also sort of shifts in his chair. And of course the minute he tries his eyeballs nearly pop out of his head. Perspiration suddenly dots his hairline. His hands don't seem to know what to do with themselves, but they're not the only ones.

I don't know what to do with myself either. Two feelings immediately bloom inside me when I see just how much pain he's in: a kind of twisted arousal that I automatically want to kick under a chair somewhere, and even more horrible … the need to care for him. I actually feel it – it's really there. I want to get up and go to him and do something impossibly sappy and stupid, like stroke his gorgeous hair. I mean, I knew I was a lost cause before all of this, but really.

'Really? Because you don't seem fine,' I say, and I try to make it as cruel as I can, really I do. I try not to think about his bright, eager eyes, or the way that he smiles sometimes – as though his heart is full of that thing and it's all for me.

Instead, I keep the pressure on.

'It almost looks as though you're in some sort of pain …' I say, but he holds it in well. He sits almost completely sideways on, hands so tight around the pad in his hand I can see white around the knuckle.

'No, really. I'm totally awesome.'

He's gritting his teeth, I can tell – and it makes me wonder why. Does he think I'm going to do it again if he lets something show? Or is it the other way around? Maybe he thinks

I'll *never* do it again if he lets something show.

It's like a test, I think, of his bravery. But oh, he doesn't need to prove a single thing to me. I know he's brave already, because two days ago he leant down and pressed his mouth to mine.

That in itself is a major achievement. After all, my strongest urge was to punch him after he'd done it.

'Are you sure? Because you know, you can tell me. If you're hurting.'

I think I really mean it this time, which is also bad. As bad as me putting my hands between my legs just thinking about his tongue flickering over the soft underside of my upper lip.

'No, *really* –'

'I mean, I would hate to think that you were suffering unnecessarily ...'

'Honestly, I –'

'Going through some sort of agony while I sit here perfectly –'

This time he doesn't wait for me to finish trailing off wistfully into some sentiment I actually probably really mean. He cuts me off, loud and sure and frantic, suddenly, and when he does he shifts in the chair. He presses his ass right to the seat and tells me clear: 'I *like* it. OK? I like it. I like feeling the pain for days afterwards, because then I know it actually happened.'

I've never seen him look so certain about anything, and it briefly makes him a different person. A bigger person, a surer person – one who knows exactly what he wants, and isn't afraid to ask for it.

Which of course just makes me think of all the things I'm afraid to ask for. I can't even say anything to him, as I stand briskly and walk to the door. And though I know how it must look – I know how crisply I snap my little jacket down; how firmly I plant each heel into the soft carpet – I don't feel that way inside.

I feel the way he looks, most of the rest of the time. I'm the reverse of him. I pretend to be hard and cool, but really I'm bright-eyed and giddy and ready to play new games.

'Uh, sir ...' he starts, because of course he knows what the door being locked means. 'I know I just said I liked it, but seriously. I don't think I could take another round just yet. Is that OK to say? I mean –'

'Drop your trousers,' I say, but I don't turn and face him when I do it. I speak into the cool wood of the door, while my hand tightens and tightens on the handle. I wait for him to refuse.

But of course he doesn't.

'OK,' he says, voice so ridiculously eager and compliant that it's almost like he'd never protested at all. I can hear him undoing that stupid belt he's worn today – with the mushroom from Super Mario Bros. on the buckle – and unzipping those flimsy trousers, before I've dared to do what I most want to.

I want to look, I realise. I'm fed up with beneath the table and under clothing. I want to see what he looks like bare, but by the time I've forced myself to swivel he has his back to me.

'Did you want me to stand like this?' he asks, when I don't immediately say anything. But really he should understand: it's because I *can't* say anything. I'm just staring at the shape he's made for me over my desk. Hands planted on the wood, naturally. Those long, strong legs spread, as though he's not six foot seven hundred and eight.

He's like me a few weeks ago – only I never asked questions like that one, and I never looked over my shoulder the way he's looking at me. He's almost raising one eyebrow, I think, and if his lips were parted I know what I'd see: his tongue curling up to touch his teeth.

'You should really learn to wait for my commands,' I tell him, but I almost lose the words on their way out. As it is, I barely hear him answering me with things like 'oh, sorry, do you want me to go back to where I was?', because as he's talking my gaze drifts down, down. And finds the gridlock I made of his ass.

'Stay there,' I say, though of course I only do it so I can get a long, long look at those marks. Some of them still red, some of them just a faint impression of the bad thing I did. All of them criss-crossing together in a way I never deliberately intended.

I thought I'd just done it in a big blurt, randomly. But now I can see that the whole thing is as ordered as me, each line meeting at some point in the middle. Each one firm, sure, straight. Nothing veering off wildly.

'Well. Doesn't that look pretty?' I say, and after it's out I kind of hate myself. The word 'pretty' is just too much, even if Benjamin doesn't seem to think so in the slightest.

'I know, right?' he bursts out, as giddy as a schoolboy. I can picture the expression on his face, despite the fact that he's turned away from me: big-eyed and big-mouthed and bright as a new penny. 'I've checked myself out in the mirror like a *hundred* times.'

'You have?'

'Totally,' he says, and then he pauses, and twists himself a little, so that he can do something I don't want him to do. I don't want him to stroke a finger over one of those mean, red lines, while telling me: 'This one's my favourite.'

'You have a favourite?'

That fond look leaves his face, and is replaced by an ever so slightly anxious one that he levels at me over his shoulder. I notice, however, that he doesn't stop touching the red line.

'Is that weird?'

My mind floods with the image of him naked, probably fresh from the shower. Water trailing down over his delicious, honey-coloured skin as he twists and turns and tries to get a better view of what I've done to him in a full-length mirror.

I can picture his expression: ever so slightly heated, with a side of open-mouthed curiosity.

'Very. I just don't know what I'm going to do with you, Benjamin,' I say. I tut as I make my way back to my desk, as though I'm not resisting the urge to look at his cock at all. I'm just going to one of my drawers, to get something specific. 'I mean, you've barely even taken care of yourself. Is that what I'm dealing with here? Someone who can't take care of themselves?'

He frowns delicately, for just a moment, then seems to fathom what I'm talking about.

'No, no – I can. I mean, I know I should have probably put something on it. But it's like I said – I like to feel it. I prefer to just ... feel it.'

He makes a little fist for extra emphasis, though of course the moment he does so my gaze just has to flick down. Of course it does. I'm a diligent student of his every little tic and gesture. It's important that I take in this one.

And if I should happen to give his cock a long and assessing look while I'm down there, well ... sue me. It deserves a long and assessing look, even if Benjamin doesn't seem to think so. He just waits and waits patiently while I indulge an urge I've never actually been able to before – to just look at a man, in the rudest way possible and without a lick of apology – before finally breaking.

'Do you want me to put my pants back on? Some girls want me to put my pants back on.'

God, I love his matter-of-factness. I'm honestly starting to think there's no limit to the things I could make him tell me, even if the things I make him tell me are the insane opinions of his obviously mad ex-girlfriends.

'That's because some girls don't know what to do with a big, fat thing like that,' I tell him, and I mean it. I mean it, even if I'm actually one of those girls too. I've never seen a cock like his outside of porn, and the fact that it's nearly curving up to his belly doesn't help matters.

It's not even one of those big dicks that can't seem to get fully hard. He's as stiff as my back currently feels, and so slick and red at the tip that my mouth actually starts watering. Even as I'm stood there, watching, I see a thin, slick trail of pre-come make its way down over the length of his shaft, and all I can think about is licking it up.

Though of course I don't let anything like that show on my face. Instead I tell him to put his hands back on the desk, the way he had them before. And once he's done it, I force myself to walk back around the desk. I give up the sight of his cock, so thick and good and God, *God*. I bet it feels amazing, sliding in.

'Are you … uh …' he starts, and though I know I should tell him to be silent, I can't quite bring myself to do it. The problem is, I suppose, I *like* the things he says. I'm just waiting with bated breath for the next one, expecting something simple and crude such as *are you going to do something with my big fat thing, then?*

But always getting something better instead. Something

hotter, something that makes me wetter.

'Are you going to get me all slick?' he asks finally, and I know what he means. I do. He's seen the little pot of expensive lotion in my hand, and clearly guessed what I'm intending. And yet the moment he says the words, I immediately think of something else.

I think of some slut writhing around on a bed. Legs spread, pussy all open and pink and already wet. Just waiting for a man to do something lewd like poke his tongue into her soft, pink hole, until she creams all over the place for him.

That's what it sounds like when Benjamin Tate asks me if I'm going to make him slick. And I think he knows it. He looks at me over his shoulder again, that near-smile on his pretty mouth. Gaze all heavy-lidded, until I actually touch my lotion-slicked fingers to his backside.

And then he just jerks forward against the desk, hard. So hard that I think I've hurt him, until he tells me all in one big breath: 'Holy fuck that's cold.'

Of course it isn't at all. It's just that his flesh is practically on fire. I can feel it burning into my fingertips through the sheen of fifty pounds' worth of lotion, and as I stroke over him that heat gets more obvious.

As do the marks. They've almost made little ridges on his soft skin, and after a while I'm no longer thinking about what I'm doing. I'm not thinking of the fundamental filthiness of coating a man's bare ass in something slippery. I'm just thinking about the length and width and weird ruffled feel of each one of these stripes, nearly rubbing over all of them.

Until I just ever so slightly veer off course …

'Oh, wow – OK. OK. Are you really going to do that?'

He's practically up on tiptoe. I think it's safe to say I'm already doing 'that'.

'I don't know, Ben. What does it seem like I'm doing?'

'It seems like you're rubbing your slippery fingers over my asshole,' he says, and despite knowing he's typically open and honest about everything, the words still jolt me. I still have to squeeze my thighs together around the sudden and startling ache that pulses through my sex the second he jerks the words out.

'You want me to stop?' I ask, but of course I know the answer. He's practically rutting back against the press of my fingers, that deep groove between his cheeks getting slicker and slicker. And when I just rub ever so lightly over the tight knot of his arsehole, he makes a lot of words that are not words at all.

'I tell you what, Benjamin,' I say, because really it's obvious he's never going to refuse. I think he's forgotten what the word means. 'If you want me to stop, you don't have to use the word no. You can just say something else instead.'

'Oh God, like a safe word?' he moans, though I've no idea what's exciting him more – the feel of my fingertip, stroking in slow circles over his still tightly clenched arsehole, or the fact that we've gotten so far and so deep into this that we actually need devices, frameworks, promises.

'I suppose you could call it that, if you want to.'

'And if I say it, you'll stop.'

'I will.'

'But otherwise I can say no, and beg you not to, but you'll keep going? You'll keep … ohhh fuck … you'll keep doing what you're doing now?'

What I'm doing now is slowly penetrating his ass with one slick finger, but somehow I don't think he wants to go into too much detail about that. I just think he wants to work himself back on the feel of it sliding in, without really admitting that he's doing anything of the sort at all.

'I don't see why I should stop otherwise,' I say, and that much is true. It feels amazing inside the tight, slippery heat of his body. Smooth in a way I hadn't imagined at all, and so much more sensitive too. He almost jumps over the table when I rub my knuckle around that tight ring of muscle, as though there were a million nerve-endings there that I hadn't even thought about.

'OK,' he says, but he's really panting now. And he's barely pretending that he's not trying to fuck himself on my finger. 'OK, uh ... what word?'

'You think of one,' I tell him, though of course I only do so because I know how hard it's going to be for him. He's gripping the edge of the desk now, hips struggling to stay still. That tight, slick little hole clenching hard around my tormenting finger.

And yet somehow he still manages to murmur the word to me, over his shoulder.

'Woods,' he says, like it just occurred to him this very second.

Though of course I know it didn't. I can tell it didn't by the way his body goes very still all over, that voice of his suddenly less shaky than it was a moment ago. He gives me a little glimpse of his expression, as sly and soft as ever I've seen it, before facing forward again for me.

'Will that do?' he asks, while I lose my breath for just a second, before roping it back in again.

'I was going to go easy on you, you know,' I say, because I can't tell him what I want to do. I can't tell him *so you've known what I've been up to all this time*. I have to keep pace with him instead, torment for torment.

'I know,' he says, and it's the strangest thing. I can tell

he's smiling, slow and syrupy, when he says it. I can practically hear the cat-that-got-the-cream note to his voice, and
it just makes me want to be more brutal than he clearly
needs me to be.

'Did he tell you he did this to me?' I ask, because that's as
brutal as I can go. It's so brutal it kicks me in the stomach,
once it's done pushing its way out of my mouth.

'No,' he says, and for a second I'm relieved. For just a
second. 'He told me he used something, when he fucked
your ass.'

I don't know which is worse: that he's saying these things
to me, or that it only spurs me on.

'Is that what you want me to do to you?' I ask, and when
I do I fuck that one finger into him so hard it makes his knee
jerk up and knock against the desk. One of his hands skids
across the wood sending papers flying in a great, white arc.

'Oh God yeah,' he groans, but he does it louder when I
get one hand into his hair and pull, hard. Then louder again
when I do something so lewd it almost sets my cheeks alight.
I'm only glad he can't see me, because in order for this
thing to have the right effect it has to be done undercover
of shameless darkness. He has to just hear me and know
that's what I'm doing, and he does, he does.

He hears me spit between the cheeks of his ass, as though
what I really need is just a little extra down and dirty lubri-
cation. Just something to ease the way for myself, as I slide
back and forth in his suddenly tightly clenching ass.

Of course, it was tightly clenching a moment ago. It
started gripping me like a fist the moment I just sort of
worked my way inside. But the intensity of the reaction is
different this time, and I know it – before he's even said a
word, it's obvious.

117

And then he goes ahead and tells me all about it anyway, just to be clear.

'Did you really just do that? Ohhhh that's the dirtiest thing ever. Oh man, I didn't know it would feel like this.'

Strangely, it's the latter that pulls me up short. I mean, I know it should be the spitting and the dirty talk and probably the fact that he apparently knows all about Woods and me, but it isn't. Instead, I just go with this: 'You've never done this before?'

I can't keep the surprise out of my voice either. He just took it all so easily, and even after I've asked he doesn't stop working himself back on the second finger I'm slowly easing into him.

'What – had a woman fuck my ass?' he asks, but he's not being funny. He sounds like he's just struggling towards the answer, as that tight ring of muscle gives for me and two fingers slide inside. 'No. No – but I mean, I want you to. Ohhh yeah, I want you to do it just like that.'

'Like this?' I say, and then I crook them. Just a little.

'Right there, yes,' he pants, but I can feel him trying to get the pressure over a slightly different place. He's almost squirming for it, those solid hips of his rolling until I can just about feel something …

'Here?'

He jerks forward a little, so I know I've almost got it. I can nearly feel it when I stroke in a long, slow way that makes him talk in short, stunted breaths.

'A little to the left.'

'That sounds awfully specific for someone who's never done this before,' I say, but he doesn't seem perturbed by this line of questioning. He never seems perturbed – unless you count his reaction when I finally make out something that isn't smooth and featureless inside him.

'Well – *oh God, there, there* – I've done it, you know. To myself,' he manages to get out, in between going up on tiptoe and shuddering pretty much all over. In fact, he's still shuddering when he finally manages to lever himself back down to the ground.

'You've fingered your own ass?' I ask, even though I know the answer. He's already told me, and now it's just the cherry on the top. It's just hearing him talk in this straining, breathless voice, while I stroke him in just the right spot.

'Mmmm there ... oh that's perfect. Fuck, you're gonna make me come.'

'That's not an answer to my question, Benjamin.'

'Oh, OK – yeah. Yeah, I've done it.'

'Tell me how.'

'I don't know – when I'm jerking off I do all kinds of crazy things. I like a lot of lube, and once I'm all slippery and messy it doesn't seem like that big a deal to just let my fingers slide in – though I swear to God, it doesn't feel the way this feels.'

'How is it different?'

'Well, for a start I can't reach my prostate the way you can. I mean, my fingers are long but *Jesus Christ.*'

This time when he goes up on tiptoe, his voice goes up with it. In fact, for a second I think he's actually going to try and climb over the desk, but he hauls himself back in admirably. And by hauls himself back in, I mean he reaches behind himself and grabs a hold of something on me, anything on me, while I stroke hard enough to make him tell me the following: 'I'm gonna do it. I'm gonna – is it OK to do it on your desk?'

I click my tongue at him.

'It most certainly is not, Benjamin. Honestly – can't you control yourself for more than a few minutes? How on earth do you think you're going to satisfy me when you come the second I do anything to you?'

All of which is grossly unfair to him, I know. I mean, I am currently stroking over something that seems to make sound catch somewhere low in his throat. And as I'm doing it, I also seem to be holding onto his hip in a very particular sort of way – one that would get me worked up if I was the person bent over the desk.

It's almost like a bit of leverage, I think. Like I need to grasp onto him and tug him back the second he tries to squirm away. And of course, every time I do it my fingers fuck hard into him, spreading him wide. Hitting that little firm spot inside of him, until he gets close to begging me not to.

Though it's not begging that spills out of his mouth once I've finished saying something I thought almost nothing of. Silly, really. The words quite clearly mean something distinct and frankly terrifying, the moment he reframes them.

'You're going to actually let me do something to you?' he asks, and for a whole long second his body is completely still. Like he's poised on the brink of the question, just waiting for the answer.

'You want to do something to me, Ben?'

His words click their way out, dryly.

'Fuck yeah.'

'And what would you do to me, given half the chance?'

He doesn't hesitate.

'I'd lick your pussy,' he tells me, of course he does. It's the best thing he can possibly offer me, and one that's likely to make me waver. I can almost feel myself wavering now, as I fuck him slow and steady, slow and steady. My clit feels like a little diamond, sharp and too obvious and just begging for some of the attention I seem to want to lavish all over him.

But of course I don't beg. I don't give in. I change the subject instead.

'Like this?' I ask him, and then I just bend over, and lick between the lotion-slick cheeks of his arse. It's not that hard to do, because after all I've got him anchored here. I've got him spread open, ready to take whatever I have to give.

And apparently what I have to give is my slick little tongue, just easing around that tight hole as it clenches down hard.

'Whoa – OK. OK, don't –' he stutters out, but he doesn't get any further than that. His words slide into harsh, guttural moans instead, and even if they didn't I'd know what he was doing. I can feel it running through his body in low, tense shudders, followed by something even prettier: the sound of his come striping my desk. It makes a very distinct noise when it spurts onto probably very important paperwork, and for just a moment I let myself revel in it.

I press my face to his back, so I can feel it going through him. So I can hear every moan vibrating up through his body – because by God there are a lot of them. He's pretty much the noisiest fucker I've ever been with, though of course the moment I've had the thought I have to roll those words over in my mind.

Been with, I think, and then I just turn my head until my mouth is almost on him, kissing his damp skin through his almost-soaked-through shirt. Just for a second, you know – a bit of contact that isn't something rude, and detached, and near impersonal.

Because that's how it feels sometimes, even if he's always pushing against that definition. He pushes against it now, in the middle of an orgasm that almost forces him into some place beyond words.

Almost.

'Oh God yeah, yeah – stay like that,' he tells me, and then he goes one better. He actually reaches behind himself with both of his too-long arms, and holds me against his back – like an embrace, only back to front and upside down and far, far too much.

Though I don't tell him to stop. I just lie there against his big, solid back, feeling his rattling breath going in and out. Barely thinking about anything, least of all what I'm going to do if he actually suggests what we talked about only a moment ago.

Because he's almost definitely going to go for it. I can feel him working up to the words, and worse, I don't think I'm going to say no. Somehow I'm at that place Woods was at – of wanting someone, of needing someone enough to just let go of all that control you've spent so many months diligently building up – after a few short weeks.

And it's only the sound of someone knocking on my office door that saves me.

Chapter Eight

'Ms Harding,' he says, once I've stepped into the elevator – like he's just a colleague, offering a curt kind of acknowledgement of me. I exist, to him, but nothing more. He inclines his head just a little, and when he does I notice his hair.

It's neater than usual. Everything about him is neater than usual, even though I haven't said a word. Woods had to tell me: *get the grey suit, wear your hair up, try heels for once.* But I don't have to tell Benjamin. He's already started letting his cuffs peek out neatly from under the far better fitting series of one-colour cardigans he's started wearing. And instead of trainers he's got a pair of briskly polished shoes on his feet.

Funny, I find myself thinking: *I preferred the Converse.* You could always tell it was Benjamin coming in those things, because they tended to squeak when he walks. And if I didn't want to give indication that I was following his approach, I didn't have to – I could just hear that sound and glance at the floor and see those far-too-turned-up hems of his trousers dancing over canvas and sloppy laces and just an ever so slight hint of *boot.*

Like he's a grown-up, only not.

But all of that's fading now. He's becoming someone else,

123

someone different, someone who can't even pick up the phone and ask all of the things he's dying to, the way that I can't. Because that's what happened about fifteen minutes ago. I sat at my desk and stared at the receiver in my hand, willing myself to just push in the numbers and call him up and say to that cool, collected wall: *I don't care how you thought you should be. I don't want to be that way*. Despite the fact that those words hadn't seemed to be the predominant ones in my head when I imagined finally having a conversation with Woods. It's just that they are now, right here, as I watch the little lights on the elevator's wall tick down one by one. Soon there'll be none left. We'll be at zero, and I won't have done any of the things I've wanted to ever since I leaned against his back and thought of being saved.

Though I realise now what I should have then: I don't *want* to be saved.

And then I just reach out and press the emergency stop button. Just like that, as though it's something I do every day – but then, that's the thing about Benjamin. He makes it easy to turn shocking, strange acts into ones I can easily perform. Even when he sounds incredulous, it's like he's not really incredulous at all. He's excited and amused and as curious as any person can be when their boss has just trapped them in an elevator.

'Oh my God,' he says. 'Are you going to do stuff to me in *here*?'

I see an image of him clearly then, always sat on the edge of his chair, just waiting for me to say the word or give the nod, before letting himself slide down, down, down into some sort of Kinky Wonderland.

Which is nice, of course it is. I like him like that, I do. And yet I can't help thinking what it would be like if he didn't have to wait for me to say *yes*. If I just looked at him, steadily, through the growing silence in the elevator, and he just looked at me back.

Those eyes, I think, *dear God those eyes*, and then oh then I don't know what happens. I just stagger to him like someone drunk on lust, grabbing at the first thing I find there – the inside edge of his cardigan, I think it is, in a fist I don't mean to bunch.

And worse than that, *he grabs me back*. He holds me like I'm falling, though I swear to God I'm not, and whispers my name in direct contrast to the way he said it earlier. It's not curt now. It's not polite. It's as desperate as I am; a reflection of me. His lips move around further words but I can hardly hear them because of the pounding in my chest and in my head and this urge in me to just yank him down, fierce and brutal.

And find his mouth with mine.

He tastes like something sharp and sweet at the same time, which just makes me imagine him eating sticky bundles of candy from paper bags at his desk. *Sour apples*, I think, unbidden, before my body pulls me back into what I seem to be actually doing right now.

I'm kissing him. I'm putting my mouth on his mouth, and I'm not doing it in the soft, sweet sort of way he did it for me in the meeting room. Instead, I appear to be eating at his face like a ravenous wolverine, tongue sliding past his lips before he's fully prepared for it, everything all hot and wet and messy in a way kisses almost never are for me.

Usually I suffer through these strange, dry, lukewarm sorts of affairs, and then do something that's expected of me. Like make a note in my diary of the equally tepid next date we're going to have. I don't call him and he doesn't call me, and neither of us end up fucking each other's faces in an elevator.

Which is what Benjamin and I appear to be doing.

Because when I really think about it, it's not just me behaving this way. He's not passively accepting my hungry kisses, or the hands I seem to have clenched around various parts of his body. He's attacking me with just as much gusto as I'm attacking him – if not more so. After all, *I* can't lift *him* off his feet.

But he can lift me. And he doesn't do it the sweet, polite, just a bit desperate sort of way either. He does it in the *I'm going to put my hands on your ass* sort of way. I can feel him actually squeezing me there, like he's waited days and days and days to get just a taste of my body, and now that he's allowed …

God, I think he's trying to get my skirt up.

I mean, it *seems* as though he's simply giving me a quick grope while the opportunity presents itself. But after a second I think I can make out the ulterior motive behind the roll and press of his hands on my ass.

He's trying to get underneath. He's trying, and he's got me shoved up against the elevator wall, and ohhhh no. I've completely misjudged his size and strength and even worse – the way that mouth of his makes me feel. His lips are just so soft and wet, which tends to make everything at least thirty per cent lewder than it actually is. And though he isn't overly generous with his tongue, I can still make it out when he darts it over mine.

It's just that I make it out someplace way, way lower than my mouth. Sensation blooms between my legs for every little slippery caress he gives me, and the feeling gets stronger the moment his fingertips actually slide underneath my skirt.

He's going to touch me there, I think. He's going to do

it, and then I'm going to die of pleasure. I have to stop this thing – for just a little while – so that any dying occurs in a more dignified sort of place.

Like my apartment.

'Sorry,' he says, the second I urge him away from me. And then he has the temerity to say it again! 'Sorry – was that too much? I didn't mean to go under your skirt, it's just … you feel so … so …'

I'm glad he leaves it hanging there, all breathless and heavy with want. It makes it easier to drag myself back under control, and frame what I want in clear, precise, well-thought-out-seeming terms.

Even if I'm the exact opposite of all of those things on every level.

'We'll take my car,' I say, and though I force myself not to look at him as I do, I can practically make out his expression anyway. It's pressing so hard against the side of my face that it'd be almost impossible for me to miss it.

It's shock, I think. Shock and a kind of thrilled disbelief.

Followed by him, following me to my car.

He doesn't say anything when we get there – but then, he doesn't really need to. He's far too busy running his fingers over all the things he previously wasn't allowed to touch, in a manner that suggests he isn't sure if I'm real or not. He touches my shoulders, and the neat crease at the hemline of my jacket. He finds the wisps of hair that have come loose from the knot at the back of my head, and just feathers over them.

All of which is somehow worse than if he'd suddenly shoved a hand between my legs and squeezed my cunt in one big fist. It's just so slow, that's the thing. So slow and deliberate, every move he makes too easy to experience in full.

127

I can make out the prickle of each little hair as he strokes over it, and I know he's getting extremely close to kissing the side of my face.

I know he is, because some sort of odd tension crackles in all the places he's not. It like there's a thin, electricity-filled barrier between our bodies, and as long as I continue doing something innocuous – like opening the car door, with extreme difficulty – the barrier remains.

Or at least, it does until I just turn my head and lick over his parted lips. After that, it's kind of hard to maintain. He doesn't seem to want to maintain it. He actually makes a noise when I touch him, and then again when he fully processes what I just did.

I lapped at his mouth, as though his mouth has suddenly become a stand-in for something else – and I don't stop there, either. I wait until he's flushed and leaning towards me, so desperate for more that he can't keep that greedy, abandoned look off his face.

And then I do it again, only with far more force this time. I think I actually lick inside his mouth – as though my tongue is a cock and I just want to feel all that lovely warm wetness inside that pretty mouth of his – and for my troubles he grabs a fistful of my jacket. He actually grabs it, before he realises how insane he's being and straightens his trembling self out.

'You are going to control yourself, aren't you, Benjamin?' I say, one eyebrow raised. Hand on the now open car door, like a suggestion – *I might not let you in if you keep misbehaving*. And then the kicker: 'Because if not, I don't think we're going to get through half the things I'm wanting to.'

He makes an expression I can best describe as biting his fist, without actually biting it. His mouth opens and near closes, that gaze of his so desperate suddenly it's near unbearable. I want to kiss him again for that look alone, but of course I resist.

'I can – I will. I ... whatever you want. Whatever you want, sir.'

Lord in heaven. Please help me get through this with my sanity intact.

'Get in the car, Benjamin,' I say, and I swear you'd never know that those things about the Lord and my sanity had just made their way through my mind. It's literally like he makes me a different person, and said person continues in this manner all the way through the car journey to my place.

I find myself gazing mindlessly out at the traffic as it streams by. Everything exactly as it always is – near darkness streaked with lights I barely pay attention to. The hum of the city fading down to an endless grey, while I think of nothing but ready meals and television shows I hate, greedily anticipating mundanity in a way most people probably anticipate wild nights on the town.

And then in the middle of all of said mundanity, I just reach to one side of myself and put my hand between his legs.

'Oh, baby,' he tells me, but the use of such an epithet doesn't bother me in the slightest. Instead I find myself fixated on his bodily reactions, like the way he seems to sit up straighter in the seat the second I stroke over that long, thick length. And when I do a little more than stroke ... when I sort of actually start masturbating him through his trousers ... he can't seem to help rocking into my touch.

I have to look. I wait until we're at a light and then just glance across at him – but the moment I do I wish I hadn't. It had seemed as if he'd made himself stiff in his seat, but that isn't the case. He's slumped in it instead, head right back against something that isn't the headrest, body making one long, eager bow down from that point until it gets to the hard jut of his cock.

Which I have to look away from quickly. I have to, because he isn't just obviously stiff and kind of rolling his hips into my hand. He's also done something that makes a thick surge of arousal go through me in a way that the obvious things don't. Hard cocks and narrowed eyes and those ever-parted lips of his are fine, they're good, they make me wet.

But the sight of his sluttishly spread legs ... that just sends me. It *sends* me.

'Is that what you call controlling yourself?' I ask, but he's long past that point now. He can't keep a handle on himself when we're in the hallway outside my door, because the second I turn to put the key in the lock he goes one better than he did by my car.

He kisses the back of my neck, all hot and wet and utterly electric. And then he *slides a hand around my body, and cups one of my breasts through my shirt.*

That's right. He doesn't do it through something safe like my jacket. He actually pushes his way underneath that particular barrier and goes for something that's so close to skin-to-skin contact that I have to clench my teeth, hard. My toes curl inside shoes that weren't designed for curling, and oh God the *throb* that goes through my clit ...

I'm not prepared for it – though I understand why. I've spent too long building it up to this, and now a little light boob touching feels like someone sticking their tongue in my ass. Most of me wants to shove that hand away immediately, but once we're in the entranceway of my apartment and I'm twisting around to kiss his pliant mouth and he's rubbing over my nipple ... I can't.

130

It's too much like all of my wildest imaginings, about actual desire and lust, for another person. Like in the movies when the heroine finally gets together with her hunk, and they're so desperate for each other they just have to start ripping off all of their clothes before they've hit the dining room.

Though granted, the latter happens for other reasons besides *because the contrived script said it must*. It happens because after a second of that same sloppy, filthy, frantic sort of … *kiss-fucking*, I just ever so slowly lever him away from me. And once he's there, mouth still gratifyingly reaching for mine … all of his focus on my lips, my tits, the way I'm staring at him like he's fucking irresistible … I say to him soft and low: 'Take off your clothes.'

And then I watch as he obeys me. His eyes don't once leave mine as he fumbles with the buttons on his cardigan, and does his best to shuck himself out of it. Wrists catching in the cuffs, shoulders standing out as round and smooth as some fruit I don't yet know the name of beneath the crisp white shirt he then reveals.

I almost don't want him to take the thing off – there's something incredibly clean-cut and boyish about it, all buttoned up like that to his throat. Only then he starts yanking on the material to get it out of the trap of his trousers, and suddenly I have to glance down. It's a necessity, because every time he pulls I can make out flashes of things I've not so far seen.

His belly, all covered in completely unexpected hair and solid in a way I didn't think it would be. I thought he'd be kind of smooth and planed somehow, like a model on the cover of *Gym Bunny* magazine. Buffed into oblivion, and perhaps just a touch bland for my tastes.

Instead he's this … this … *man* beneath his clothes. He's … *burly*. There's hair just about all over him – as toffee-coloured as the hair on his head, but still impressive somehow – and bits I don't quite understand. Like his shoulders, which don't go straight across in the way I'd probably expected them to. They've got these slopes of muscle instead that slide upward into his massive man's neck. His collarbone is like something archaeologists unearthed at the nearest dinosaur's graveyard, and his chest ... oh dear Lord his *chest*.

I can't help wondering about the sound it would make if you were to punch him somewhere on that vast expanse of flesh. Would it *thwack* in that dense, meaty way a fist does, once it's connected with something incredibly heavy and solid?

I imagine so, but that doesn't make the reason for my imagining any clearer. Even he looks perturbed when I finally manage to drag my eyes back up to his face, and he's the one who let me fuck his arse with my fingers. I doubt much truly unnerves him – particularly with a body like the one he's got.

He could wrestle for a living. Maybe in a damp basement somewhere, with many other sweaty, possibly horny men. And then once they're done fighting, they could ...

'Am I ... not what you were expecting?'

Of course, my immediate instinct is to say no. *No, you're not what I was expecting. You're so heavy and solid and masculine that I just want to climb you like a tree, and maybe live on your face for a couple of decades.*

But I refrain. In some respects.

'Get the rest off,' I tell him, just as cool as you please, while inside great waves of heat roll their way down between my legs to settle in my swollen, maddening little clit. I have to clench my nails into the palms of my hands just to keep myself from doing some of the things my brain had threatened, when he finally strips out of his trousers.

I mean, I've seen his long, strong thighs before. And I can recall the shape and size of his cock almost exactly. But once everything has been put together in a single glorious tableau, it's extraordinarily hard to help myself.

In fact, it's so hard that I don't really bother at all. I just step forward and start running my hands all over his solid body, until he says something half-amused like 'are you actually groping me, Ms Harding?'

I am. I'm actually groping him. And I'm not ashamed of that fact either because he feels amazing. His nipples are taut little points beneath the stroke of my fingertips; all of his flesh so warm and firm. When I run my hand over his belly I can feel every muscle there, jumping, and the more I go on, the worse it gets.

By the time I've gotten a handful of his ass, his mouth is back on mine – or at least it's trying to be. Mostly he's just missing due to his simultaneous efforts to get me somewhere other than the entrance to my apartment.

'Where's your bedroom?' he blurts out against the side of my face. Then realises he should probably modify a comment like that. 'I mean – if you're wanting to.'

He'd have to be mad to imagine otherwise. I practically writhe against him when he finally lifts me off my feet again and starts in the direction of the nearest dark room. It's lucky, really, that we don't end up in the bathroom or a random cupboard, because I'm not paying the slightest attention to anything other than his meaty shoulders, and how easily they give beneath the press of my teeth.

And he's not paying attention to anything other than how that feels, to have someone biting down hard.

'Fuck, that's so …' he tells me, then gets no further, probably because of the contact his cock is suddenly getting with someplace strange like the underside of my ass. The second he stumbles onto the bed with me still tangled around him, I can feel him rutting himself against me. He doesn't try to hide it, until I manage to get some words out.

'Is that what you're going to do, huh?' I ask him, between mouthfuls of his body, his face, good *God* he smells incredible. Like that American-boy-perfume but like something else too, something heated. Something ready to fuck. 'You're just going to rub yourself off on me like that?'

'No, no,' he says, but he doesn't stop exactly. He just keeps on rocking against me as he kisses and fondles his way down my body, mouth always seeking the sweetest thing he can find – like the smooth curves of my breasts beneath my shirt.

Of course it's obvious that he wants my clothes off. And I feel for him on that score, I really do, because he's all vulnerable and I'm all covered … but I can't let him do it. For a moment I'm so overwhelmed by him – by his size and his heaviness and most of all his eager, greedy need to get at just about every part of me – that I can hardly do anything at all. I just kind of twist beneath him, awkwardly, as though maybe I'm trying to reach for a drink on the nightstand.

While he buries me beneath his body. He doesn't wait for me to say yes or no or possibly, he just kisses wetly down over me, lingering on parts I don't want him to – like my embarrassing stiff nipples. They're sticking out through two layers of material – a thin lacy bra I shouldn't have worn, and this wretched blouse I seem to be trapped in – and he just homes right in on them, licking and licking until I'm only half-heartedly trying to wrestle back control.

In truth I'm far more interested in the sensation it produces, which is somehow worse than if I'd been completely naked. Every time he just sort of … tugs at one stiff peak with those soft, clingy lips of his, I get a double burst of pleasure. First from the pressure and heat of him, and then from the feel of the material sliding just ever so wetly against those sensitive points.

By the time he's moved onto less intense areas of my body, I'm barely conscious. The heat blooming between my legs is an inferno, and it's wiped me out. My arms and legs are like syrup. My face feels like it might burn someone if they were to touch it, and the longer this goes on, the worse it gets. It's not like I'm going to get a last-minute reprieve. I can't really get myself a glass of water.

And in all honesty I've done this to myself, with seven hundred kinky games and an equal amount of nights in when I gallantly refused to masturbate. I am an *idiot,* and he takes full advantage – even if I can't really call it that. When normal people take advantage of another person's paralysed-with-lust state, they don't seem half as grateful and wildly horny as he does, I know.

His cock's so hard it's almost hurting me whenever it shoves into someplace soft, like my inner thigh. And I can feel how slick it is at the tip too. When he eases his way down my body and actually does something crazy – like poking his tongue into my belly button through my shirt – I can make out the slick trail his cock is making over my skin.

But he isn't trying to rut against me any more. Oh no. No, no – I think he's got something a lot more selfless in mind. And I can tell I'm going to like it because the second he starts trying to shove my skirt up, I almost *help* him.

That's how desperate I've become. I'm a woman who helps some guy push her skirt up so that he can get at her slippery, too-swollen pussy. I'm breathing as hard as he is, and I'm twisting around on the bed in a way that's not like escaping at all, and when he finally exposes my cunt to his waiting gaze I'm the one who needs to rut.

I actually rub my ass against the sheets, like an animal in heat – but he doesn't make me feel bad about it. He's too busy staring and staring at my spread pussy, eyes all heavy-lidded and lost.

'You're all *bare*,' he tells me, and it takes a second to understand what he means. Probably because I'm lost too, in the thick sensation between my legs. He hasn't even done anything yet, and I can feel my clit pulsing. I can make out my own wetness trickling down between the cheeks of my arse.

And all of it intensifies when I realise: he's never seen a completely waxed pussy before. He's seen everything all hidden away and veiled with hair that I just don't have, and oh *God* this must look so rude by comparison.

'Did you do this to yourself?' he asks, and then it gets even ruder. I can tell what he means without inquiring. He's thinking about someone doing this to me – maybe lathering up my soft sex with something that feels just so … *delicious* over my stiff little bud. And then when it's done, the sharp edge of a cold razor cutting through my curls …

It excites me to imagine it, God knows what it does to him. The expression he levels at me looks caught somewhere between a kind of bitterness and an inescapable sort of arousal – and both feature in his words.

'Or did someone do it to you?'

I raise an eyebrow at him.

'I don't know, Benjamin. You're the one with the inside information. What do you think?'

Of course I know we're both thinking of Woods, and not the beauty expert who removes every hair from my body, once a fortnight. But he has no idea about the latter and seems to know a great deal about the former, so let's go with that, shall we?

Only he doesn't go with that. He won't answer me.

His gaze drops too heavily, instead, back to the smooth expanse of flesh he's now definitely stroking. I can feel him gathering just a bit of wetness with his thumb to spread over the outer edges of those slippery folds, and he's making a mess, I think.

But ohhh, it's a good mess. I want him to smear my slickness all over my body, and all over his body, and just everywhere, everywhere.

'I think your pussy looks very pretty,' he says, finally, decidedly. 'I think it's amazing to see everything all bare and exposed like this.'

'Really?' I ask, and it comes out a little bored and sardonic, though that's the opposite of how I'm feeling. My pulse is beating in my clit again. Everything seems slow, so slow, in a way that makes me think we're just kind of falling into this, instead of actively doing it. We're falling through honey, into a sort of sex I don't fully understand.

'Yeah, yeah. God, you're sooo wet … and your clit …'

Said part of my body responds to its label. It jerks, as though he put a little hook in it and pulled, rather than what he's actually done – left me hanging on the edge of his words, all of me waiting breathlessly for the rest.

'It's all … stiff and swollen. You want me to …?' he asks, and I consider for maybe five seconds. Though in truth, consider is perhaps the wrong word. Really I don't do anything of the sort. I just put my hand between my own legs, two fingers sliding down, down over my plump sex lips, parting everything as I go.

And once I'm more rudely exposed than I already am – clit

standing proud and unmistakable amidst my slick folds – I tell him what I want him to do more than any other thing.

'Lick me here,' I say. 'Lick me right here.' It's a mistake, however. The moment he goes ahead and obeys me – that wicked tongue of his just flicking ever so lightly over my clit – I know it's going to be too much. I can feel it burning into me before he's even begun, and it burns hotter when he licks more firmly. He just curls his tongue over the underside of my too sensitive bud, and lashes upwards, and then after he does it I come apart.

I make a sound, too loud and not like me at all. Usually I'm as silent as the grave in bed because really, who knows what a person might say in the throes of passion? But here, now, I can't be. He's looking up at me with those eyes as he gets up a slick rhythm, and I can feel his hands digging into the backs of my thighs.

And then he asks somewhere in between it all: 'Is that good?' and I actually want to answer. It feels so good that I'm almost rubbing myself against his face, and there are words in the back of my throat, and when he just slides the tips of two fingers over the entrance to my cunt, I let them out.

'Yeah, do it,' I tell him, though I don't mean it. I really want to say *no, don't*, but something gets mixed up in the translation. Instead of no I'm saying yes, and I'm now definitely urging myself against his face. I've even got a hand in his hair, squeezing too tight for his probable comfort – but it just makes him lick faster, harder.

He gets the flat of his tongue right on my straining little bud, and just sort of ... rubs it over me. Those fingers easing into my clenching cunt as he does it, everything about him so patient suddenly. Apparently he can't wait when it's him getting all the attention, but when it's me he can wait for-ev-er.

He just eases his fingers into me, twisting as he goes. Those hubcap knuckles of his running over a million nerve-endings that didn't previously exist, all of my wetness so apparent now that he's sliding around in it. I can almost hear how slick I am – that's how bad it is – and that little dirty clicking sort of sound gets louder the more insistent he gets.

He pumps those fingers in and out, in time with the stroke of his tongue over my clit. And if that wasn't bad enough on its own, he's moaning too. I can hear him over the slippery noises I'm making, caught somewhere between a breathless gasp and a hum of pleasure, and of course every time he does it I can feel it.

It starts in my stiff little bud and works its way up through my body, until it connects with all the sounds I want to make too. I want to moan more than anything, to tell him how this feels: like someone's squeezing a fist between my legs.

But instead I do something very bad indeed. I put my fist to my mouth and whimper into it – though that's not the bad thing. No, no … the bad thing comes after I've realised that I'm not going to be able to take this, and in response to the overwhelming sensation coiling in my belly I just sort of … maybe … dig my heel into his shoulder.

My sharp stiletto heel, right into that flesh I've already bitten and marked.

Of course I don't mean to do it. I'm sweating and shaking and heaving on the bed, hips no longer just rocking. Now I'm almost making a kind of arch, and I'm definitely forcing his face right up against my creaming sex.

So it's not quite intentional, this move. It just sort of happens as a result of everything else, and if it only makes things worse, well … that can't be helped. I don't mean to force a thick gush of pleasure through my body because of something so brutal and cruel. And I certainly don't mean to make him push out the sound he then does – like a grunt of pain, only not.

It has an airy, open note to it that I can't explain or deny, and his body jerks when he makes it. His mouth works harder, sliding messily through my slit, and I can feel his hand squeezing and relaxing on the back of my thigh. He's getting as close to orgasm as I am, because of a heel in his shoulder and maybe the sense of me shaking and shaking as my body gives in.

Of course I try to hold it in, and maybe push it down a little to some point in the near future. But unfortunately it doesn't want to be stopped. It wants me to jerk unsteadily into my orgasm right now, while saying things I don't want to say like *God, yes*.

And I don't feel resentful about any of it. It feels too good to be resentful – intense in a way I'd always imagined an orgasm should be. I actually grit my teeth at some point through it, and dig my nails into his back, and it's only when he gasps that I become sensible of what I've done.

I've made him a pair of wings, from just above his ass to the nape of his neck. Four lines on either side, not quite bloody but not quite painless either – though he doesn't make me feel bad about them.

On the contrary.

He makes me feel bad about something else, instead.

'Did you *seriously* just come?' he says, incredulous frown in place, mouth as wet and rude-looking as fuck. And then I glance at the clock on my bedside table and realise it hasn't been an eternity of pleasure after all.

It's been about the time it takes to boil a kettle.

Chapter Nine

I halt about three paces from the inside of my bedroom, all the things I thought of to say to him in the bathroom now sliding away from me. They just go in one big rush, and I'm left transfixed by the sight of him, stood in front of my full-length mirror.

It's all right, though. He can't see me making a girlish fool of myself like this, eyes on him as though I can't bear to ever look at anything else again. He's too busy looking at his own reflection as it twists and turns before him – in just the way I'd imagined, when he told me he couldn't stop checking out the marks on his ass.

His big body just eases around at the waist, and then he can see what I've done to his back. Four distinct marks on either side, all not half as vicious as I'd thought they were a second after I'd made them. They'd seemed very red and cruel through the sagging daze I'd found myself in – so much so that I've spent the last five minutes in the bathroom trying to think of a way to apologise for them.

I mean, he asked for the other stuff. He had the opportunity to do vital things, like say no or use that fucking safe word he so spontaneously thought up.

141

But he didn't have a chance to do anything about this. I just did it, like a reflex, and now he's marked from the nape of his neck to the backs of his thighs. I've left a trail of destruction everywhere, and though I know how normal people feel about that I can't see any evidence of such on his face.

He doesn't look disturbed, I know. He looks proud that I did that to him, and proud that he can wear it so well, and all I'm left thinking after that is: I never felt that way. I didn't look at myself in the mirror, as though the marks had somehow made me more beautiful. I don't know what that emotion's like, in truth, or if I'm capable of it.

I don't know if I'm capable of feeling anything at all, when I really think about it. Most of me just seems frozen the second he finally catches me looking, next to his reflection in the mirror.

'Have you seen what you did to me?' he asks, voice some sort of unholy mixture of disapproving and delighted. 'I'm like a hot griddle pan.'

Of course my immediate instinct is to laugh, because really – what a ridiculous thing to say. And it's just so typically *him* too, to talk like that while his cock sticks out at me like an accusing finger.

He hasn't had any fun yet, my mind reminds me, but doing so just makes me go over to the bed and start doing something odd, like smoothing my hands over the sheets. By the time his focus is all back on me, I'm actually primping the damn thing. I'm making hospital corners, and fussing over the edges of things, and as I'm doing so I'm becoming more and more aware of the robe I definitely shouldn't have put on.

It's very thin, and flimsy. And the second I bend over I know what he's looking at. I can practically trace his sightline all the way down to the open V over my bare breasts, and though he just spent a good two minutes with his face buried in my cunt, there's something very … exposed about that.

I'm not in my jacket and skirt and shoes any more. I'm barefoot and I'm doing a series of very weird things, and all the while he's watching me. He follows me all the way around the bed to my alarm clock, which I pick up and fiddle with.

Despite the fact that it's already at the exact right settings.

'Are you OK?' he asks, but I really, really need to concentrate on changing the time my alarm goes off at from 6:00 to 6:03. It's of vital importance to my mental wellbeing. 'Do you maybe want me to go?'

I stop then and glance up at him, alarm clock and mental wellbeing briefly forgotten, because it's a question I'm not sure how to answer. I mean, it's hard to come to a decision on something like that when he seems to have stretched himself out on my bed, one long leg crossed over the other, cock still jutting up at me all thick and faintly glistening.

It doesn't help that he's kind of pointing at the door and looking at me all guileless, as though he really might just leave if I said so. He didn't really think I'd mind if he made himself comfortable, and now that he knows I am, he can go.

He can save all of that delicious, rampant horniness for later.

'I don't …' I start, then somehow end up taking a big breath in between. It's pathetic really. 'I don't know what I want.'

He leans towards me, just a little. Winces on my behalf.

'Kind of a deal-breaker for a Dom,' he says, and I don't mind admitting that I jolt a little on that last word. I have to. He called me a *Dom*, and I'm guessing the real end of that word isn't *-inic*. He doesn't think I'm secretly a man with a three-syllable name.

He just thinks I'm awful at this thing I'm not even sure I'm trying to do.

'Am I ... am I really that bad at it?' I ask, but he doesn't respond the way I think he should. He doesn't get out a five-point plan of how I could possibly improve – number one being *don't start fiddling with your alarm clock because you're terrified out of your mind.*

He almost laughs instead. A little sound comes out of him, and he's smiling in this kind of gentle way, and somehow that's worse than the imaginary five-point plan. He's better at this than I am, I know. He's better at it just because he knows exactly what he wants, and isn't the least bit fazed by anything.

'Actually, you're kind of awesome at it,' he says, while I wring my hands around the stupid clock I'm *still* holding. He's naked on my bed and I'm doing ... *this* nonsense. 'Pretty sure it's not sexually dominating me that you're nervous about.'

He's also way, way too astute for his own good. God, what a mistake I made, thinking he was big and goofy and kind of a mess. He's actually much more like some sly Parisian whore who gets you to give her all your money. Or all of your feelings, if we're really going to be honest about it.

'What do you think it is about, then?' I ask, though as soon as I've said it I wish I hadn't. He could go with just about anything, after all – accusations, further criticisms of my BDSM abilities, the truth ...

'I don't think it'll make you more comfortable if I advance some of my theories.'

Or, you know, maybe just some kindly vagueness that makes me more unnerved than I was before. I burst out something I don't intend to, and do something crazy like put a hand to my head while I'm going about it.

144

'Jesus, this was all just so easy before.'

'What – you mean back when you were letting Woods stand on your head in some kind of weird silent sex agreement?'

My hand drops from forehead all on its own, but it's not really a step in the right direction. Moving it just seems to make my face sag, as though that one slight pressure was holding everything together. Now my mouth's open and words are coming out of me, and none of them are the right ones.

The right ones would be something to do with the silent sex agreement that Benjamin apparently knows about, I think. Whereas I go with the following: 'I never let him stand on my head.'

Like some idiot who's been caught out in open court. I didn't do it, your honour, I swear. I'm perfectly innocent, even in all the ways that I'm totally not. It's obvious that I'm not. He knows I'm not, because after I've spoken he raises an eyebrow, and said eyebrow hauls me right back to something like honesty.

'OK. Maybe ... maybe I let him do it *once*,' I say, and then I wait for the recriminations. Strong women aren't supposed to let men do things like that to them, etcetera etcetera. You've set the feminist cause back three hundred million years with your sexual fantasies, and so on.

How dare you want to explore the entire gamut of your own weird desires!

But of course he doesn't give me any of that. He doesn't look mildly perturbed to discover that I'm less of a Dom than he thinks. He just shrugs instead and goes with something effortlessly breezy.

'It's not a problem for me, if that's what you're thinking. I don't mind.'

Seriously, how is he this easy-going? How? How does he *do it*?

'So maybe *you* want to stand on my head, is that it?' I ask, though I can see by his expression that it's not. For a start, if he did something like that he'd probably pop my skull like a grape.

'No,' he replies, and when he does he's near-laughing, incredulously. 'Don't you know by now? I want *you* to stand on *my* head.'

Yeah, I probably wouldn't pop *that* like a grape. Unless I was maybe wearing stilettos, and accidentally caught him in the eye.

'I just meant ... if that's the kind of thing you really like, it's OK. I mean, that is what you like, right?' he says, but he's got to be kidding with this. Does he honestly think I know the answer to that question? I don't even know whether I should go over to the bed and sit down, instead of standing here with a clock in my hands like a moron.

'Do you like it?' I ask, purely to turn the conversation back on him. Yeah, I'll make no bones about that. I want that heat *off* me.

'Do I like what?'

'Someone standing on your head.'

He actually narrows his eyes, as though he's thinking real hard about it. That mouth of his going up in the middle in a way I'm coming to know too well. It's like he's almost shrugging with it; it's like he's using his lower lip and part of his chin to aid rumination.

And Lord, it's cute. He's just much too cute for his own good.

'I guess I might. I don't know. I didn't really think about all of this until Woods started talking to me.'

I want to roll my eyes, but fail hopelessly. Fucking *Woods*.

'He has that effect,' I say, and when I do I picture my former lover with his hands out, several strings attached to each finger and all of us mere mortals dancing below.

But apparently Ben doesn't see it in quite the same way.

'No, no – it wasn't the effect *he* had. It was the effect *you* had. At first I just thought it turned me on because he went into all of this … detail. And he was obviously trying to make me go all … you know. The way I do.'

Dear God, did he really just say that? He did, he definitely did. And so casually too!

'But then I realised – I wasn't fantasising about him doing it to you. I was fantasising about *you* doing it to *me*.'

Or maybe Woods doing it to him.

Because let's be honest here, that's what he's just hinted at. And though I really, really want to concentrate on the parts that make this happy, soaring sort of feeling go through me, I can't. I've got to skip right by the idea that he's been thinking about me for a long, long time, and go directly to the scarier stuff.

'Did he … actually *aim* to get you worked up?' I try, while my heart beats far too hard, somewhere really high up in my chest.

'Well … yeah,' he says, and for the first time he looks just a touch embarrassed. 'Come on – you think he was telling me that stuff because we were best buds for ever?'

I don't know, in all honesty – but I do know I can't ignore that unfamiliar flush on his face. Or the slow ache that's starting up again between my legs. I mean, it's one thing for Woods to have shared some salacious detail with a colleague in a way that's probably designed to humiliate me. It's quite another if he was using said salacious detail to turn someone else on.

Someone who is not a woman.

'Did you ever …' I start, but I've got no idea what question I want to put on the end of that. All I can see behind my eyes is Woods getting Benjamin over a desk. Woods forcing his cock into Ben's incredibly tight and extremely hot little arsehole.

And I pray, dear Lord I *pray* that Benjamin can't see it all over my face.

'Are you asking if he fucked me?'

OK, so I guess he can maybe see it all over my face.

'Maybe.'

'Oooh, do I have, like, a little dirty secret? Are you excited to hear it?'

He's practically bouncing on the bed, which makes this whole matter much more comfortable than it probably should be. I should be mad, I know, that he had these conversations about things I thought were private, but instead I'm just suddenly wet and wanting, eager for more.

'Just tell me. You owe it to me.'

'Oh, because he told me about you? Now you get to hear all about him and his secret proclivity for big, clumsy men?'

'Is that what you think you are?'

'That's what I know I am.'

I wonder if he also knows how beautiful he is right now. He's telling me all of these terrifying things, and most of them seem to be about how little he thinks of himself, but he hasn't stopped being lax and loose on my bed. He's still smiling in this soft, faint way, and it's touching his eyes so keenly I can almost feel the light in them running over my skin.

And it prompts me to say something I don't mean to.

'You're not, you know. You're more than that,' I tell him, then can hardly believe I've done it. The urge to vomit

148

rises almost immediately afterwards, and really it's only his suddenly gushing and obviously excited words that keep it down.

'I think you totally just gave me goose bumps. Was that a compliment? Can I give you one now? Your breasts look *in-fucking-credible* in that robe – I mean, seriously. Those jackets you wear don't do your body justice … you're like Bettie Paige or something –'

Good Lord, his babbling. I have to hold both hands up and cut him off at the pass before it swamps us both entirely.

'Stop. Stop, all right? Let's just … return to what we were talking about previously,' I say, but he's not entirely content with that. He has other things to point out for me first.

'You really don't like people telling you nice things, do you?' he says, and I'll admit – I kind of hate him for it. I mean, so what if it's true? He doesn't have to go ahead and state it outright. And if he does state it outright, he has to know that I'm going to respond in a rather indignant sort of manner.

'I like you telling me whether or not my former lover shoved his cock in your ass,' I say, and then just for good measure, I strap a little bolshy '*That's* what I like' on the end. I jut my chin out, and wag my finger at him, and feel kind of stupid about doing both, afterwards.

Though naturally, he doesn't seem to think I should feel that way. He almost licks his lips on the words *cock* and the word *ass*, and when I get to the part about me *liking* it, his hips jerk upwards, just once. Like I was saying I actually enjoy thinking about him getting fucked, rather than what I actually meant, which was … fuck knows. I can't remember now, and I recall even less when he gives me a little heavy-eyed suggestion.

'Make me tell you,' he says, and of course I picture the marks on his ass. The marks on his back. The marks that are probably now all over my immortal soul.

'I'm not going to spank you again,' I say, but I know I don't really mean it. I'd mark him from head to toe if it meant he told me what I think he's going to anyway.

'You don't have to. Just –'

'I'm not going to finger your ass either.'

'Really? I was kind of hoping you would. Felt so good when he … well. I guess you'll just have to figure out the rest.'

I clench my fists at my sides.

'You're a goddamn tease.'

A roll of pleasure seems to go through his big body when I say it, followed by a grin that shows his just ever-so-slightly too pointed incisors. They don't ruin the effect of his perfectly white, perfectly straight smile, however. They just give it a little edge, that goes very well with him fucking with me.

'Ohhh that's right. Call me names.'

'You like names?'

'You know I like names. Call me a cocksucker – I've always wanted to hear that one. Sometimes, when he was stood over me, I used to imagine what I'd do if he told me to get on my knees and suck him off.'

I think I'm holding my breath. I don't want to be holding my breath, because that means I've somehow gone all the way from his Boss to someone he can effectively hold on the edge of astonishment with barely any words at all.

But it's happening anyway.

'And would you have?'

He licks his lips, slow and slick and so unsubtle I want to chide him. Doesn't he know it's better if you keep it reined in, just a little bit? Just eke it out, one tiny thing at a time.

Keep me waiting, keep me begging for more, oh God which way around are things now?

I don't know. I just want to hear him say: 'Yeah. Yeah, I would have,' while my mind floods with the visual.

Strangely, however, it isn't Woods I imagine fucking his cock down Benjamin's throat. It isn't anyone at all – the man doing the honours is faceless, formless, nothing but a driving, thrusting force. Rough hands tight in all of that lovely thick hair. Words on his lips that Woods would never utter, like *fuck* and *yeah* and *oh you little whore*.

You little cocksucker, I think, and then my legs don't want to hold me up any more. Even after he's put the idea to rest with an unsurprisingly disappointed sounding 'but he never did', I can't help being a little breathless when I next speak.

'He never fucked you?'

'Never. No. I told you I hadn't had anyone touch me there. I wouldn't lie.'

'And you never … touched him … or … or … did stuff with him of any kind?'

'Apart from the talking, no,' he says, with just a hint of disappointment in his voice again. Lord, I'm going to be thinking of that low tone for a long, long time afterward. 'But then, I understand that's pretty much how he was with you too. Never tried to fuck you, or go down on you, or have you go down on him. Right?'

It's strangely sad that I wish I had something else to tell him. But of course I don't.

'Yes,' I say, simply, and then he shakes his head. I understand why, however, I mean, it's the kind of thing most people would shake their heads over. I had an odd, detached sort of relationship with Woods, and now he's going to tell me that I'm an odd, detached sort of person.

It's why I can't be with him the way he wants someone to be with him. He probably wants a girl who's much more open and warm, and who can do something other than just stand there while he lies on her bed.

Or at least, I think that's what he wants until he says:

'It's the only thing I never understood about him, that he had you … he had you right in the palm of his hand. And yet somehow he didn't want to spend every second of every day touching you all over. He didn't want to make love to you.' He pauses and flicks his gaze back up to me, genuine confusion all over his perfect face. 'Don't you think that's weird, Ms Harding?'

Chapter Ten

'I can't help noticing that you haven't said anything for a really, *really* long time.'

He's right, you know. It's been at least a minute – probably roughly around the amount of seconds it took me to come all over his face. There's nothing I can do about it, however. He's just said something that plucked at heartstrings I don't have, and he doesn't seem to know he's done it.

He's just ... laid there, cock still impossibly hard. And when I say impossibly I mean the actual literal meaning of the word because seriously, how is he still aroused? Shouldn't it have gone down by now? I just stood here in silence for an eternity – it's not right that he's still got an erection.

Even though I still seem to have my ladyboner. I keep counting down all the things he's just said in my head: me and Woods, him and Woods, him and me ... *making love.* And then something just sort of clasps my pussy in a warm, wet hand, and everything I wanted to do or say runs right out of me.

'You OK? Where did I lose you? It was the word "love" in there, right?' He points at the door and near-mouths his next words. 'I'll just get my coat.'

I swear, I actually let out a little amused sound when he does it. And though it's funny – God, he's funny – it's also sad at the same time, because I can't remember any man making me laugh. Literally: I can't name one.

It's just him, with his too-big gestures and his future career in mime. He makes me grab his leg and say, 'No, no', while doing something weird, like *giggling*. I'm giggling like some girl I never was, and reeling him back in even though he's still trying to escape. He's halfway over the edge of the bed when I finally manage to get a grip on his body – though the grip isn't exactly a good one.

I've just sort of curled myself against the back of him, arms around his middle. And he takes note of this, in a very particular sort of way.

'Oh, so you *are* going to fuck me – oh OK then,' he says, and here's the thing – I laugh again. It's easy to, when I get to hide my face in his shoulder-blades and listen to him laughing too.

It vibrates against the side of my face when I press said place to him. When I hold him for just a second, like this, and feel how soft his skin is. How furry he is in front, and so big too. It's sort of like hugging a really lovely bear, only without the word in there that I'm absolutely not doing.

I'm not hugging him, all right?

'Are you ... holding me?'

I'm not doing that either.

'No. I'm just getting ready to fuck you through the mattress.'

'I see. Building up to it, huh?'

'I'm drawing it out until you go insane.'

'Well, you're pretty close to that right now. *Fairly* sure I can feel your breasts pressing into my back.'

154

'You can't. I just have really weird elbows.'

He tries to glance at me over his shoulder, but it's hard because I barely make up half of him. It's like he's got a knapsack on his back, in all honesty.

'I don't think it's healthy to have such pillowy arm joints. Plus, you know, I think I can *see* your elbows. They're right here with the arms you've got wrapped around me.'

'They're not my arms. They're someone else's.'

'Oh yeah? Are we playing sexy stranger now?'

I rub my face against his back in a way I can only describe as *contented*. Even though I don't want to describe it as anything of the sort.

'Is that what you want to do? You want me to be some chick you picked up in a bar?'

He laughs, long and low.

'You think I pick up *chicks* in *bars*? My God, you don't know me *at all*.'

'OK then,' I say, as something very specific flutters through my mind. Something very specific that he said – about how he didn't, with Woods. But that he *would have*, if asked. 'Some dude in a bar.'

'That … that wasn't exactly what I was saying.'

'No. You were saying that you're about as smooth as granite and couldn't pick up a girl to save your life. But I'm saying: so would you fuck a guy, if the opportunity arose?'

I almost feel him hesitate – just like he did when the topic first came up. Just a hint of embarrassment there in him, even if it's not enough to make him silent, to make him dodge the question the way I probably would if he asked me just about anything.

'If you told me to, yeah,' he says finally, and Lord I don't know how to respond to that. I was imagining a simple *yes*, and had planned my reply accordingly. Now I have to come up with something way, way better.

'Would you do anything I told you to?'

And that was *totally* not it. I should have said something more sensitive, I think. Something with poise and understanding, that encompasses the depths our relationship has apparently gotten to.

Instead I just jerk some words out and hope for the best.

'Yes.'

'You know how badly I could take advantage of that, right?'

'Yes, *sir*,' he says, and ohhh that word he practically purrs, on the end. It still has the ability to make me absolutely boneless, even after we've cuddled and laughed and been generally more relaxed about things.

'I could just ... I don't know ... make you take off all your clothes ...'

He lets out a little amused breath, as though to say – *huh, that's not so bad*. But I have a feeling he's going to regret doing so in a moment. Oh, he's going to regret it all right.

'And then once you're naked, I might ... tease you a little,' I continue, and as I do I give him a little preview of that said same thing. I just ... slide my hand down his solid belly until I encounter the thick root of his cock, and encircle it with my thumb and forefinger. Gentle enough to get him to buck, tight enough to make him hold back just a little.

And of course he moans. He always moans. He moans so loudly that the urge to push myself against the curve of his ass becomes a bit too much for me to take – so I do it, slow and like I'm hardly doing anything at all. I'm really just scratching an itch or making myself more comfortable, and if either of those things ruffles the silk of my robe up between my legs and just kind of strokes it over my clit, that can't be helped.

Not even if he says to me that he knows exactly what I'm doing.

'Yeah,' he tells me. 'Rub yourself on me.'

And then I don't know. Maybe I die or something. I certainly lose track of what I was saying, at the very least, and I've just got to chastise him for that. How dare he throw me off with his catalogue of wildly arousing things to do, said in that syrupy, lowdown voice of his!

'Did I say you could talk, Ben?'

He shakes his head once in lieu of a real answer, but I know why. And it's not because I've just told him he needs to be silent either. It's because I've just found the sensitive and very slick spot just underneath the head of his cock, and am currently circling it with my thumb.

'Where was I again? Oh – that's right. You're naked, and probably slippery with oil, and definitely very aroused. None of which should be very hard to achieve, because as you've told me before: a stiff breeze could get you hard.' He trembles violently against me, but this time I can't tell why. It could be the humiliating things I'm saying. It could be the fact that I'm now rubbing all of the lovely pre-come he's produced over the slit at the tip of his cock. 'And then once I've got you like that, I'll just … I don't know. Maybe invite all of my friends over for cocktails, with you as our diligent waiter.'

'You – OK. OK. Can I talk now?' he asks, and oh the urge to grin is huge. I can't get enough of the way he makes mistakes – blundering into them before attempting some sort of rectification five minutes too late. It's like he wants me to collar him for stuff, though even as I'm thinking such a thing I realise how stupid it is.

Of *course* he wants me to collar him for stuff. No one could forget that they're not supposed to talk ten seconds after being told just that. He's not stupid. He's as clever as fuck.

'No. In fact, I'm not sure you should ever be allowed to talk again.' And yes, I'm absolutely lying when I say that. If he was suddenly rendered mute tomorrow I'd be devastated – where else would I find someone who actually enjoys telling me about that one time he came all over himself? 'Which is why I'll probably gag you before everyone comes over. You know – just in case there's something filthy you want to say to a group of refined businesswomen.'

This time he just gives me a long, low groan, in response to what I've said – though I can't help noticing that it directly coincides with the word *businesswomen*. Which just makes me wonder what he's picturing exactly.

Is it the same as the image I've got in my head? Several stern-faced women in tight little suits as crisp as a new day … all of them sat around with drinks in their hands. Some discussion about something inconsequential going on between them.

As my glistening, nude little man-toy serves everyone margaritas.

'But by then I think I'd have you well trained anyway. Even without the gag you wouldn't dare say anything to anyone – not when one of them fondles your undoubtedly stiff cock as you do your best to pour her another drink.'

I'll be honest: I doubt he could say his own name while a stranger jerked him off. But we'll leave that for now, because oh this fantasy's so *delicious*. And I know it is for him too, because when I tell him about the fondling he stops pretending he's got any restraint at all. He just turns his face into the bedspread and starts fucking my hand in earnest.

'Yeah, you like that?' I ask him, but of course he can't answer. I honestly didn't realise how delightful that could be, considering how good he is with the talking. 'You like the idea of some anonymous women smacking your bare ass as you pass by, or maybe … maybe giving you a little lick, huh?'

I make the circle I've got around his dick very loose now. I have to, because he isn't just jerking into it any more. He's rolling his hips and rubbing the swollen head against my palm and if he carries on he's going to come.

I can almost feel it building, somewhere around his lower back. And even if I couldn't his desperate, guttural moans are an absolutely massive clue.

'Yeah, I think one of them leans over as you stand at attention, awaiting further orders. And then she pokes out her tongue and just tastes the strand of liquid that's trailing down over your stiff cock. What do you think, Benjamin? You think that sounds nice?'

He breaks, this time. It's definitely not a moan that comes out of him – I know it isn't. It's a breathless, panted 'please', and judging by how close he's getting to just rubbing himself off on my bedspread, is aimed in the direction of my teasing hand.

'How about if one of my friends is a guy?'

'OK, I have to talk because you clearly don't want me to come, but I am *definitely* going to come if you keep telling me this stuff. It doesn't matter how little you touch me – I'm going to do it anyway,' he blurts out, quite suddenly. And ohhh I know I should be mad at his disobedient ways, but fuck it – I can't be. I can't be. I just want to make him worse than he already is, instead.

'If you come, I'll punish you,' I say, then just for good measure I slide my free hand down over his back, to those marks he still has all over his ass.

159

And I *rake my nails right over them*.

'Ah, God. God – *OK*. I'm calm, OK? I'm calm.'

'You'd better be, because now I'm going to talk about how much my friend … "David" really, really wants to suck your cock.'

'Is this seriously an actual person?' he gasps out, and good *Lord* he sounds frantic. I can't tell what the franticness means either, but it doesn't seem of consequence. Nothing's of consequence when he's got a hand between his legs and is doing something I initially want to tell him off for.

Until I realise what he's actually doing. He's getting a good, firm grip on his balls, so that when I say things like *suck* and *cock* he can yank on them hard enough to make me wince.

'No. But you can still picture him, can't you? You can still picture him slowly easing his mouth down over your big, stiff cock.'

'Yeah. Yeah.'

'In fact, I'm betting you can picture just about everyone there, taking turns to suck you off,' I say, and I swear for a second I can see it so clearly *I* almost come. I've never been this aroused so soon after an orgasm, and it's definitely the fault of this perverted story I've thought up.

And maybe also his fault, for being so turned on by it that he has to yank on his balls to stop himself coming. He has to actually push my hand away, because apparently brushing his cock with my palm is just too, too much.

'They take *turns*?' he asks.

'Of course they take turns. It wouldn't be fair if only one person got to try out your delicious cock, would it?'

He's practically sobbing, now, and the incredulity in his voice has reached fever pitch. It's like he can't believe that someone could actually come up with this stuff – which only makes me wonder what he was like with Woods. What happened when Woods told him that once he tied me naked to his desk?

'You seriously think my cock is delicious?'

'I think if all of my friends saw you naked and aroused, they wouldn't be able to keep their hands off you. I think they'd want to touch you all over – and you know what? You'd let them. You're such a slut that you'd let them suck and rub you everywhere, all of those women, all at once. Two of them licking your nipples, one of them sucking and playing with your balls. And then the man ...'

'Is he sucking my cock?'

'Is that what you want?'

'Yeah. He could force me. He could force me.'

'He could force you to let him suck your cock? Or he could force you to suck his?'

Of course, I expect him to hesitate here, just like he did before. I mean, this is definitely a step up from some vague, theoretical question. He's close to orgasm and the whole scenario is really, really clear in my head, at the very least. And judging by how rigid his body's gone, and how tightly his eyes are closed, I'm guessing it's fairly clear in his.

But he doesn't pause for even the smallest moment.

'I want him to force his cock into my mouth.'

'And then what?'

'And then he could fuck my face. He could hold me down and fuck me like that, while you suck me off.'

Now it's my turn to hesitate. Though really the word 'hesitate' doesn't quite encompass everything that happens to me. I think I go numb below the waist, once the electro-magnetic pulse of pleasure has finished wiping out my groin.

'Is that what you want, huh?' I ask, but I already know

the answer. He isn't just squeezing his eyes shut now. He's got a hand over them as he rocks against whatever he can find, helplessly.

And I can't really blame him for that. I'm the one who's supposed to be in control, and I don't want to hold back any more. I want to clasp my hand around his cock instead, and feel him shudder and gasp as he jerks through that tight circle. I want him to imagine exactly how it would feel to be pinned and fucked so completely, and I want it so much that I don't stop at some sloppy, largely passive hand-job.

I make him turn onto his back so I can just lean over his body and lick his stiff, solid length, from root to tip.

Of course, a bunch of other stuff happens when I do. His hips jerk up, a sound escapes his mouth, his hand leaves his eyes. But I think the thing I like best is his dazed expression when he glances down his body at me and finds what I sort of meant to fix the moment it occurred.

My robe is open. And I mean *open*. It's practically off my shoulders and I'm finding it very hard to care about that fact when he's looking at my breasts like he possibly wants to drown in them. I can see him just kind of … inching his hand in their general direction, as though maybe I won't notice he's groping my tits if he does it really, really slowly.

He doesn't get there, however. He's too busy being stunned by the fact that I'm almost bare, and am currently flicking my tongue over the swollen head of his dick.

'Oh you're naked,' he says, only it comes out all in one big breath. It isn't like words really, but he doesn't try to clarify. He just eats at my body with his eyes in a way I don't think anyone else has ever done, taking in all the parts he hasn't yet seen.

God, I can't believe he hasn't yet seen me. I can't believe

I feel self-conscious about it, even now. But I do, I do – I swear, it takes all my effort not to flinch when he just strokes his fingertips over my shoulder until most of the rest of the robe slides down.

'Uh, don't do that,' he says, and he does so because I've gone a little way beyond some teasing little licks. I'm not quite sure when it happened, but I seem to be kissing the silky smooth tip of his cock in a very wet, rude sort of manner. 'Don't – Jesus. I didn't think you'd look this way.'

This time when I give him a little kiss, I do it with pretty much all of my mouth. All over the head of his cock, greedily, messily, before returning to the matter at hand.

'How did you think I'd look?'

'I don't know, I don't know. More – *ooohhhh that's so intense* – more severe. Angular, I guess. Your suits don't do you justice.'

And by 'that' he means the long, strong suck I give him as I ease down over his cock, then all the way back up again. In fact, I do it so hard and so long that my cheeks hollow out as I go, something which he sure seems to appreciate. He almost fucks up into my mouth in just the way we discussed some guy doing to him not a moment before.

'I see.'

'You're so soft ... oh, your tits ...' he moans, but he's pretty much lost it by now. His eyes are just those hazy little slits again – like they were on the table when I lashed his ass. And I can see the hand he wants to put on me clenching at the sheets somewhere to the right of his body.

'You want to touch them?'

'Are you kidding? Yes. Yeah –'

'You want to lick them?'

'Fuck, *yes*.'

'And how about if I let you stick your cock between them, fuck me there, like that, then come all over my chest and face?'

'Ohhh man, you're messing with me, right? I'm sorry, I'm sorry –'

'Sorry for what?'

'Sorry I want to cream all over you. Sorry I want to fuck your tits and your pussy oh please just let me come. Can I come?'

There's a moment where I'm pretty sure I'm going to let him. He's struggling to keep his hips on the mattress and the head of his cock feels oh so tense and slick. Every time I make a slow circle with my tongue around and around it, or maybe ease my lips in a nice tight circle down over it, I can practically make out the effect it has on him. It's like an electric charge goes through his body, and he has to clench hard just about everywhere to keep it in.

But then the moment passes, and I find myself saying something else instead.

'I don't think so, Benjamin.'

His fingers wriggle and twist around the handfuls of sheets he's gotten hold of. Like a little kid, I think, unable to contain himself at the sight of a sweet shop, though what sweet shop I've just shown him, I don't know.

'I think I'm going to use you to get off instead.'

And then it's clear. He wants to be denied. He wants to be tormented. In fact, he wants to go one further than all of that – and he isn't afraid to tell me so.

'Oh God yeah, do that. Say that word again.'

I give him a little lick, right on that sensitive spot just below the head.

'And which word might that be?'

I genuinely have no idea. His face has gone all flushed and

he doesn't seem capable of closing his mouth – his lips look like some soft, wet fruit that's been split down the middle – but it could just be due to the grip I've now got on his cock.

Or you know. It could be this: '*Use*,' he says, and then again, just for good measure. 'Use me up. Use me like I'm your toy.'

Oh, Lord. Lord, how does he know? How can he be so perfect like this, and not see it? He seems a little ashamed of himself for saying something so vaguely ridiculous, even if its very vague ridiculousness is what makes him breathe all shaky and weird when I crawl my way up his body.

'Are you … are you actually going to do it?' he asks, when I get to his mouth – but he doesn't really need to. Before he's gotten the words out I'm kind of answering them for him, and I'm not doing so by drawing him a diagram.

I'm doing it in a way that makes him go all still, those misty-blue eyes of his fixing on my face in a kind of delighted, wondering sort of manner that excites me almost as much as what I'm doing does. He looks like he's figuring me out, I think, as I rub my spread sex over his deliciously solid belly. He looks like he's so aroused that his words have gotten caught halfway out of his mouth, and though I think he wants to stop himself from touching me, he doesn't quite manage it.

Instead he just slides his hands down over my hips, over the curve of my ass, and once he's there he grips me, tightly. Tugs at me, just a little bit, until I'm *really* sliding my swollen clit against him.

Though it's not that taut little bead he notices particularly.

'Ohhh that's really slippery,' he tells me, as though I really might have no idea. I was wet enough after the licking he gave me – fuck knows what I'm like now. I'm guessing someone could take a swim in my pussy, if they so chose.

Or you know. Maybe they could just rub all of that wetness all over Benjamin Tate until he goes nuts. He can't seem to keep it together when I cut him off, though of course I understand why now.

I think he actually *prefers* being denied.

'Put your hands above your head,' I tell him and he just does it. He even clasps his left wrist in the circle of his right, just for good measure, and oh the way it all looks ...

I can't get over the heavy curves of his biceps, framing his head like that. Or how shuddery he seems with anticipation, despite the tense and sure hold he's got on himself. He's almost a maze of contradictions in that moment, and all of them are almost as exciting as the slick sound of my cunt sliding over his skin.

As the feel of his perfectly soft lips, when I stroke my tongue over them.

'I'm going to ride that thick cock of yours now,' I tell him, in between a million little licks that seem to send him almost out of control. He gasps every time I do it, and bucks his hips, and when he does both I can feel his cock butting up against my ass. I can feel how wet it is at the tip, how ready he is to fuck, and though I know I should maintain my calm that fact makes it hard.

I think my hands are shaking as I lean over and fish a condom out of my bedside drawer. And then I know my hands are shaking, because it's obvious when you're trying to unwrap a rubber and slide it down over someone's cock. I expect him to comment on it – on my fumbling, sloppy efforts to get the thing on him – but he doesn't.

He just lies there, squirming, as I do my level best to squeeze his immense cock into something that's clearly two sizes too small for it. By the time I'm done it looks like its cutting off the blood supply, but he hardly seems to mind.

He's busy mouthing at that smooth curve of muscle that's just in reach of his teeth and tongue, little tight groans of pleasure escaping him every now and then. All of his attention on his body and everything that's happening to it, until I do more than just touch him.

I take that big, thick cock of his, and slide it through my slippery folds. Like I'm just trying him out, I guess, though it ends up being more than that. Once I've felt the soft-but-hard head of his cock against my clit, I don't really want to do anything else but rub it there, nice and slow.

Which he doesn't particularly appreciate.

'Oh come on, Elea–' he starts, then seems to come to his senses before he finishes the word. However, once he's done so he doesn't seem to know what he should go with instead, and I have to say – I'm no help to him there. I don't know what he should go with either. 'Sir' seems too formal, at this moment, and he's hardly being obedient. 'Ms Harding' is for the office; 'baby' is something you reserve for your girlfriend.

So he plays it safe and goes with nothing instead.

'Come on, don't tease,' he tells me, but I'm in the teasing business now. My clit feels so stiff, and even stiffer against the solid tip of his cock. Every time I stroke that thick thing back and forth these sweet little almost-aftershocks shudder through my body, like a reminder of the orgasm I had not so long ago.

And the promise of one I could have right now, if I really wanted to. I could come all over his cock, fast and hard, and afterwards let him have what he so clearly needs. He's so eager for it he's practically jerking up into my grip, and every now and then he holds his breath, like he's just on the verge of it and wants to feel it fully.

But that would be just too easy, I think. Far, far too easy.

'If you come before I do, I'll never let you do this again,' I tell him, and just as his eyes widen and his mouth opens to let out a bit of outrage, I find my wet and waiting hole with his hard cock and just ease down over it.

Though in all honesty, I've no idea how I do it. He's so big that I actually gasp, and I don't get much further than the halfway point. In fact, when it gets to the halfway point he actually jerks his hands down and grabs my hips, as though he's the one who's afraid of where he's going to end up.

And then he apologises too, just for good measure.

'Sorry,' he says, but he doesn't explain why. Is it for the hands he's now got on me, even though I told him to keep them above his head? Or is it for this absolutely incredible thing that's currently spreading me open, in a way that seems to be making me flush and say some pretty stupid things?

'Oh you're soooo big,' I think I tell him, like I've just found myself in a ridiculous porno of my own life. Though to my credit, I'm not certain I've ever felt anything quite like this before. It's hardly a shock that it's making me flush all over and gasp incoherently, and I'm just thankful that he doesn't want me to feel bad about it.

In fact, he seems more concerned with the effect it has on him than anything else.

'Seriously? You're seriously going to say stuff like that? And you're gonna also look like that while you say it? But I'm not allowed to come. You say stuff and look like that and I have to somehow not come.'

I test him out just a little – just a little rock back and forth, so that the big, thick head of his cock almost rolls against something awesome inside me – and watch him jerk as though stung. *Then* I answer.

'Why? What's so bad about saying that? I mean, you *are* big. Ohhh you're so big that I can't even take all of you into my tight, wet cunt.'

'That's ... OK. That's not cool.'

'Mmm, baby – you feel so good. Here, watch. Watch your cock sliding in and out of my little pussy,' I say, and then it's quite possible that I actually show him. It doesn't take much to do, after all – I just brace myself on his crooked legs and lean back a little, and everything's made nice and clear. The split of my sex around his solid cock. Everything all slippery and silky and so, so swollen with arousal.

I can make out the tight bead of my clit, and as he watches with something like incredulity on his face, I just reach between my legs and rub it a little. You know – just enough to force a moan out of me, in a way I'm sure he's going to appreciate. Ohhh, I'm sure he will.

'Are you *kidding* with this? I think I'm going to die. I am literally going to die if you don't stop. No no no – don't fuck me like that. Don't, don't!'

I'm fairly certain he's referring to the slightly more vigorous fucking I'm giving him, but the truth is I can't help it. It feels too good to stop, and especially when I just kind of rock myself against him. Every time I do it something very thick and very solid urges itself against that bundle of nerves inside me, and the resulting sensation is strong enough to make me take my hand away.

Though I don't do so because I'm close, and want to draw this out. I do it for a different reason, one that occurs to me when I roll my hips and hit it just right.

I could actually come like this. I don't need to rub my

clit or have him do the honours. I think I could really get myself off on his cock, with just a little bit of help from the way he looks – all glossy with sweat and desperate to do it – and the hot little sounds he's making, most of which go right through me every time they spill out of his mouth.

Even the weird things he says excite me, though that isn't anything unusual. Yesterday I got aroused when he told me about the copier being on the fritz, so him saying, 'Oh God I can't watch' is something of a no-brainer.

He just pushes the words out, then after them covers his eyes – as though he's watching a horror movie, instead of what he's actually doing. Namely, fucking up into me while pretending he's not doing that at all. No, no, he's just casually minding his own business, one hand gripping tightly to my hip, the other shielding his eyes from the sight of my bouncing breasts and my flushed throat and the rolling contortions I'm putting my body through, to get the best possible pressure on my G-spot.

And if he just so happens to shove up into me while doing those things, well, I'm not going to criticise him for it. I wouldn't criticise anything that helped along that heavy, pulsing sensation that seems to be developing in my lower belly – not even if it's him bursting out with something even stranger, after a moment of prolonged and largely silent bliss.

'You're not doing it right!' he says, and I swear, he's so fierce about it that for a moment I almost stop to check. Did I accidentally start fucking his elbow when I wasn't looking? It's true that I'm barely paying attention to anything at this point. The sensation has gotten so intense that I've started fearing it, and instead of pushing towards it I'm sort of backing away. I'm almost covering my own eyes, and I'm definitely shaking all over.

I don't want to be, but it just can't be helped. I might actually come from penetration alone, which had previously seemed like some mythical thing that only sexual gymnasts ever achieved.

Whereas I, on the other hand, am not a sexual gymnast. Instead, I'm apparently someone who gets so worked up during sex that I fail at it hopelessly, and have to be told off by my almost-beside-himself boy toy.

Seriously – he's beside himself. There is another him next to the one I'm fucking, and this version is *pissed*.

'No, no – here. Move back,' he says, but I haven't the faintest clue what he means. I don't think I've ever heard him be so forceful, even if that's not quite the right word for how he's behaving. He's more agitated than anything else – with maybe just a hint of pleading in his expression – and both make me want to do something very odd.

I want to put my hands on his face, and just … I don't know. Soothe him a little. Tell him that it's all just a game really, and if he comes I won't do as I promised. I won't forbid him to ever be with me like this again, because in all honesty I don't think I could stay away.

How can I when he's like this? When he looks at me with those lust-stoked eyes and takes a hold of my hips in his big, broad hands, and then just oh God then … I don't know what he does because the short, sharp shock of pleasure is so fierce it briefly blocks out all rational thought.

I think I cry a little. I didn't even cry when a car ran over my childhood pet, but something in that general area comes out of me when he shoves me into a very particular sort of position. He just kind of tilts my hips, and angles my body, and then suddenly his cock isn't just rubbing against that place inside me, in a slow, leisurely, *polite* sort of fashion.

It's jerking against me, hard, in a way that makes me do something mad like try to escape.

'Little too much, huh?' he murmurs, and I can't fault him for that smug note in his voice. He should feel smug when he can apparently make me grab reflexively onto his shoulders and grunt like a man.

'No, it's fine,' I say, but I'm lying. It's not fine. I can't bear it, and especially not when he's got his hand over my mound and he's just kind of pressing and pressing there, as though maybe he can mould that sensitive front wall around his cock from the outside in.

Which he absolutely can. Ohhh Lord he can. He can so much that I have to dig my nails into the shoulders I'm definitely not gripping, just to stop myself from jumping seventeen feet in the air then running out the door.

'Yeah, yeah like that,' he says, but I swear to God I'm not doing anything. I'm simply kneeling here, dumbstruck, as he just kind of urges me into orgasm. As he just kisses my mouth, and tells me I'm beautiful – all of which he can now do because I'm pretty much past resistance. I'm shaking almost as much as he is and I'm moaning with an alarming frequency, and when he say, 'You wanna make it even better?' I utterly fail to say no. I should slap him really, or pull his hair. Do something to prove I'm this wonderful Dom he seems to think I am, rather than this trembling mass I appear to have become. But the most I can muster is an abrupt little 'what?' when he makes his next suggestion, followed by yet another frisson of pleasure.

'Turn over,' he says, and I think of a million delightful things. He's going to fuck me while he fingers my ass. Or maybe he's going to fuck me while he does incredible things to the bundle of nerves that barely existed before right now.

Either way, I only hesitate long enough for him to tell me something delightful, like *don't worry, we can go right back to me being your fucktoy a second after you've come all over my cock* before doing as he's asked. I slide myself jerkily off his cock and clamber around clumsily until I'm on all fours on the bed.

And then he just gets behind me and spreads my legs with his good, gentle hands. Tells me he'll take it easy, because oh Lord he feels even bigger like this.

The blunt head of his cock is like a fist trying to work its way in. And although he fondles me a little first – those long fingers sliding into my pussy, briefly, in a manner that's definitely not all about easing the way for his big prick – I can feel myself clenching, when he tries for it.

Then less so, after he's whispered in my ear.

'God, you're so tight,' he says, and then everything just sort of opens for him. As though today we're in Oppositeworld and once he's stated something, I have to go in the other direction. I have to let him slide inside, slow and easy and oh so good.

Though not so good that I can make out why he's done this. I mean, sure – he feels a little bigger like this. I'm a little more spread open, and I like having the headboard to put my hands on instead of his shoulders. It's less intimate, more straightforward, and the clasp he gets on my hips is like that too.

But it's not all that different.

He just wants to work me back on his cock, and I don't see why he shouldn't do it. He's still as faintly awestruck as he was before, still my toy, when he draws that delicious cock nearly all the way out and then –

And then –

173

'Oh my God. No. *No*,' I blurt out, in a voice that almost sounds panicked. I think I sort of twist and try to maybe push him away a little, because seriously, seriously. No. I can't. I can't do whatever this feeling is, and especially not when he sounds so gleeful about it.

'Yeah, it's there, right? You like that?' he says, but I do *not* like it. It's making my body cave in on itself. I'm no longer holding onto the headboard, I'm *hanging* on to it, and then he does it again and oh Jesus *Christ*.

'Ohhh Ben, yeah. Do it there,' I tell him, but I swear it's not me doing the honours. I'm somewhere outside my own body looking down on the sobbing mess I've become, disapprovingly.

While said sobbing mess gets thoroughly fucked, hard. Oh God he does it so hard. He holds back for just a little while – just long enough to make me beg a little, for more – but once I've moaned his name and put my hand over his and made some stupid attempt to jerk myself back on his cock, he lets it all go.

'Yeah, yeah you like that? Ohhh I can't believe how wet you are. Oh seriously – you're just creaming all over my cock, baby, just tell me. Are you gonna do it? Are you close?'

He sounds desperate, I think. More so than before, because there's a shaky edge to his voice where there wasn't previously, and he's getting very near to digging his fingers into my hips. He slows his thrusts, just a little, like maybe he needs to take some of the pressure off – but I can't have that.

I don't tell him so, but I think I *am* actually close. Every time he fucks that thing into me a little burst of sensation radiates outward from the contact point, and it's definitely building to something. I'm going to come, and I'm going to do so while he holds me and fucks me, and despite all of these things I don't really give a shit.

For the first time in my life, I don't care. I just tell him to fuck me harder, come on, fuck my cunt, and when he finally, blissfully does I moan his name *again*.

'Ben,' I tell him, then even worse: 'Oh you fuck me so good.'

Because, well ... it's the truth. He *is* a good fuck. He's so good that the second he does pick up the pace, that bursting sensation – that blooming sensation – coils tight, low down in my belly. It's coils so tightly that I have to bite my lip and make some sort of wholly embarrassing keening sound, a moment before he tells me exactly what I'm doing.

'Fuck, you're coming, aren't you? Are you really coming? Oh my God, oh Jesus your pussy's gone all tight and no, no – you're gonna make me go off. Easy ... easy,' he pants, but I can't be easy. I've never had an orgasm like this, and it isn't a simple thing to navigate. It's like a fist, squeezing and relaxing somewhere inside my lower belly. And once that sensation's done with, all of this warmth just spreads through my thighs and my pussy until I can hardly take it.

It's too lovely. I don't deserve something this lovely. I have to tell him to stop because it's going on for far too long and besides, I'm pretty sure my cunt is cutting off his blood supply. It feels like I'm trying to clench his cock to death, and once I'm calm and sort of limp, he confirms this suspicion.

'Thought you were going to squeeze my orgasm right out of me then,' he says, in that good good way he has. I don't think he means to, exactly, but he so often offers me just the thing to put me at ease, once I'm all wrung out and so unsure about everything that just happened.

Though of course once I've considered this, I also have to

consider something else swiftly afterwards. Because I think …
I think he just implied that he *still* hasn't climaxed. In fact,
I'm fairly certain he hasn't, due to several pretty big clues.

He's shaking, for one. And when a little aftershock goes
through me and my pussy flutters around his cock, it's obvious
he's still incredibly hard. Plus, he makes this sound: 'Ah-huh,'
the second I do it.

Somehow, somehow, I've had two amazing orgasms, and
he's had *zero*. Not one, not two, *zero*. Nada. Nothing. I've
had relationships where guys have gone over before we've
even gotten to the bedroom, then fallen asleep. I've had relationships where I've *asked* for things, and still been denied.

But I told him to do this, and he obeyed me to some kind
of insane point of madness. It's like he's simultaneously ready
to faint, and go nuts – or at least, that's the way it looks
when I finally manage to ease myself off his jerking cock
and turn myself around.

'Was that nice?' he asks, as though he just took me for a
pleasant walk in the park.

'What do you think?'

'I think it's really easy to make you come.' He pauses,
but when he's trying to be perfectly calm and just consider
things, he's still vibrating like a maniac. His face is all flushed
right down to his collarbone. His nipples are two tight little
points, and his cock … Lord, have mercy.

It hardly surprises me when I offer what I do. It should,
really – and later I'll probably feel strange about it. Like this
whole thing was too flipped, and outside the parameters of
where it's supposed to be. But when I look at him like this,
all trembly and half-crazed, it's easy enough to do.

'I want you to come on my face now,' I tell him, and he
hesitates – but he doesn't do for so long. Not half as long

as he probably would if I'd just flat out ordered him, in my office, three minutes after he'd entered.

Currently he's past the point of not-being-sure, and the second I spread myself out on the bed he just looms over me – so big, God, he's so big. I think of all the things he could do to me in that moment. All of the things, in a strange, lurid succession – how he could manhandle me if he really wanted to, and force me to do all of the things he just kind of coaxed me into.

Though that's the thing about him, isn't it? That he could do all of that stuff, but doesn't. He seems conflicted about taking his now bare cock in his hand, right over my face. And after a few strokes over that swollen length, I know what he's trying to do.

He's trying to aim it somewhere other than the rudest possible place someone could do it – like maybe over my tits instead, or possibly the bed sheets. And it's not because he's making an effort to be polite, or like a gentleman, either. It's just the way he is. He's just lovely like this. Considerate, in a way I've never known a man be before.

Which of course makes it absolutely easy to tell him to do it, and oh so much more arousing, too, when he finally does. It's like pushing someone over the edge; it's like sticking my finger in him and twisting everything around. *I'm corrupting him*, I think, and then he groans for me, loud and long. He tells me he can't help it a second before he jerks and groans and finally does it, all over my face.

And when I say all over, I mean all over. He fills my mouth, coats my cheeks and my eyelids in long, thick ribbons of delicious come. By the time he's done I know what I must look like – utterly debauched, utterly satisfied, and so filthy that for a second he doesn't seem to know what to say.

I'm pretty sure he's about to apologise. He's practically melting and his shaking thighs don't seem to want to hold him, but yeah – he's about to take a moment to be sorry. So I cut him off, as gleeful as he was, earlier on.

'Now gimme a kiss,' I tell him – but here's the thing.

He actually *does*.

Chapter Eleven

I think it's around four-thirty, or maybe five. Reasonably it could be any time at all, because I've got my eyes closed and I'm promising myself that I won't open them. Not even if he says something all soft and tender, I won't open them. I'll just lie here on the barest edge of the bed – as I've done all night, like his massive body somehow grew cooties when it hit someplace past midnight – and wait for him to retrieve the rest of his clothes.

And though I want to say something to him, I won't. It's better this way, with him just leaving. I mean, let's not pretend here. We're not going to have breakfast together and chitchat over the morning paper, and then hold hands on the way to work.

That's not what this is.

Instead, it's him leaning over me while I brutalise myself into fake-sleep, to leave a barely-there kiss on my cheek. You know – the way that normal people do when they have those things called feelings, and want to express them.

I think the one he's trying for is called 'affection'.

I think the one I'm trying for is called 'denial'.

Because although I tell him that we really need to establish some better boundaries once I get to work, it's not exactly what I'm thinking as I look at him, stood there on his spot. I'm thinking of how sharp and sweet his come tasted on my tongue. How smouldering his gaze seems, when he levels it at me.

And most of all I'm thinking about how cold I need to be to combat all of these things.

'So I think we'll try something a little different today,' I say, but a calm, still tone seems to make no difference. His expression practically overflows with pleasure – eyes narrowing to slits, that smile as slow and sweet as syrup.

'What*ever* you want, Ms Harding,' he says, in a voice that affects me almost as much as his position does. I didn't have to ask him to put his hands behind his back, or stand with his shoulders nice and straight. He just did it all, for me. All for me.

'I want to really ... test the limits of your control.'

'Oh, you mean the control that I don't have?'

My mind tromps on the button marked denial for me, over and over and over again. He does not make me so crazy that I just want to take him home with me again tonight, and probably listen to romantic music with him while taking a bath. He does not, he does not.

'Yes, that's the control I'm talking about. I mean, you *did* come all over my face last night, Ben. How on earth am I supposed to forgive something like that?'

'But you *told* –' he starts, in one big burst of righteous indignation.

Before he realises, and reins himself back in. He doesn't *need* to do something like protest his own innocence, of course, because all of this is just a lovely, lovely game without any real consequences at all. Things can shift within the parameters of it, and I can lie and he can lie and we can tease and protest and do whatever we want.

But no one gets kissed on the cheek with something like exquisite tenderness afterwards.

'I'm sorry, Benjamin. Was there something you wanted to say?' I ask, but he just grits his teeth. Gives me a lovely long lick of ruefulness in his gaze.

'No, *sir*.'

'Excellent. Come and have a look at your present then, would you?' I say, and though I lean back in my chair and act as casual as I can – meaningless paperwork is a blessing, it really is – I can't help the flicker of delight I feel to see him hesitating a little. He just kind of stops about six inches from my desk, almost up on tiptoe.

A question on his lips that he's clearly unsure about asking.

'Are you seriously wanting me to …?'

'Walk around with a sex toy deep in your sweet little ass? I think that's a given. I mean – unless you have another orifice I could shove this thing into.' I pause, as though I'm really considering. 'Your mouth might be nice.'

'I couldn't walk around the office with a sex toy in my mouth! That would be … *obscene*.'

I have to say, I really appreciate the way he purrs the latter. It's like he believes it, oh of course he believes it. Yet at the same time maybe he also appreciates how that word feels on his tongue.

'But as for the other thing I just mentioned – that's A-OK,' I say, and though I expect him to look caught out or unsure, he doesn't this time. He leans over the desk towards me instead, that syrup-smile back on his face.

'I think I could be persuaded, sir,' he murmurs to me, all

soft and low and good. It's so soft and low and good, in fact, that I have the strongest urge to flick things back to the other idea I mentioned.

You know – the one he wouldn't do, under any circumstances. If I'd demanded it he would have refused, I know he would, and then where would we be? Back to him being just an assistant, most probably, with me as his internet-surfing, Woods-obsessing, tightly boxed-in Boss.

'I have to persuade you?'

'Well, no. Mostly I'm just going to do it because it sounds awesome. But you know – I just wanted to seem cool and seductive and like I understand what we're doing here.'

I don't think he means to do it, but those last words definitely stomp all over the lines I'm trying to draw. In fact, I think they scrub them out with the heel of an old boot, before kicking dirt over their shallow graves.

We might *play* games, but we can't go back to *being* a game. It's too late for anything like that now. We've cuddled, and laughed together, and he thinks it's OK to say something cute to me in the middle of me telling him to lube his ass and fill himself with a sex toy.

'You want to watch me do it right here?' he asks, and ohhh I've definitely lost the rulebook on this. The second he says something like that my heart starts beating a little harder, and my toes kind of curl inside my shoes, and then I just have to watch as he picks up the thing I've given him and examines it with excessive enthusiasm.

His eyes are way, way too big for something like this. But I understand, because my eyes got big when I found it in the sex shop I visited not so long ago.

It's not just a plastic dildo, or a butt plug of some description. It's thin and curved and at its base it has an extra little tongue that could, say, lie comfortably along that strip of skin just behind his balls.

The one that's unbearably sensitive and just waiting to be buzzed, courtesy of the remote control in my hand.

Because that's the other feature that this little item has. And when I press it he almost jumps right out of his skin before he's gotten it anywhere close to his ass. Currently he's just holding it in his hands, and apparently that's enough on its own to make him nuts.

He's never going to survive this.

'You can … you can make it do that, at any time?'

I lean forward over my desk, as he does his best to hold onto the thing.

'What fun would it be if I couldn't?' I say, but he doesn't seem to know how to answer that. He's too busy marvelling at what could well be my evil genius as he works to get his trousers off.

'You know, Benjamin,' I say, in that way I've reserved for things I don't really mean at all. 'It's more than a little unseemly to be so eager.'

The words don't appear to affect him, however. Quite the contrary. He only shoves his pants down faster, seemingly unable to decide between hanging onto that magnificent toy and using both hands to get the job done.

'Is it OK if I don't care?' he asks, and oh the urge I get to tell him yes. Yes, it's more than OK. Be as eager as you like, be as crazy as you like, oh Benjamin, my lovely Benjamin.

But of course I don't actually reply with any of that.

'I suppose it will have to be,' I tell him instead, one leg crossed casually over the other, hands in my lap as though I don't want to grab anything that he's just revealed.

Even if I absolutely do. His cock's so hard it's almost as

though I've just spent the last half an hour sucking it – and it's as pretty as it had seemed the night before. It has that deliciously steep curve, as though it doesn't understand things like weight and gravity. It just wants to push up towards his belly in a way that tests my resolve, to be this calm and aloof sort of person.

'Do you have some lube?' he asks me, almost as though I might not. Instead of anything so considerate, I'm just going to make him force that thing into his ass without any help at all.

Lord, I must really seem like a wicked, wicked person.

'Here,' I say, and then I'm given front row seats to the kind of show I've only previously seen in my wildest dreams. And if that makes my wildest dreams very odd – far odder than they'd seemed before – there's nothing I can do about that.

I want to see him do this, and he doesn't disappoint. He even makes the act of lubing his fingers seem sensual, because after a moment of him coating them I can tell he's enjoying it. He's actually enjoying the slippery feel of it on the sensitive webbing between thumb and forefinger, between fore and middle – and I can tell he is, by the way he reacts when everything slides around everything else.

'You realise I'm totally going to make a mess here,' he says, but his voice isn't steady or even amused any more. It's just breathless, and he's all flushed, and when he finally gets around to reaching behind himself, he's shuddering just a little.

'I'd expect nothing less from someone as clumsy as you,' I say, though after I've done it I regret it. I'm not trying to push him away – I'm really not. It's just happening ... but here's the problem:

It has absolutely no effect whatsoever.

'Yeah, talk dirty to me,' he says, and he isn't being sarcastic. He's actually taking my mean words and turning them into something else altogether, and once he's done it I have to accept the fact that I probably wasn't trying to be cruel at all.

I was just trying to make him be the way he currently is: so full of amusement, and pleasure, and all of the things I probably barely understand. I can't even process the simplest of feelings, whereas he's more than able to turn boneless right in front of me the second he finally manages to work one finger inside himself.

I know that this is exactly what's happened without seeing it for myself. I can tell by the way his head goes back, and the way his eyes drift near-closed, and the way his lips part to let a little gasp out. It's always the same with him – that slow sink into abandonment the second anything even mildly sexual happens.

And this isn't even mildly, at all. He's fingering his own ass in front of me, in my office, while I watch with breath that is bated. It has to be because I swear if I breathe out I'll never be able to take any oxygen back in again.

I'll just suffocate, right here at my desk.

'You want to know what I'm doing?'

Ugh, I hate him, I hate him. Where are my boundaries, for God's sake? Where are the lines I had thought to draw around all of the feelings that are currently trying to blurt right out of me?

I'll tell you where: they're in the goddamn toilet.

'Yes, tell me,' I say, like some breathless whore he just met five minutes ago – and oh Lord, he knows it. He's seen my true face now – the one I've never shown to anyone, the one I keep under this cool, cold mask – and it's turning him into the biggest tease in all the world.

185

'Not as good as when you do it.'

Did I say biggest tease? I meant to say bigger than that. Way, way bigger.

'When you do it, it's smoother. Less awkward – though I kind of like that too. Is that weird? I like it being awkward, because when I actually manage to hit it just right it's like I've worked hard for it, you know?'

I almost resist the urge to respond to that. Almost.

'And you like to work hard for something, Benjamin?'

'You know I do,' he says, as though it's almost amusing to hear me pretend otherwise. Why, a fool would understand how intimate we've now become! It's really quite preposterous that I'm sat here trying to squirm my way out of the fact that we're lovers.

We're lovers. I have a lover. A someone. A one in particular.

Thank God he then distracts me from this revelation with mindless sex talk.

'Oh man, that's ... oh that's really good.'

'Right there, huh?'

'Yeah, right there,' he says, and then I just have to watch as he does something unbearably sweet and sexy – like sinking his teeth into his lower lip. Plus the sound he makes, to follow it up ... oh it's nearly my undoing. It's not quite a grunt and not quite a sigh, and underneath it I can just make out the slick-clicking of his finger in his ass.

He's not going about it calmly now. He's fucking himself, hard, and after a few seconds of this treatment he has to put his free hand on my desk – you know, just for the extra support just for a bit of solidity beneath him as he works himself back on what has to be more than one finger.

It's probably three now. He's probably getting close to filling himself, which in all honesty is just one thought too far for me.

'Stop,' I say.

Then have to take a moment to gather myself. That one word came out like a foghorn, blarting, and though it's jerked him back to reality it's also made him raise one eyebrow. I can't have him raising one eyebrow over my total lack of self-control. I mean, wasn't this whole thing supposed to be about *him* controlling himself? And now here we are with me practically drooling all over myself, words snapping out of me without my permission, one of my hands unbearably close to his on my desk.

'You do recall what I asked you to do, don't you, Benjamin?'

He glances at the gleaming plastic toy on my desk, like he has almost no idea how it got there. I doubt he can even recall letting it go, once fingering himself and holding something at the same time proved too hard.

'Uh ... yeah,' he says, but he's lying. He has absolutely no clue, which of course only means that I have to explain it to him again, in explicit detail.

'Take that plastic cock and slide it into your ass,' I tell him, and it's good, it's good. Orders make me firm and resolved, even if the content of them turns my insides to syrup. Even if words like those close a little hand around my sex, and squeeze, tightly.

While I wait for him to obey.

And he does. It's just that he does it in a slightly different way to the one I expect. He doesn't oil the toy first before making an attempt. He holds my gaze, nice and steady, and then tries the very thing he refused to do a moment earlier.

He eases it into his mouth and sucks. And licks. And generally puts on the lewdest act he possibly can for me, so that I can't imagine anything but what he'd look like if that thing were real. That's how he'd suck someone's cock, I think – all slow and half-smiling, as though it amuses him to tease in such an obvious, brutal sort of fashion.

I'm not even the man he's doing it to, and arousal is currently pulsing through me. It goes through me hard, which is bad enough on its own. But then he just curls his tongue out to lick the tip and says a whole bunch of words as he does so, and I realise I don't even know what bad is.

'Think it's wet enough?' he asks, after which my face actually heats. I mean, I knew he could be this rude. I've seen him be this rude before – he got pretty close in my bedroom, and more than close when I sucked his cock.

But I don't know. There's just something different about it here now. Like he's been given permission to run with whatever he wants to, and to hell with my orders. To hell with everything. We're past petty parameters now, and oh I don't mind admitting it: That thought is terrifying to me.

'I think you need to do what I've asked you to,' I say, but that little hint of behaviour correction doesn't hit. He just grins at me, all pointed incisors and stormy eyes, and then he takes that sex toy I should never have bought and slowly, oh so slowly eases it into his ass.

Though of course he does it in the worst possible way he could. He doesn't just stand there and squirm and work it in. He actually puts one knee up on the desk while he does it, because he knows exactly how thrilling such a thing looks.

It looks like he's a naughty little whore, and his words back that assessment up.

'You know what I love best? I love the slipperiness. I love feeling something just … gliding in, nice and slow. Is that what you like, too?'

I can't answer. I'm too far gone for that. If I move a muscle

I'll do something insane, like have an orgasm without one single, solitary finger laid on me.

'Or do you like the feeling of being filled? Because you know this thing is really ... it's, oh, it's a lot bigger than it looks.'

His eyes flutter closed, briefly, and though I think it's unwise I can't help picturing what's making him react like that. Is it too much for him to take, just that little slender toy? Or has it recently pressed against something sweet inside him and now I'm looking at the fallout of that?

His chest isn't so much rising and falling as jerking through each breath. And I'll be honest, I'm pretty much in love with the way he's touching his tongue to his upper lip. It's like the whole thing is hard, very hard ... but at the same time he could carry on feeling this way until somewhere around the end of time.

And then his eyes flick quite suddenly open, and his mouth curls up at one corner, and I know what's happened. I know, even though I ask him anyway.

'Are you done?' I say, but before he can respond I do something very bad indeed. Oh, it's so bad that I almost feel sorry about it, after the fact – though when I say almost, I *mean* almost. It's not like I punch him in the gut or anything. I just hit the button on the remote control, then watch that victorious expression slide all the way off his beautiful face.

* * *

By the time I get to point twenty-seven on the agenda, he's close to a nervous breakdown. I know he is because when everyone takes a moment to read over the section in some new contract I dare to glance up at him, sat in his corner.

He isn't scribbling down the minutes to the meeting any more. He's just sat in that weird hunched-over position that I suspect was all he could manage, with one hand actually over his face.

And every time I press the button on the remote control he loses just a little bit more of his composure. In fact, when I hit it for the seventh time he almost slides right off his chair – to the point where someone other than me notices.

Oh yeah, Aidan notices this all right. He notices it so much that once Ben actually gathers himself a little, my second in command decides to ask him if he's all right.

In a decidedly suggestive sort of tone.

'Would you maybe like to get yourself a drink of water, Ben?' he offers, but that's not what he's really saying. He's not really being kindly or thoughtful to a colleague who probably appears to be losing the plot.

And he obviously knows he isn't really losing the plot either. Or at least, I hope he knows. Because after he's asked and Benjamin has bolted for the door, he turns his glacial gaze on me.

Then *winks*.

He actually has the gall to wink, though in one way I'm glad he does. It makes it very easy to hardly care once the meeting adjourns, and it's just me and Aidan in this stifling, stiff little room.

'Oh *Harding*,' he tells me, like a teacher expressing his disappointment in an otherwise exemplary student. They just did this one bad thing, you see, this one terrible thing, and the teacher can't resist shaking his head at them.

And Aidan can't resist flashing that shark's grin of his at me either – though in one way I'm glad he does. I'm glad he's sitting there in his swivel chair, trailing himself back and forth, back and forth. Beautifully manicured fingers laced over his even more beautifully manicured suit jacket.

He's so smug and so smooth that it's almost easy to puncture his bubble. In fact, it skates very close to victory, when I just let the words slide out of me.

'As though you wouldn't do the same,' I say, and as I exit the room he laughs, oh how he laughs. I can hear him laughing in that deliciously wicked way of his all the way down the hall.

Chapter Twelve

He doesn't react the way he did before, when I tell him we should probably cool it for a while. He doesn't try to provoke me into anything, with a dirty shirt or a misspelled letter. He just waits for the perfect, most excruciating moment – which just so happens to be 12:35 in a fairly busy break room – and presses a slow, low trail of words against the side of my face.

Like the glances he used to give me, in elevators and stationery cupboards and other enclosed spaces, all of that heat pushing and pushing against me, even when I refused to look. Only now it's spelled out in explicit detail, each letter a little brand pressing into my cheek.

I go red before he's finished talking, and I haven't the faintest clue why. He's said ruder things before. He's told me about how it feels to get fucked, and what my pussy tastes like, and whether I enjoy watching him debase himself ... and none of those things had any real impact.

But this ... this is different.

'I want to make love to you again,' he says, and he does so in such a proprietary sort of way. Like we really are lovers now, and because of that fact he gets to suggest stuff and ask for things.

Things that make my insides run right out of my body.

'We'll discuss this later,' I say to him, because that seems like the best way to go really. It keeps things neat and ordered, and it takes note of one very important fact – that we're currently in public. That people are looking, as I pretend to get milk from the refrigerator and he pretends to finish nuking something in the microwave, and though none of these people are Aidan Harcroft, I can't help thinking about him.

He's different with me now, and I know it. He gives me knowing looks that seem both amused and oddly … proud, I suppose, and all of it is just a little much for me. Aidan's glacial eyes and Benjamin's proprietary *make love to you* and oh, Lord.

I've made this awful mess, I think, and the worst part about it is – I don't exactly want to stop. I mean, I've told Benjamin that we should cool it a little, and we're doing well on that front so far. It's been four days, without any kind of touching or game playing or kissing or any of the things I so desperately want to do with him.

But then, that's the problem, isn't it?

I desperately want to do all of them. Desperately, crazily. I hadn't realised how much I'd started craving all of this, but now that I do – it doesn't bode well for Benjamin. It can't possibly bode well for him, because the moment I really start considering all of this I feel a strange coolness flood through me.

It replaces all the insides I've just lost, one by one. And by the time he's worked up the courage to say something more to me, I've got something very specific to say to him.

'Six thirty, in my office,' I tell him. 'And we'll just see about that.'

* * *

By the time it gets to 6:25, I'm almost beside myself. My leg keeps jiggling up and down all of its own accord, and I think I'm actually sweating inside my clothes. I'm made nervous by too long without him and too much pressure from Aidan's iceberg eyes and too much thinking about those words: *make* and *love*.

Though of course, all of those things only make the ideas I'm currently dreaming up worse. I started out with innocent, tame sorts of activities, like maybe I could tie Benjamin to a desk and leave him there for a little while.

But since then I've progressed into a different sort of territory, and I don't know what I'm going to do about it when he gets here. I'm not sure if I'm really going to order him to behave that way, because of course I know why I'm wanting it. It's the ultimate in keeping things ordered. It's the perfect way to press the reset button, all the way back to the beginning, when things were simple and straightforward.

The idea almost has a kind of symmetry to it, and I like that. I like thinking about how Benjamin's going to handle it, though as per usual he doesn't do what I expect him to the moment I say the words.

I just tell him that I'd like him to pin me to the desk and fuck my ass.

And he just tells me to lift my skirt.

No really, that's what he does. 'Lift your skirt then', he says to me, and after he's done it he actually puts his two big hands on my body, and starts … rubbing all over me. One goes to my belly and one goes to my ass, and once they're there I can feel him just sort of … fondling me, until my clothes start rucking up and near-disappearing.

And all the while he murmurs things in my ear, like in the break room, only worse. So much worse. I didn't think it could be worse, but apparently he's able to achieve it.

'Can I play with your pussy while I do it?' he asks, but I can't answer a question like that. I'm too busy marvelling over whatever's happening right now, because it's the exact opposite of what I was intending. I thought about things being clinical and cool, and somehow we're making out against my desk, and his mouth is all hot and wet and warm, and when he finally turns me around and starts pushing up my skirt in earnest, I'm not the least bit detached.

And neither is he.

'You seriously go around without any panties on?' he asks, while my heart tries to hammer its way through my chest. It's very like something Woods would say to me, true enough, but it's missing a rather crucial element.

Disdain.

'You know, you should really be silent when you do this,' I say, and wince after the words are out. But it can't be helped really – it has to be this way. It has to, before I go insane.

'You want me to not talk?'

I try to focus on the words he's saying, but it's hard, very hard. He's already got a hand between my legs, and he isn't just clasping or making sure I'm actually as panty-less as my naked ass seems to suggest I am.

He's sliding one finger through my slit already, and after a second of gentle stroking he finds my clit. Of course he does. I'm so wet it's like gliding towards that little bead on a water chute.

'Because I think I'm gonna have some trouble, considering how slippery you are – oh my God, look at that. My fingers just slide right on in. Ohhh that's soo hot, that's sooo –'

I crack down hard, before he can finish.

'Yes, I want you to be silent. I'm ordering you to be silent. Don't say anything, don't touch me – just fuck my ass. All right?'

I feel him go a little still, then, though I daren't turn around for the expression to match it. Is he put out by what I've just said? Does it disturb him just a little? And more importantly – is this the thing he's going to refuse to do?

And then I realise … he's taking so long to reply because he isn't doing so with words. He's not talking. He's just nodding his head against the nape of my neck, and he follows that exquisite bit of obedience by bending me over the desk. He actually does it, slow and steady and like he just knows exactly what I'm asking for.

I won't lie. A great flood of something like relief goes through me when I finally feel that cool wood against my cheek. When things are, at last, back to that sweet simplicity, and I don't have to think about anything any more.

I just have to think about his hands on my inner thighs as he spreads them with a deliberate sort of slowness. And if he kind of caresses me at the same time, well, that's all right. I can bear that. I can even bear him kissing the curve of my lower back, because a moment after he gives me that little bit of tenderness I feel the slick, lewd shape of his tongue, running between the cheeks of my ass.

And he doesn't do it sweetly either. He's not nice about it. I can hear his breathing, harsh and guttural, and his hands are on me, spreading me open. It's obvious what he's after, I think – more. More of the taste of me, more of the squirming I'm doing.

More of me coming apart in his hands.

Because I absolutely do. I'm just not prepared for a

sensation like that against something that shouldn't be so sensitive – though I soon learn how wrong-headed that opinion is. I think I actually sob when he finally licks and licks at my tightly clenched asshole, and I *definitely* do for the finale:

His finger, just stroking ever so lightly over the place his tongue just was. Like a threat, almost, of something he could do if I'm prepared for it. But if I'm not, well ... maybe he'll just wait until I beg him.

Or not *beg* him, exactly. Really, when I think about it, it's much more like an order.

'Do it,' I tell him, and he doesn't need me to explain. He simply eases that one maddening finger into my ass, as slow and deliberate as anything like that can be, and once I've taken him all he licks again, around the place he's opened up.

It's unbelievable. It's delicious. But most of all it's making me realise how much I actually enjoy the sound of his voice when we're together like this. I miss him telling me all the things I barely dare to think about – like how something feels or tastes or looks – and for the briefest moment I almost tell him so.

I can take the imaginary gag off if I really want to. I can do anything if I really want to – and that thought, for some strange reason, makes me hold the request inside.

Instead I go with something clear and practical.

'There are condoms in my desk drawer,' I say, though of course I don't tell him what else is in there. I just watch him in the exact way he watched me when I first spanked him – through slitted eyes, with my cheek against wood – and revel in the reaction when it comes.

It's probably the strap-on that's making his face flush like that. Or maybe it's the handcuffs, or the ball gag, or any other number of delights I've got in there for occasions like this.

By the time he's managed to fish out a rubber, he's the colour of a tomato and obviously dying to say something. He tries to sort of mime how he's feeling at me, with an expression best described as 'a flash of widening eyes with a hint of open-mouthed delight'.

Though his delight could just as easily be outrage, or a kind of amused disapproval. There are whole worlds on his face, and I want to live in every one of them.

'Don't make me wait, Benjamin,' I say, but I ensure my tone is fierce when I do. I don't suggest any of that nonsense – about worlds and living in him and what have you – though I suspect it wouldn't matter if I did.

He's so excited now that he can barely get the condom on. He doesn't have anything left for figuring out vocal inflections and hidden feelings – and that's fine by me. I'm practically clawing at the desk by this point, and all I want is to feel his hands on my hips, pulling me back and back onto his big, thick cock.

But thankfully he doesn't make me wait long. There's a lot of under-his-breath cursing from somewhere behind me, and a lot of rubber-snapping sorts of sounds, and then finally, finally the blunt head of his cock pressing against a place I've never had penetrated by another person.

I've had plastic, but plastic just isn't the same. It's not heated and it isn't just ever so slightly yielding, and most importantly: it isn't attached to anything with feelings. It doesn't send a million sensations through the point of connection right up to the other person standing behind me.

Who can't seem to help moaning the second my body gives under that firm, unrelenting pleasure.

'Didn't I tell you to be silent, Benjamin?' I ask, but I'm

just being cruel now. He clearly needs to let something out of his body, because squeezing at my hips and my ass with perspiration-slicked hands just isn't doing the trick.

It's not keeping him calm. It's making him dig his fingers in until I actually let out a little shocked noise, though of course he's sorry once it's happened – and I know this without any words from him. He tells me in the way he soothes over the marks he's just made, with the back of his hand.

And in the way he just lets his cock ease into me, one slow, slippery stroke at a time.

'Ohhh God you've no idea how good that feels,' I say, then almost laugh after I've let the words out. In the absence of him I apparently supply my own little rundown of what's happening, and what it does to me.

Namely: it makes me rut back against the press of his cock, until he can't help making another surprised sound.

And this time, I don't punish him for it. I can't punish him for it, because his hands are on my hips and he's starting to maybe fuck into me a little, and the sensation is so intense I forget to remain measured and still on the desk. I forget about him pinning me, or being restrained in any way, and just reach behind myself to grab at him.

Though once I do, it gives him the perfect opportunity to grope me a little more thoroughly. I lift up off the desk and he just does it – one hand stroking up over my body until he finds my left breast. And then once he's filled his hand with it he squeezes, and uncovers my taut nipple beneath the material, and strokes it in a way that drives me almost out of my mind. Just the pad of his finger – slightly slick for reasons unexplained – right on the tip, then working back and forth … ohhh.

It's good enough to loosen my tongue further, into asking

for all the things I suppose I always wanted to – because that's the thing, isn't it? With him, I *can* ask. I can tell him to pinch that stiff little bud, and fuck that big cock into me harder, and when he does both for me without question I stop holding back altogether.

What would be the point in doing so now? There isn't a slither of space between our bodies. He's pretty much pulled me right back against his chest, and though that hand he's worked inside my shirt is ostensibly about fondling my breast, it's also fairly clearly about crossing his arm over my body, on the diagonal.

He's holding me, I think. And I'm not hanging onto the desk any more – I'm definitely hanging onto him. I'm clinging so tightly to that crossed arm I'm practically cutting off his blood supply, and when he pushes his face into the side of mine I know I'm lost. Any second now and I'm going to start making out with him, and then it's just a short hop, skip and a jump to cuddling in front of the television.

Or at least, that's what I'm thinking when the door to my office abruptly opens.

After which, it's very hard to think of anything at all.

* * *

I suppose the problem is not that we've been caught doing something extremely rude in my office. I mean, for example – if another person had walked in on us doing this, I'm fairly certain they would have squeaked a 'sorry and' exited the place immediately.

No, no, the problem is not that someone has found out our sordid little secret. The problem is that it's *Aidan Harcroft* who's done the finding. Aidan Harcroft, who does not turn around and walk back out again, or offer his apologies, or express any kind of shock or outrage like a normal person.

Instead he strolls right up to the sideboard in my office and pours himself a large Scotch. As though what's really happening here is some sort of insane invite to a cocktail party, and the attire was just listed as 'smart/casual/anal sex'.

I can't move. Or breathe. And Benjamin certainly can't make up for my shortcomings in that department. He's so far from breathing I'm beginning to fear for his life. If he doesn't take in oxygen soon he's going to die for sure.

'Well, you two certainly look like you're having a good time,' he says, and though I try to think of a way to say *actually, no we're not* without sounding like a complete imbecile, it quickly becomes clear that there isn't one.

Benjamin's cock is deep in my ass, and he's got a big handful of my left tit.

The jig is up.

'How kind of you to notice,' I say, then don't know how I dared. Words like those are only going to make things worse, and this fact becomes obvious when Aidan actually takes a seat by the sideboard.

Yes, that's right. *He pulls up a chair* and then he *sits down*.

'It's been extremely hard not to, all things considered,' he says, as he crosses one leg over the other. Swirls the Scotch I've never touched around in the glass I've never drunk from.

'And what are these things you've been considering?' I ask, though it comes out a little less indignant than I intend, and a little more like I'm wondering where this is going to go. And if it ends up a certain place, well …

Benjamin's reaction to that might be interesting.

'I think you know. I think Benjamin knows too, though he's being awfully quiet on the matter.'

202

And then of course it hits me, all in a big rush of who the fuck knows.

Benjamin *can't* speak.

Because I *ordered* him not to.

'He's taken a vow of silence,' I say, but naturally Aidan knows exactly what I mean. He runs the point of his wicked tongue over those shark's teeth of his, and takes a little not-casual-at-all sip of his Scotch.

'That I'm assuming you gave him.'

I try to turn a little, then, to see if I can catch the expression on Ben's face. But when I twist, all I can see is one shoulder and half an arm. All I can feel is the juddery up and down of his chest, as he does his best to keep to what I told him to do.

And it's that struggle, I think, that forces me to answer.

'What do *you* think, in all honesty?' I say, aiming for flippant and hitting shaky. I can feel Ben's hips going, just a little, and it isn't making any of this easier to figure out. Every time he does it I'm reminded of how hard he still is, how excited – and of course I get a burst of sensation as that stiff thing rubs over the nerve-rich rim of my stretched hole.

'I think you look beautiful with a cock in your ass.' He pauses, that sharp gaze of his just a touch sultry, for the briefest moment. 'That is what he's doing to you, right? He's fucking your ass.'

'You're good at this guessing game, I have to say.'

'I'm good at a lot of things,' he says, and oh the slow curling smile he gives me ... it's almost a relief in the midst of all this terrifying talk and laser-gazes. It makes it easier to answer, though I don't say what I intend to.

'Like watching people fuck?'

His smile broadens to epic proportions.

203

'Oh, yes. I make an excellent spectator – and especially so when the view is so delightful.'

Of course I immediately wonder what sort of sight I'm making. Half my clothes off, legs spread, that slick cock buried deep in my ass ... I must look like the rudest thing anyone could ever imagine. Or at least, that's what I think until it hits me.

He isn't really looking at me any more.

He's looking at Ben.

'Does he usually get this flushed when you let him fuck you? Or do you think he's just embarrassed that I'm watching?'

It's a combination of both, I know – but I don't tell him that. I don't say anything,

'God, that cock of his. I mean, everyone in the office knows what he's got underneath those ridiculous trousers, but still ... it's something else to see it buried to the hilt in your ass.' He takes another little sip of Scotch, as though he's just ruminating over all of this. He's not really talking about cocks and asses at all. He's having a polite conversation about a fascinating political topic, and I just have to avoid the pitfalls and minefields of such lively debate. 'How does it feel, Harding?'

Though of course, I fail to avoid this one.

'Thick,' I say, and when I feel Benjamin shift restlessly behind me I'm sorry to report that I go one better. 'Like he's filling me – almost hurting me.'

This time the shift is big, and for the first time he gives me something like a signal through the hand he's still got on my breast. He squeezes, just a little, and it's to his eternal credit that I know exactly what he means.

Am I really hurting you?

And I suppose it's also to his eternal credit that *this* is the comment he wants to discuss, through the medium of minute shifts and little touches. He's not bothered by Aidan, talking on about this bizarre situation we seem to have found ourselves in. He's not fazed by my reaction, so calm and ready to take whatever there is to come.

He's just concerned that he might be hurting me, and once I've reassured him that I'm not – through the hand I've still got on his arm, and the little squeeze back I then give him – he goes right back to the state of breathless, over-excited acquiescence that he was in before.

And I go right back to watching Aidan's eyes close over the things I've just said.

'Mm. That's perfect,' he says, after which I understand what his expression means. It's not like Benjamin, when he lets his expression sag in that same way. Benjamin can't control his reactions, and if something turns him on he just lets it show all over his face.

But Aidan … Aidan can control himself. It's obvious he can. And it's also obvious that what he's doing now is *imagining* how that very thing I've just described would feel.

If maybe Ben was doing it to him.

'It is perfect,' I say, then just for good measure, just to really rub it in: 'You want to see what it looks like when he really goes for it?'

He flicks that cool gaze to Ben, though I understand why. The moment I say the words I can feel the reaction going through the man behind me, all shivers and grasping hands and oh that sweet little sound he makes, right on the end.

It's not quite a protest. But then again, it's not quite anything else either.

'I had nooo idea you were so kinky, Harding,' he says,

but he finishes with something sweet for afters. 'Though I'll be perfectly honest, I like this version of you. And I have absolutely no objections, if you want to give me more of her.'

I do, oh Lord how I do. I want to be that person he's so clearly seeing, so cold and aloof and perfectly in control. I'm in control, all right? I know what I'm doing and if Ben doesn't like it, well ... he can just say the word.

Say the word, I think at him – but he doesn't. He doesn't.

'Fuck me hard,' I tell him, and he just obeys me, utterly. Those big hands slide down my body until they're resting on my hips, and then he simply pulls me back onto his now impossibly hard cock. It's like being nailed by an iron bar, but I can't complain about that. I can't complain about any of this, because oh good Lord it feels so good when he finally lets it all out.

It's all I can do to hold on, once he really gets going – and ohhh the sounds he makes. I can tell almost exactly what he's doing – holding his breath, then letting it out, holding his breath, then letting out – but breaking it down into its component parts doesn't make it any less arousing.

He's past the point of easy control, and now he's deep into trying to hold off his orgasm. He's so deep, in fact, that after a moment of these delicious, pounding thrusts his hand comes up and thumps right over my shoulder, as though he needs me for something other than frantic sex.

He needs to hold onto me, desperately, while his body shudders through what I'm sure is his climax.

And apparently Aidan has the same theory.

'Did you just fill her ass with come?' he asks, like he's reading out the football scores. It's remarkable, it really is, but it's something else at the same time: exciting. Thrilling. Enough to make my clit swell and my body tremble minutely from head to toe in a way that says my own orgasm isn't far off.

I mean, for God's sake. He just said: 'fill her ass with come.' Lately I've been getting turned on over the sight of someone's trousers, so it's not a surprise that comments like those almost put me over the edge.

Or that I hardly realise what they're designed for, until long after he's said them.

'Did you?' Aidan asks again, and *then* it occurs to me.

He's trying to get Ben to talk. In fact, he's not even doing something as simple and straightforward as *trying*.

He's cajoling Benjamin into talking. He's making his voice like the slither of a snake, and he's just worming it across the carpet and up over Ben's obviously overheated and extremely shuddery body.

If he hasn't come yet, he's going to soon. And Aidan obviously knows it.

'Or are you just hovering on the edge, waiting for her to say the word?'

Still no reply from Benjamin – though I'm not sure how much that is to do with his obedience any more. It's hard to say if he *can* talk, in the middle of all this crazy, kinky sex.

'Maybe you're just being a gentleman, waiting for her to come first,' Aidan says, before delivering his final one-two shot: 'Though I suspect you don't have the restraint for something like that. I bet you've coated her in come a thousand times before now because … well. Just look at you. You look like an eager, flushed little slut.'

I can't hold back my gasp, once he's said the words – they're just too close to things I've thought myself a million times over, and I'm sure they're going to have the right effect on Benjamin. At the very least I'm certain he's going to protest.

But he doesn't.

Dear God he doesn't, and once I realise that he's not going to – not ever, not for anything – it's like all of whatever he's not acting on transfers itself to me. A big surge of feeling goes through my helpless body, and I just blurt it out.

'You can talk,' I tell him, breathlessly. 'Talk, please talk, it's fine – just do it.'

And oh it's glorious, when the first thing he does is laugh. I don't know why, to be honest, because I know now that I'm pushing and pushing him and I'm not doing it to be kind. I'm doing it because of the *make* and the *love* and the *kiss*, and if he's not saying no I shouldn't be happy.

So why does it make me so, when he purrs: 'That's because I *am* an eager, flushed little slut,' as though it's the most obvious thing in the world?

I just don't know myself any more. I don't understand what I want, or what I'm doing – I only understand what the most visceral part of me needs right now. And it's not anything to do with emotions.

It's just these two men talking, while Ben's cock eases back and forth inside me, slow, slow.

'I see. And was I right? Did you come in her tight little ass?'

Those thrusts get just a tiny bit jerkier.

'No. I'm close, but no.'

'And is she close?' Aidan asks, which just seems like the weirdest thing. They're talking around me, like I'm not here – though I can hardly say anything about that. I talked around Benjamin as though he wasn't here, a moment earlier.

And besides … it's getting me close just hearing it.

'Probably not. I'm waiting for her to ask me to do something else – you know, like maybe stroke her clit, or finger her pussy.'

'But you won't do it unless she orders you to?'

I actually feel Ben shrug, in that lovely boyish way he has of going about it.

'Is that so weird?'

And then of course Aidan shakes his head, in a manner best described as 'filled with inexplicable danger'.

'I wouldn't say that,' he murmurs, and for the first time he offers us just a little hint of what he's feeling – though when I say hint, what I really mean is that he stretches like a cat in his seat, and we get a glimpse of his actually and obviously very stiff cock. 'In fact, I'd say I appreciate a man who can take orders very much.'

Oh, Lord.

'Seriously?' Ben asks, but it's the wrong thing to say – and I think he knows it, about five seconds later.

'Definitely. It just makes it so much easier when what I really want to see is your fingers on her clit.'

At this point, Benjamin has to slow the erratic thrusts he's going with altogether. But let's be honest here ... it's kind of obvious why. An idiot would know what forces him to grind to a halt, because the moment Aidan says the words Ben moans, unsteadily.

If he wasn't close to orgasm before, he *definitely* is now.

'Rub her clit,' Aidan says again, and this time ohhh this time Ben actually does it. He just obeys, wordlessly, one hand sliding around my body until he finds my very wet and very swollen slit.

And then he simply works his way through all of the mess I've made until he finds what he's looking for.

'Ohhh man, her clit's all stiff,' he says, while I think: *yeah, tell me something I don't know.* Or at least, I try to think it. Mostly I just jerk forward against the desk, one hand skidding on the papers there in the exact way Ben's had, all that time ago.

'And you like that?' Aidan asks, but really, what on earth is he going on about? Of *course* he likes it. He sounds like he's about to die, as he regales Aidan with one hundred and one tales from my various body parts.

'God, yeah. Yeah, I love it. She gets so wet, and so excited … you think she's all aloof, but underneath she's absolutely dying for it.'

Did he seriously just say that? And more importantly: is that actually how I seem? Cold and aloof on the outside, sluttish and horny on the inside – despite all my best efforts to get the two sides of me to match up?

Man, I'm just failing at everything lately. Being normal, having a relationship, not fucking somebody in front of my second-in-command.

'I've always suspected as much,' Aidan says, and when he does he winks at me. Dear God, I'm never going to be able to scrub the shame of Aidan's winks off me now.

Though even worse – I'm not sure that I want to. In fact, I'm certain I don't want to, because the combination of all of these things – Ben's fingers circling and circling my clit in messy spirals, Aidan's amused and delighted reaction to just about everything, those words about me being full of desire – is shoving me into the biggest orgasm of my life.

I can't even moan when it hits. All of the sounds I want to make and the words I want to say hit hard against some impossible barrier, and I'm left in a very embarrassing sort of state. Mouth open, with nothing coming out. Most of me trying to get away from Benjamin, as the sensation pours through me.

Though naturally I don't succeed. If he wants someone

to stay close to him and experience every little last drop of pleasure, they don't really have much choice in the matter. His arm turns vice-like around my middle. The heel of his palm presses harder against my slippery mound, that finger working and working over my clit until I really can't take any more.

I have to tell him.

'Enough,' I say, but this time he doesn't obey immediately. He waits – he actually waits – until Aidan suggests the same, which probably just makes matters worse. I'm very aware of how disastrous I look, how little power I now have, and I can't deny that those things contribute to the way I then behave.

Even if I don't want it to be the case.

I don't want to slow my breathing so quickly, or drag myself up off the desk. Most of me just wants to fall asleep right there and then, while they most likely fuck each other to death on my office floor.

But I can't do that. I have to order Benjamin away from me instead, and once he's gone I do something ridiculous, like snap my skirt down. I straighten my jacket, as though doing so is going to make me look like a completely ordered and totally aloof person again, instead of the horny mess everyone in this room apparently knows I am.

'Tidy yourself up, Benjamin,' I say, but really I've no idea if such a thing needs to happen. I daren't look at him, for reasons best left untouched. And after I've sat myself back at my desk all nice and calm and without a single wince what-soever, I still can't quite bring myself to take in all of him.

I have to do it in sections, starting with his right elbow. And then maybe I can progress to his chest – which is still practi-cally heaving – and the clothes he's rezipped and straightened over his-stripped-of-a-condom cock, and that lower lip I so often dream of kissing, or licking, or any number of other things I shouldn't do.

Then finally, his gaze. His blazing bright and beautiful gaze, that's so the opposite of Aidan's ever-still and quite amused one. It's like he's trying to push every ounce of feeling in him up and out through his eyes, and I can't bear it. It's too much like a challenge, which I unfortunately have to meet.

'You know, Benjamin, it's very impolite to leave a guest waiting,' I say, while straightening things on my desk that don't actually need straightening. It's practically become a habit now – this return to something that looks like mild uninterest – but it doesn't have quite the effect I was expecting.

And nor do my words.

I'll be honest – I thought they were just cryptic enough to invite hesitant questions, maybe give a little space for refusals – all of which are bound to be coming. They're bound to be, because I have a very specific order in mind.

It's just that I don't actually have to give it.

'You want me to suck his cock?' Benjamin says, and of course I realise then: I don't have any power whatsoever. I was fooling myself in ever thinking I had.

He has it all, all of it, all of me, and there's nothing I can do about it.

'That is, if you're agreeable, Aidan,' I say, though I can think of a million other things I'd rather go with. I'd rather tell Benjamin that he's more fearless, more amazing, more everything I've always wanted than any other man I've ever known.

But it's easier to turn away from his perfect face, to Aidan's clearly shocked one. Somehow, in the last hour I've managed to propose marriage in my head to Benjamin, and actually almost stun Aidan Harcroft.

It's been a strange day. And it's getting stranger.

'Let me see ... would I like to get a blowjob from this walking Calvin Klein ad in front of me?'

Benjamin's not a walking Calvin Klein advert at all, but I see what he means. He's like a walking Calvin Klein ad, if Calvin Klein had been a fat nerd in high school – because that's how Benjamin looks. He's just ever so slightly excessive, just ever so slightly edging over into weird, with his too long eyelashes and his pretty mouth and the rest of him so big and masculine.

And of course, those eyes ... those eyes that are almost a colour that doesn't exist. If you cupped your hands around them, I suspect they'd glow.

'It's a hard one you've posed there, Harding, I'll grant you,' Aidan finishes, finally, just on the end of what seems to be some sudden and completely unseemly drooling on my part. Next thing you know I'll be painting nude pictures of him while aboard the *Titanic*. 'I'm not a fan of posing easy ones,' I say, but it's Benjamin's gaze I hold. Benjamin who tells me with his eyes: *go ahead and try. Go ahead and give me a challenge you think I won't meet. You'll come away the loser, every time.*

Or the winner, depending on your view of man-on-man action.

'You want me to go over there and do it to him like that?' Ben says, and he doesn't stop there either. 'Or maybe you'd prefer it if he stood over me, and just forced his cock into my mouth.'

Of course I know why he's wording things this way. I've heard him respond very well to similar ideas before, so really it's sort of obvious what he's doing, here – he's suggesting things he likes. He's giving me little reminders, under the guise of being an obedient little submissive.

And I'm only too happy to oblige him.

'Fuck his face,' I tell Aidan, and then all I can do is watch with something like a gutful of impatience as Aidan slowly gets to his feet.

In fact, he doesn't just stop at being incredibly, annoyingly slow. He also removes his jacket and folds it with exquisite deliberateness over the back of the chair he's just been seated at. Removes imaginary fluff on his near-pristine shirt – the perspiration circles under his arms spoil the perfection some-what, but I feel I can forgive him for that – before finally getting around to facing Ben.

Who's the exact opposite of the way Aidan now seems. He's lost that bit of steel he had a moment ago, and now he's just right back to being a panting, shaking mess again.

'Get on your knees, kid,' Aidan says, and I flashback to all the times I've called Ben *boy*. It isn't the slightest bit true – his personnel file lists him as twenty-nine, and he'll be thirty in January – but oh it so fits for occasions like this.

It makes it seem less like Aidan's a good six inches shorter him – though of course, other things help with that, too. Like Aidan's cool gaze and his immaculate suit and oh then oh then … the way he unbuckles his belt …

It's like he's going to lash Ben with it afterwards.

And I think Ben is thinking the same thing, because he can't seem to take his eyes off Aidan's thin-fingered hand as it works. Everything so slow, so deliberate in a way that should probably remind me of Woods.

But it doesn't. Woods would never have smiled while he did it. He never looked like he enjoyed any of the things we did, and he certainly wouldn't have said the thing Aidan then does.

'I can't *wait* to feel that sweet mouth on my cock.'

I mean, it just reeks of eagerness. It speaks to the person Aidan actually is – which isn't half as cold as those glacial eyes suggest. He's fleshy, I think … *visceral* somehow. He reacts in swift, passion-filled spurts, and even if his various shenanigans around the office weren't backing me up on that, I'd know it.

It's in the way he quite suddenly grabs a fistful of Benjamin's jumper, then jerks him forward. And maybe also in the way he smashes their mouths together in a manner that makes Ben's hands fly up and his body jolt.

Followed by some very similar reactions from me.

At the very least I have to grab a hold of my desk to stop my body from sliding off my chair. And though I do my best to keep any and all response soundless, I know a little gasp escapes.

Benjamin Tate is making out with Aidan Harcroft, in my office. It's like the plot of some teen movie, if teen movies featured a lot of intense gay sex. I could almost put a camera on them both and sell the footage on eBay, because oh the sight is something else.

Ben isn't so much kissing Aidan as melting all over him, and it's a testament to Aidan's composure and wiry strength that they remain standing. I'm starting to think I'm really going to get them fucking on my office floor – though with the added bonus of a front-row seat.

Seriously, I have a front-row seat to Aidan thrusting his tongue into Ben's mouth – because that's what he does. He gets a hand in Ben's hair and then he just *uses* whatever he can lick or bite at, until Ben actually starts moaning.

He moans into Aidan's mouth, in the exact way he's done for me a dozen times before. Helplessly, desperately, and oh so ready to do anything – though I can hardly blame him. I can see how hard he still is inside the trousers he so neatly zipped up.

And I can see it better when Aidan's kind enough to outline the whole thing with one grasping, groping hand.

'Still stiff, then,' he says, and I get the strongest urge to laugh. As though he's going to fall down on a matter like that, when he's getting mauled and rubbed by another human being!

Clearly, Aidan doesn't know Ben at all – but that's OK. That's good.

It's OK for it to be good, isn't it?

'Get on your knees,' he says, and the only thing that seems to make Ben hesitate is that hand on his cock. I can tell he doesn't want to give that up so easily, but the pull of actually getting to do what he's only ever confessed to me before is clearly too much.

He gets on his knees.

And I almost cover my eyes with one hand.

In fact, I get so close to doing that very thing that I end up touching somewhere schoolmarm-ish, like the collar of my shirt. And when Aidan puts a too-fierce hand in Ben's hair and tugs him roughly to the long, lean cock he's just exposed, I get even closer to my eyes.

I put my fingers to my lips and press there, hard, as my no-longer-just-almost-boyfriend blindly rubs his face against whatever is presented to him in a way I recognise. It's that eager, seeking heat sort of thing he does, for far more typical things like the side of my face or the inside of my thigh.

And now he's here, doing it to someone's cock.

Until said man yanks on that fistful of hair and gets him back on the right track—which in this case is Ben using his mouth and his tongue to slick that stiff length from root to tip.

'That's it, baby,' Aidan says, and I swear I don't know what's worse: the fact that Ben is greedily going at all of this, or the fact that Aidan just called him 'baby'.

And oh lord, Benjamin *likes it*. I can tell he does because the second the word is out he loses some of his focus. That eager lapping becomes a stuttering sort of fumble, and he caps it off with a long, low moan, right into dark fur that surrounds Aidan's cock.

It's almost like he's fallen face first into the man's groin, but I understand why. I wouldn't be able to stay upright either with someone above me saying the things he is.

'Here, here,' Aidan tells him, and then he just takes his cock in one hand and Benjamin's face in the other, and does exactly as he had promised: he eases his now glossy and extremely swollen dick into Ben's mouth.

At which point I let the breath out that I hadn't realised I was holding. Unfortunately for me, however, it comes with a little side order of gasping – or maybe moaning – and when I break the silence in the room with it, Aidan turns his head and looks at me.

All I can say is: thank God I didn't really cover my eyes. His expression is painful enough on its own, without me exposing myself any further – because I have exposed myself. I'm flushed so red I could pass for a postbox, and I'm leaning right over my desk like a maniac. I'm practically a gawker at the scene of some crime, and the scything grin he gives me only confirms this.

'Surprising how arousing it is to watch someone fuck, isn't it?' he says, but he's not done yet. I'm starting to think all his sentences need a little kicker on the end, just to polish the listener off. 'Though I'll be honest, it's not half as good as getting this sweet mouth around my cock. Dear Lord,

Harding – you could have told me how good he is.'

All I can think in response to that little doozy is: *how could I?*

I don't *have* a cock to judge just how good Benjamin's blowjob technique is – though in all fairness to Aidan, I do have eyes. And I can absolutely see the hollowing of Benjamin's cheeks as he sucks hard on the swollen head of Aidan's cock. I can make out the slight flicker of his tongue as he slides back up that length, lapping and licking as he goes.

And I remember how all of those things felt when applied to a sort of similar body part. I can recall the feeling of him just sort of … *rubbing* at my clit with his tongue, and it makes answering easier.

'I wanted him all to myself,' I say.

Which has the virtue of at least being true.

'And now that you're watching someone fuck his mouth? Now how do you feel?'

Again, the truth collars me.

'I've never been so aroused in my life,' I reply, but he doesn't make me pay for it. In truth, I don't think he's going to make me pay for any of this, because Aidan isn't like that. He's always discreet about everything, even when 'everything' is him getting sucked off while he says a series of very dirty things.

'Ah, me neither. His mouth is unbelievable – so hot and wet and ohhh yeah, that's it. Just like that. Stroke it while you suck me.'

Benjamin obeys, but not with any sort of ease. He's shaking so hard now that each little shudder is practically passing through him and into Aidan, and when he finally gets a hold of the base of that cock he has to cling to something with his other hand.

Like the tight little curve of Aidan's ass.

'You want to come too, kid – huh? Get that big dick of yours out,' Aidan says, in response – and it's obvious why. Benjamin's so far gone he doesn't seem to know what day it is, and that eager sucking he's doing is getting sloppier and sloppier.

By the time he actually fumbles down his zipper he's almost drooling, though Aidan doesn't seem to mind.

'Uhhh yeah. Yeah. I'm gonna shoot – if you want to do it too, you'd better hurry,' he says, and I almost feel like telling him: there's going to be no problem on that score. Ben's so hard and so aroused he can hardly bear to touch himself, and from all the way over here I can see and hear how wet the head of his cock is. He's practically dripping on my carpet before he's finished a stroke, and Aidan's moaning declaration that he's coming only gets him closer.

And then Aidan actually does it – spurting thickly over Ben's tongue – and it's enough. It's enough to make him cling to Aidan again, and jerk at his own cock just that little bit harder, and finally, finally …

He shudders and gasps and locks up tight, before striping my carpet with thick, lengthy ribbons of come. It goes just about everywhere – all over Aidan's trouser leg too, before finishing with a thick dribble over his own fist – but he doesn't seem to care. After it's done he actually sort of sprawls back like a young maiden, swooning, and if it wasn't for his sleepy but open eyes I'd suspect he'd lapsed into unconsciousness.

Even Aidan seems to imagine the same, because once he's gathered himself a little and laughed about how awesome all of that was, he asks if Ben's OK.

And in reply, Ben murmurs: 'Are you kidding?'

Which is just awesome of him, I have to say. He deserves

219

a round of applause for that performance, and he seems to know it – in fact it's almost like he's asking me with his eyes if that's what I wanted from him. I can almost hear the words coming out of his mouth – and probably would have gotten them if it wasn't for Aidan getting there first.

'Is that what you had in mind?' he says, but in all honesty I have no clue. I don't know anything any more – I'm just oddly drained and mostly conflicted, and I can't see my way out of either of those feelings.

Plus it makes it all just that little bit harder, to see Aidan be so casual about everything. He doesn't care, I think, but then – he doesn't have anything invested. He can just turn before he gets to the door and survey us – me still at my desk, Benjamin spread like butter over the carpet – and say something blasé, like: 'Call me, if you ever feel like doing this again,' before taking his eminently cool and collected leave.

While I sit here, shell-shocked, in the rubble of my life.

Chapter Thirteen

If we sit like this any longer, in complete silence, I think I'm going to go insane. All I can hear is the rain drumming against the roof of his car, and the occasional swish of the windscreen wipers. I don't know why I agreed to get in here, to be honest – but now I am I have to make the most of things.

It's pretty clear that the rain's not going to stop any time soon and allow me to get out and go to my own car. I have to do this instead, though thankfully when I actually work up the courage to look at him he doesn't seem anxious, or disturbed.

He seems content.

He's leant his head back against the seat, and his eyes are near-closed. There's a little wistful smile on his lips, as though he's just happy to be in here with me, enveloped in this strange silence.

Either that, or he's remembering everything that's just happened – all the craziness and that thing and then that other thing ... oh God. God.

'I'm sorry,' I blurt out, though after I've done it I've no idea what I'm aiming it at. It doesn't seem like pleasure should be something I'm apologising for, but then again … there's all this other stuff underneath.

Stuff that he's apparently aware of.

'You hoped I'd say no, right?' he says, and then I can't quite bring myself to look at him. It sounds so ridiculous once he's said it out loud, and even worse – cold. Really, really cold, and unnatural.

I'm unnatural.

'Sort of,' I tell him, but that comes out like there's something wrong with me. It's not even a comfort when he's kind about it either, because in a way I don't want him to be. I want him to tell me that I'm no good, and that maybe I should get out of the car and walk in the rain like the tragic heroine of some melodramatic novel.

Even though I'd reject something like that out of hand if it landed on my desk.

'I wish I could tell you it would work, as a way to get rid of me. But you have to know by now that it won't.'

Something bright and sharp bubbles up in my chest. And unfortunately it makes the words I then try to babble come out very strangely indeed. They're so high they're practically attracting bats, and I even do something mad like clutch pearls I don't have, as I'm trying to force them out.

'I wasn't trying to get rid of you, Ben. I'm not trying to get rid of you – I just –' but he cuts me off before I can finish. He puts a hand over my hand, and that's enough to silence me.

His words just kind of finish the job really.

'It's OK. I'm not exactly great at making kinky games turn into a relationship either,' he says, and after that I have to look away. I glance out of the window at the industrial park across the road, and pretend to be really interested in the way corrugated steel looks, washed in rain.

'Is that what this is?' I say finally, but he doesn't balk at answering.

'Yes. I'm pretty sure we're in a relationship. I think you might even be my girlfriend – though admittedly one who invites dudes into her office to do things to me.'

Of course once he's done so, I can't help throwing up my hands.

I mean really – is that what he thinks? That I invite guys into our … our … thingie in order to force him into saying no? I'm pretty sure he does, but have to be sure.

'I didn't invite him! It just … happened,' I say, then I wait for his response. I wait for him to tell me he doesn't believe me – frankly, I don't believe me and I'm the one who had to process Aidan just waltzing into my office to fuck my boyfriend's face – and when it doesn't come, I don't know how to deal with it.

He just says: 'Are you serious? Whoa. Wish you'd let me know that before it got going – I'd have probably come in my pants the second he got a hold of my hair.'

And I'm left stranded, back in Over Complicating Things Land.

Because really, none of this is a big deal. It's all pretty straightforward: he likes me, and he likes to do any of the kinky things I seem to need so desperately, and all of this should be easy, so easy.

Except that none of those things sound straightforward at all to me. I'm wrong inside and I know I am, because the second he says that he wants to be with me, all my feelings just kind of rush out, in one big glut.

'You don't get it, Ben – I don't even understand what that means. All of those things that other people do all the time

223

– the normal things, like going on dates and holding hands and taking baths together … I've never had any of that. Sometimes my life is like looking through glass at everything that everyone else does so easily, and I don't … I can't …'

I can't change that, my mind finishes for me. It has to, because my voice is actually starting to crack a little and I haven't a clue why. My life isn't so miserable really. I'm not sad. I'm not.

But I let him take me back to his place anyway.

* * *

There's something about the silence he seems to have sunk into that's very comforting in a way I can't quite explain. I suppose it makes it hard to ask questions or offer protests – which is useful when he wants to do something that makes my insides turn to honey.

Like carry me slowly up the stairs inside his actual house.

Because he doesn't have a sloppy, grimy apartment in a neighbourhood that reeks of patchouli and students, as I'd always somehow imagined. It's not even an apartment – he has a narrow three-storey house on the kind of street most people are intimidated by, with the railings around each neat little square of garden and all the doors painted a glossy, bold colour.

His door is red, and it has a brass knocker.

And those are all the things I concentrate on, while I hold onto him tightly and maybe press my face into his shoulder. I mean, I can't actually look at him, as he does a thing like this. I can't focus on it as it happens, or ask him questions about it, or wonder what exactly is going on.

Though that's mainly because I kind of know already

what he's doing here. I know, and the idea is persuading my heart to pound in this heavy, sickly sort of manner. I can almost feel each beat shuddering through me, and it doesn't get any better when he sets me down in his neat, warm little bathroom, and starts slowly peeling off my clothes, one item at a time.

First the jacket goes, neatly folded on top of the wicker washing basket he's got in here. Then he works on my skirt, easing down the zipper in such a deliberate, careful sort of fashion that I almost stop him right there.

It's a proud moment for me when I manage to resist. I'm breathing in this strange, shaky sort of way and I know my face may well be wet, but I don't tell him to just leave it at that. I let him kneel on the black and white tiled floor – so pretty and modern and clean, in a way I never imagined him being – and lift each one of my legs to take off my punishing heels.

Like Cinderella in reverse, I think, and then I have to hold onto him just a little bit. I need the support of his broad shoulders to help me stand here in just my panties and half a shirt while he holds me close inside that lovely, low gaze of his.

But it's OK. It's fine. I'm allowed to do this now because although parts of me are freaking out, I understand where this is going. I know what he's trying to do, and it's silly and probably too sickly for my palate and rationally speaking it's not going to help anything.

But oh, it's too lovely to turn away from. It's the contrast, I think – between something so tender and loving, and the cool, silent way he's going about it. As though he knows that I couldn't bear to hear a thousand gooey words on the subject before it all happened, and understands that this is the way it has to be.

I need borders, I need rules, I need things to be calm and still. And though he does a million things that should be anything but – like kissing me, gently; like running a bath for me; like pulling my back to his chest as we lie there, floating, in the warm water – I can bear it. I can take it, because it's Ben, my Ben.

Plus, the first words he says to me after my little outburst are these:

'So that's the main one. What were the others you mentioned, again?'

* * *

I think I actually fall asleep like that, with my cheek just resting against his chest. It's easy to, really, in the muggy heat of his bathroom, surrounded by him and the water and the soft scent of the ridiculous bath salts he's put in here.

I can see why people like doing this, I really can. It's certainly more impressive than coming home after a long day of intense threesomes, to a nearly cold shower and a thin sliver of soap and a bitterly hard towel that only reminds you of what you should have done yesterday instead of staying at work until 10:30 at night, again: *Buy new ones.* 'Are you awake?' I ask him, though it seems strange that this is the first thing I've said since he decided to put me through my normal relationship paces. I didn't answer him about the *other ones*, and he hadn't seemed to mind – which is good.

I'm not ready for dates just yet. I'm not ready for holding hands during long walks in the park, and whatever other normal stuff he has in mind for me. I just need to ease into this one first, and I can make a good start at it by asking an innocuous question.

226

Or at least it seems like an innocuous question, until he answers.

'I don't think I could fall asleep while you lie all relaxed on top of me. Did you really just fall asleep? I think you did, but hey – I won't tell anyone.'

He whispers that last bit in my ear, while doing something warm and good like smoothing a hand over my hair. And though I know it should panic me, though I know I should be desperate to get out of this tepid water right now and away from his gentle hands and his soft words, I find myself doing something very strange instead.

I laugh, and press myself closer to him.

'Yeah,' I say. 'I think you're doing it with hypnotism.'

'You think I'm hypnotising you?'

'There's no other explanation for what I'm doing right now. I think I'm actually cuddling someone, in a bath tub.'

He considers, briefly, before offering me a possible explanation.

'Maybe it's just my intense charm. Or my willingness to suck some cock in front of you.'

OK, now I *really* laugh. I laugh like I did when we were together on my bed – only this time I don't feel strange about it afterwards. I don't get the urge to pretend I'm asleep on the edge of the mattress, or reset everything back to the beginning again.

Instead I find myself doing something else I know couples do, without any help from him at all. He's taking my training wheels off, and now I'm riding the bike on my own, it seems.

'How do you have this big house?' I ask, but he's onto me immediately.

'Was that an actual question about me? You're doing awesome at this.'

I pinch him, somewhere just below his right nipple – though of course it has the opposite effect to the one I intend.

'I don't think hurting a masochist is the right way to get him to stop being a jerk,' he says, so I pinch him again, and demand he answers me.

Which he does, after a moment of what I think is a comfortable silence.

'It was my grandfather's place. He left it to me in his will,' he says finally, and suddenly the comfortable silence is not so comfortable any more. It's just him not wanting to share something sad with me, in a way that makes me ache for him to continue.

Go on, I think at him, *go on*, but when he does it's no better than if he hadn't spoken at all.

'I used to come and stay with him in the summer, every couple of years or so,' he says, and then I just have to picture his probably idyllic childhood. Long hot days spent with Grandpa in the garden – on top of his boyhood adventures in Hawaii. Next he's going to tell me about the Werther's Originals and the Roald Dahl bedtime stories, and I'll have to just give up on being a human being for ever.

'You must have loved him very much,' I say, but I only do it because I can sense something coming from him. He's going to ask me about my childhood, and then I'm going to have to explain to him what *council estate* and *alcoholic absent parent* mean.

So it's a relief when he just gives me a rueful laugh.

'God no. He was *horrible*. Everyone hated him – he was mean, and rude, and he used to jab at the neighbourhood kids with his cane. I think I was pretty much the only person in the world who could tolerate him – which is probably why he left me this awesome house.'

He obviously means it all as a punchline, but that's not how I take it. Instead I find myself thinking of this old man that secretly cared for Ben, even when he seemed mean and rude – and I comment accordingly.

'Sad,' I say, softly, and Ben agrees.

'Yeah.'

'That he was ... that he couldn't relate to other people, I mean.'

He laughs so abruptly I almost jump right out of my skin, though I have to say I don't exactly come back down to earth when he shares the reason why.

'Eleanor, you're not like my aged grandfather. He used to try to poison the neighbours' cats. The only TV programme he liked was something called ... *'Til Death Us Do Part*. He was awful. Is that what you think you are? *Awful?*'

I can't help shoving out an annoyed breath.

'How do you know I was in any way reflecting back on myself?'

'Oh, come on. It's obvious!' he cries, and then I just feel busted. I honestly didn't intend for my words to come out that way, but now they have and he knows and oh Lord he's still talking. 'What's not so obvious is why on earth you think you're like some sour old man. You're just a little ... closed off. That's all.'

'I didn't ... I mean I ... I spent a lot of time alone, when I was younger,' I say, but I'm embarrassed about doing it. He just pours everything out so easily, while I stutter and stumble like a fool.

Though part of what makes him so wonderful is that he never makes me feel bad about any of this. He just kind of chuckles, and pushes his fingers through my hair in a way that almost turns me to goo.

'I think a blind idiot would know that much about you, baby,' he says, and then everything's all right again. We can go back to comfortable silences instead of tragic ones, while my mind ticks slowly back through the conversation to more pleasant topics.

'Do you think that's what you are? A masochist?'

Or you know. More kinky topics.

'Was that *another* question? Don't go too crazy, El, I might start thinking you like me.'

I don't pinch him this time. I dig my knuckle into his side instead, until it hits just the right ticklish spot and he squirms, and laughs. Does his best to bat me away from that sensitive area, before caving.

'All right, all right! I'm sorry, I'll be cool. What was the question again?'

'Something about masochism. With an added incredulous – *did you just call me El? Seriously?*'

I can feel him nodding before he answers, all big and too giddy and oh just perfect for my frazzled nerves. He's like some sort of grand champion at putting people at ease, to the point where I'm actually starting to cuddle him, all on my own. I've literally turned onto my side, in the space he's made for me between his legs and on his big broad chest.

And now I've got my arm around him and my cheek against him and in another moment I'll be writing love poems to him and spelling out his name in sky writing.

But that's OK. It's OK.

'I totally, totally did. I was going to go with Eleanor but backed out at the last second. One syllable's far easier to force out than three.' He shifts a little beneath me, runs a hand down over my now slick back. 'Plus, you know – I can't go with *sir* while we're being romantic together.'

230

'Is that what we're doing?'

'Sorry to have to tell you this, but I think it is.'

'You still haven't answered my other questions, you know.'

'I know.'

'Are you avoiding them?'

'No.' He kisses the top of my head, soft, soft. 'I'm just trying to think of impressive answers, like: yeah, I go hardcore on a Saturday night at the local gimp club.'

Of course I burst out laughing, all over again – but it can't be helped. It's not just the things he says, all easy and without a care in the world. It's the way he says them. It's that note of sardonicism that's sometimes in the back of his throat, and how warm he somehow makes it.

It gives me so many inroads. So many ways into him. I don't feel weird about teasing him back, despite the fact that I don't think I've ever teased anyone in my entire po-faced life.

'Really? Because your idea of impressive sounds a lot more like ridiculous.'

'You don't want me to tell you about my rubber all-in-one suit?'

'I want you to answer my questions with a straight face.'

'OK – yeah. I'd say I was a masochist. I like pain. I like being spanked, being bitten, being bruised, though I've never done any of that with anyone else.'

'So basically you've just been punching yourself in the dark, while masturbating,' I say, and I fully expect him to laugh or roll his eyes or tell me I'm now being the ridiculous one.

But he doesn't. He just shrugs, before finishing with a little: 'Pretty much.'

In a way that makes me feel foolish for even asking. I mean, it's not as though he hasn't told me before, in a myriad ways. The wings on his back and the way he'd admired them, his reaction to things like spanking and hair pulling and pinching – all of these things tell me as much.

It's pretty clear. It's just that it's not pretty clear inside me, and all of this just flashes that fact up in neon until I have to go ahead and ask. I have to know what he thinks, even if I'm sort of sure already.

'And what do you think I am?' I say, and then I wait with bated breath. I wait for him to tell me that I'm a secret sexual sadist, or a dominant on the inside, or that I have deep-seated issues about fucking that I should really address before we go any further.

But he just laughs, nice and easy.

'I can't believe how little you understand yourself – you know it's obvious, right? You're a switch.'

My mind draws a blank. Should really have spent more time on those BDSM sites before I got into a conversation with the sexpert over here.

'A what?' I actually say, but he doesn't hold it against me.

'You like both. You like being spanked, you like doing the spanking,' he tells me, and of course he's right. Of course he is. It's obvious, once he's put it that way – though I can't help being curious about one little element of what he's said. He just seems so naïve in some ways, but so sure in others.

'How do you even *know* terms like that?' I ask, but I understand once I've done it that I've set myself up for a fall. He's half-laughing before I've finished speaking.

'I told you. I'm real big on the BDSM scene. My handle is StandOnMyHead359.'

'You're an ass.'

'I know. But I'm kind of enjoying behaving like one right now. It's a whole new world of you being unsure, and me being the worldly-wise relationship guru.'

232

'I don't think being StandOnMyHead359 makes you Dr Phil, in all honesty.'

'True. But I'm not afraid of knowing and understanding what I want,' he says, which takes me a good long moment to process. Is he saying that I am? Is that what this is?

Because I'm not. I'm not.

'Neither am I,' I tell him, only once I've done it I get the strangest little cold feeling running down my spine.

It's probably the bath water, which is, by this point, absolutely freezing. I have to make him finish the rest of this conversation in his bedroom, which is much more like the sort of thing I'd imagined him living in. Books spilling out all over the place, clothes strewn over every available surface … about the only thing in there that looks clean and tidy is his bed, but it's one of those too-cool-for-school modern ones, without anything as conventional as a frame.

In fact, I'm starting to suspect it's just a mattress.

'I can never decide what to wear now,' he offers sheepishly, when he takes in my aghast expression. Seriously – there are actual islands of clothes growing in this bedroom. He could sell one of them to Richard Branson. 'I'm aiming to impress, and I don't think a jumper with dancing penguins on the front really achieves that professional sheen.'

He's right. It doesn't – but the point he's just made leaves behind some questions.

'It's not me you're trying to impress, is it?' I ask, because let's face it. I'm currently a bedraggled mess, sprawled all over his bed. And yes, true, he keeps glancing at my breasts and my pussy and occasionally my face, as he tries to make things a little more presentable in here. And maybe he's also stupidly hard while he goes about it.

But still. I've never felt less impressive in my entire life.

'Well ... yeah,' he says, but not in an embarrassed sort of way. More in an *isn't that obvious* kind of manner.

He turns to look at me, hands full of immensely silly clothes. T-shirts with cartoon characters on them; pants that are neither long enough to call them trousers, nor abrupt enough to imagine they are shorts.

It's no wonder he says what he does next, really.

'But I like it,' he tells me, then rushes on before I can interrupt and possibly spoil the party. 'I like you straightening me out. I even like imagining you going further – telling me what to eat, how to behave, how to handle myself in sudden threesomes. It's very ... relaxing.'

He pauses, as though unsure as to whether he's got the right word. I don't feel like interjecting to say that he has, however.

'And of course when I do as you've commanded ... that's very relaxing for you too, right? Knowing that someone will do what you've asked, without question. That things are ordered and safe, and nothing's going to spiral out of control.'

I don't say anything then, either – though this time it's because I can't. I just have to lie here instead, while he smiles his soft smile at me, and wanders over to the bed. Runs a hand up my side as he joins me there, so that he can murmur words in my ear.

'Yeah, you like that, huh?' he tells me, and I do, I do. I do so much that I'm having to press my lips together to keep any untoward and highly embarrassing sounds down.

But it's OK, because his kisses cover it too. They help with all of the weird surging emotions that are going through me, even if his words don't.

'You know what we're going to do now?' he says, in

between a kiss to my left temple, and a kiss to my still tightly closed mouth. 'We're going to make love.'

And in response I nod, helplessly. I put my arms around his shoulders all on my own, and rub my naked body up against his, and actually ask for the tangle I refused before. I want our legs to intertwine and his hand to go into my hair and most of all I want him to tell me, I want him to.

'I love you, El,' he says. 'I love you.'

And after he's done it all I can think of is all the ways he absolutely shouldn't. I'm closed off, I think, and strange. I don't know how to behave like a person. I'm almost crying because he told me something so simple and basic like that, and once he's done it I can't say it back.

Instead I kiss him and kiss him and kiss him, until everything turns just a little more passionate than it was before. His hands go to my ass, to slip and slide over the smooth and still slightly damp skin there. And after a long moment of rolling around and moaning into each other's mouths, he starts rubbing his stiff cock against me – right into some sweetly sensitive place, like the little cleft between my thigh and my tender mound.

Of course it's then that I realise I'm still a little raw from earlier. Not hurting exactly, but just a little more on edge than usual. The grip he's got on my ass reminds me of where his cock has recently been, and the impact of that intense orgasm hasn't quite gone away.

It doesn't take much to make me cry out.

'Still feeling it, huh?' he says, because he's a genius. He's a sexual genius, and this very real fact is confirmed when he slides two fingers through my slippery slit to find the most recently neglected part of my anatomy. 'That any better?'

It is, but I don't say that. Instead I go with the following:

'Fuck me. Just fuck me, Ben,' while he continues to pump his fingers in and out of my greedy cunt.

'Like this?' he says, but he's just being a bastard. He knows I want more; he must be able to tell I want more. I'm shoving myself against that slow back and forth before he's worked up a rhythm.

'No. No. Fuck me – fuck me like you did before,' I tell him, restlessly, and for a second I almost think he's going to. He reaches for a condom from his bedside cabinet. He puts it on, diligently, while I do my best not to replace his fingers in my pussy.

But when it actually comes to it, he doesn't make me turn around. I'm not going to get it like that again, apparently, because what he wants to do is cup me against him in one sweet curl, almost on my back but not quite.

And then he just slowly, slowly tugs me down onto his big stiff cock, until I can't escape him on any level whatsoever. He's holding me too tightly to him, and his mouth is feverish against my throat, my breasts, my lips – not to mention the feel of him, filling me so completely.

It's just as I remember from the first time he did this – like being deliciously stretched from the inside out. Better, in fact, because that sounds stupid when I really think about it, and this … oh this is bliss.

'I'm gonna work you on my cock now,' he says, which really only adds fuel to the flames. I can feel how broad his hands are on my ass, and in this position he's got me totally at his mercy. He can literally just manoeuvre me until my pussy slides over and over the thick head of his prick, almost as though he's trying to rub an orgasm out of himself.

Though I won't deny it has almost the same effect on me. Every time he drags me back down onto that solid length I moan for him. I claw at his back until he pants out something in response.

'Yeah,' he tells me. 'Yeah, do it, hurt me – fuuucckk you're getting so wet. Is that good, huh? You wanna come on my dick?'

I've no idea why he asks such ridiculous questions during sex. I mean the answer's completely obvious – I'm almost beside myself. I'm clawing and biting and shoving at him, and when he finds one stiff nipple and just plucks at it with his thumb and forefinger as he fucks into me hard … I definitely cream for him. At the very least I jerk and sort of try to get away in the face of such extreme pleasure.

And yet somehow I find myself answering him anyway.

'Yeah, oh yeah it's so good. Make me come, baby. Oh please, please,' I say, as though I've become a babbling maniac version of myself. I can't think, I can't breathe, I can't make proper sentences about normal things.

I'm just pure feeling for a long moment – like a held note before the rest of the song can continue. And when it does, when it sings out inside me in low, pulsing waves, I do something bad.

I tell him I adore him oh how I adore him, as he follows me down, down into oblivion.

Chapter Fourteen

I get a little deeper glimpse into him later on, courtesy of the pictures that are all over the walls of the narrow hallways in this place. Unlike my own home there's evidence of him just about everywhere here – some of it neat and tidy, like the bathroom and the kitchen. Some of it sloppy, like in the magazine-littered living room.

As though he's managed to get about half of himself in order, but the other half is still spilling out all over the place. It's spilling out in the pictures of him, stood next to an elderly gentleman outside this very house. The older man is neat and tidy, and so sour-looking he can't be anyone but the legendary cane-poking grandfather.

God only knows what such a miserable old man thought of the boy stood beside him, because in all my days I've never seen such a chubby, ridiculous-looking kid. His hair's too long and his grin's too big, and of all things he's got a skateboard under his arm.

It's a wonder his grandfather didn't kill him during one of these inexplicable holidays – though when you know Ben you don't really need the *in* on that word. It's entirely explicable.

239

He's just a lovely, lovely person, who manages to find some good in everyone.

Even me.

Because let's be honest here: I don't think I have any family pictures in which I am smiling. In fact, I don't think I have any family pictures full stop. I didn't have the kind of life that's revealed in the third photograph on the left, in which he's stood with his handsome and obviously proud father on some beach somewhere, in what is likely Hawaii. I didn't have a grandfather that I gradually won over with my slow-dripping love. I didn't have any of those things.

In truth, the only person who's ever really been kind to me is the one who's smiling out at the world, from those pictures.

Which is a bit too overwhelming a thought to be having at six o'clock on a Saturday morning, while wearing a gargantuan T-shirt of his with the Sprite logo on the front. I feel like a skulking, pathetic fraud in the house that his love built, and so make my way to the kitchen.

The kitchen will be safer, I reckon. In there he's just got a fridge full of bizarre American food and a pinned note on the front of said appliance: *get stuff E.H. can actually eat.*

Which makes the tone I've suddenly found myself in somewhat lighter, I have to say. By the time I've snooped my way back into the living room, I'm almost feeling good again. He called me *E.H.* He had plans, to bring me here and maybe cook me an appalling dinner of things he only thinks I like.

He's perfection.

Or at least, I think so until I see the pile of papers on his coffee table. Just like at the office, I think – his desk at work is still covered in mounds and mounds of God only knows what, and apparently it's starting to spread to his home.

I see contracts that should have been forwarded. A memo

from someone about something, that he probably hasn't paid any attention to, and then finally, finally …

There's a letter. There's a letter, with Woods' handwriting on the back of it.

Of course, I realise at this point that I could be wrong. I can only see a tiny corner of it peeping out, from between one massive pile of shit and another massive pile of bollocks. But even so, I'm pretty sure I recognise that *E* of his.

Like a backwards three, I think, and then I do something I'm not entirely proud of. I mean, this is Ben's stack of papers. Most of it might not even be office work – it could be his private stash of secret love letters from Gregory Woods, for all I know.

Or it could be that I'm looking at a letter to me. *Eleanor*, it says on the back, even though I don't want it to. I try to will it into saying something else, and then when I've managed to draw out the obviously read piece of paper inside, I will it even harder.

My stomach turns over, somewhere too low down inside me; my heart attempts a three-hundred-metre dash; my brain doesn't want to process the single typed line right in the middle of this single, solitary page.

I'm sorry that I'm this way, it says.

And it still says it five minutes later when I float back into my body, and read it again.

In fact, it still says it when Benjamin comes down the stairs to probably see why I've passed out standing up. Though of course the moment he sees me with this … this *thing* in my hand, he has some rather illuminating points to make.

'OK, I can totally explain.'

Or maybe not illuminating, exactly. More like something that makes me punch him with my heavy, disbelieving gaze.

'You can explain why you kept a letter like this from me? A private letter. From Gregory Woods. To me.'

He can tell he's in trouble here, I think. He doesn't shrug effortlessly, or smile in that good good way of his. For the first time in the entire length of our 'relationship' he looks almost grave.

'I just … I just didn't want you to feel like …' he says, but he's not talking fast enough. He's not. I have to grind words out from between gritted teeth to make him go faster.

'Like *what*?' I demand, which seems to work.

He barks out something almost immediately after, at least.

'Ashamed! That's what that letter is – *shame*.'

And oh God, he sounds so fierce when he does it. So disgusted somehow, as though the very worst thing he can imagine is that this feeling that's starting to rise up inside me – this panic, that I've done the wrong thing all along, and just didn't know it without this fucking *letter* – should put a stop to all of the blissful things we've done together.

That it should make me say what I then do.

'And you think I shouldn't be? You know, I was his subordinate. You're *my* subordinate.'

He rolls his eyes, but that just makes things worse. Now my panic is like a tidal wave, and pretty soon it's going to crush me.

'So that somehow makes me something other than a consenting adult,' he says, while I fumble for how I'm supposed to be feeling about this.

'Yes. No – it just …' I try, but I'm not really getting anywhere. I can't say yes and no at the same time, and the word *just* isn't helping matters at all. Plus, I kind of wring my hands afterwards, which is definitely the wrong thing to do.

It makes his face kind of sink, and then he delivers *this*

doozy: 'Don't use this as an excuse to run away.'

I flick my gaze up to him, and when I do I see myself reflected in his eyes. Not strong and powerful at all, but nervy. Ready to bolt at a moment's notice, because apparently real life is just too damned hard for me.

It's an ugly image, and one I try to refute.

'You think that's what I'm going to do?'

Though let's be honest, here. I don't exactly succeed – and he seems to think so too. What other explanation is there for what he says to me next?

'You did it to Woods.'

I think *my* face sinks then. Is that really what he thinks? That I abandoned Woods in some kind of conflicted time of need, instead of what actually happened?

'*He* left *me*,' I tell him, but I'm aware of how over-adamant my voice sounds. It's like I'm hammering up a sign with the words painted on them in bold black lettering: I AM NOT GUILTY, YOUR HONOUR.

'Did he?' Ben says, but I can hardly blame him for that now. I'm the one running the campaign entitled 'No Honestly, She's Really Innocent'. He's just being rational about things, even if those things sting like a bastard – and his next words are a prime example of this. 'Once he was out of there you didn't try very hard to find out what happened.'

God, I wish he didn't sound so kindly while saying these things. It's like he really is Dr Phil, and I'm his hysterical guest.

'Because you hid this from me!' I cry, while actually waving the thing aloft. Any second now the audience are going to start chanting, at which point I'm going to have to change the channel. I need to change it now, before we've gotten to the meat of the matter.

Which he then supplies.

243

'And what would you have done if I hadn't? Would you have called him? Gone to see him?'

Oh it's *bitterly* unfair for him to say these things to me – especially when my strongest urge is to blurt out something absolutely awful, like: *he never meant what you do, to me. He never meant anything to me, oh God, I didn't love him.*

But I love you. I love you.

And the worst thing about it is: this is the first time I realise how much I do. Right here, in the middle of the only argument we've really had. In fact, I'm not sure if it qualifies as an argument, because at the end of it he says something that almost makes me swoon.

'I'm not like he is, you know,' he tells me, but that isn't the part that stirs my cold, dead heart. It's the words he follows it up with a second later, as though it barely takes him anything to let them out: 'So if you want to run, run. I won't sit on the side-lines and wait for you to slip away, like you never existed.' He pauses, thickly. Takes a second, in a way I can understand. 'I'll fight for you, El. I'll always fight for you.'

Funny, really, that the most romantic thing I've ever heard anyone say makes me sob, once I'm safe in the back of a taxi.

* * *

I don't think I expected him to look any different, exactly, and yet it's a shock when he doesn't. It's 11:35 on a Sunday morning, but he's still in his immaculate suit, with his immaculately polished shoes, sat immaculately, on his immaculate leather sofa.

In fact, this whole room seems like it's made out of leather – though taking that notion in only makes me realise how weird it is that I've never been in his apartment before.

We did all of that kinky stuff together, and I never even knew he had a gigantic stag's head on one of his walls. Though I'll confess: it might have made me think twice about a lot of things if I had.

The whole place is just so … clichéd. He's a cliché. The first thing he did after he'd opened the door to me was pour himself Scotch, but I suppose it's kind of funny, now, to see him do it. Instead of other things reminding me of Woods, Woods reminds me of other things.

I think of Aidan, and then of course I think of my Ben.

Ben would never swill Scotch before midday. In truth I'm not even sure if Ben drinks at all, which somehow makes Gregory look even sadder.

'To what do I owe this pleasure?' he asks, once I'm settled in the armchair opposite him. Though I'll be honest, the word 'settled' is overstating it somewhat. I just sort of perch on the edge of the cushion and hope for the best.

'I recently received a rather interesting letter,' I say, but the funniest thing happens when I do. I get the urge to laugh, because really – I even start to sound like him, in his presence. There's no easy back and forth like there so often is with Ben. I have to hedge around the subject with lots of *rathers* and *recentlys* before finally coming to my point.

'From you.'

His expression doesn't change, once everything is on the table. I don't know why I expected it to.

'Ah yes,' he says, like he's considering a particularly interesting crumb, that's somehow found its way onto his tie. 'I'm assuming that young fellow didn't actually give it to you.'

'He didn't.'

'And now I suppose it's too late for it to have any sort of impact on you whatsoever.'

My breath catches in my throat, but I plunge on regardless. You have to catch him quick, that's the thing. You have to grab his tail and hang on, before he slithers away.

'Is that what you wanted? Impact?'

He regards me coolly, which somewhat lessens the power of what he says next.

'I wanted to offer you an apology.'

In fact, once he's said it I find myself snorting with something like derision.

'Is that what you think that was? An apology? You weren't sorry about anything other than how you felt about yourself,' I say, and this time I get a reaction. It's not a big one – just a flicker of one eyelid, a smoothing of a non-existent crease in his trousers – but on Gregory, it looks immense.

He really is ashamed, I think, and it makes him pitiful.

'And you think I should have been? I should have been remorseful for giving you exactly what you wanted?'

Suddenly I understand how Ben felt when for one brief moment I agreed with what the letter said. Fierceness just blooms through me, and it comes out in my words.

'No, *Greg*,' I spit, and oh I'd be lying if I said that using his first name doesn't thrill me. I'd be lying if I said it doesn't sound awesome when I let it out in that contemptuous, patronising manner. It's like sticking my finger in a wound somewhere on him, and I cap it off with words I've been longing to say since for ever.

'You should be sorry for just walking away without a word.'

But of course, no real explanation comes.

'I had an opportunity somewhere else, and felt it best to

246

make a clean break,' he says, which just about sums him up.

Silence, cryptic notes, and self-service.

'You know, Greg,' I start, and this time I actually see him wince, on that use of his first name. It's satisfying in a way it probably shouldn't be, but what the hell – he tried to leave me mired in shame-filled confusion for absolutely fucking *nothing*. 'I kind of suspected that it was you holding me back all of this time. Your example that made me this way. But now that I'm here, looking at you ...'

I shake my head before I can continue, and when I do I think some of the bitterness drains out of me. You can't be bitter in the face of this – it's too sad. *He's* too sad, somehow, in a way that makes me realise something heartening.

I'll never be like him, because I actually *do* know myself. I know myself so well that I have no problems laying it all out for him.

'It wasn't you at all. It's been me, right from the start. I'm the one who wanted those games, I'm the one who cut you off, like a limb I didn't need any more. And I'm the one who's pushing away a man who's worth a thousand of you, for no reason at all.'

Now those grey eyes regard me with something that could almost be emotion, though I can't read it exactly. If I had to guess I'd say it was amused wistfulness, but reasonably it could be anything.

'And is it working?' he asks, finally, softly.

'Is what working?'

'The pushing away.'

The rest of my bitterness goes with those words. It can't possibly stay when he's looking at me with actual gentleness, and the answer is rising up inside me like the crescendo at the end of a long piece of music.

247

'No,' I tell him, and he nods, as though that's how things should be.

'It's different when you care for someone, isn't it?' he asks. 'Unfortunately, I just don't have that in me. Whereas you, Eleanor, you … well. You're filled with all the love in the world, and just waiting for the right person to coax it out.'

Is it weird that I have to hold back tears, then? I didn't expect to be upset – I expected to be angry. Though I suppose all of this crying is something of a recurring theme lately.

'You're wrong,' I tell him, though I only do so because I suspect the opposite. I've known it for some time, but it's crashing hard over me now – that knowledge of how easy it could be, oh so easy. 'I can't even say the words.'

At which he laughs in a way I don't think I've ever heard before, and raises his glass to me, his once-was-protégé.

'Put it in a letter,' he says.

Because I guess some things never change.

Chapter Fifteen

I know what his expression means, when he walks into my office. He doesn't try to hide it – that sweet look of sadness that says he knows which way this is going to go. I'm going to tell him that all of this is over, and then maybe I'm going to take up some 'other opportunity', and finally I'm going to be an aloof asshole, in a leather-lined room.

We can't be a couple, you see. It would never work out with someone like me.

No matter how insistently he stands on his spot with his arms behind his back.

'I have something for you,' he says, but he doesn't step forward to give it to me. Of course he doesn't. He has to wait until I say it's all right to move from the position I like him to stand in.

He has to wait for my command, and oh he's right. It *is* relaxing to know he'll always obey me no matter what. I don't have to worry about him causing a scene or making a fuss. He just waits, and waits, and waits – as patient as the tide – for me to tell him he can leave it on my desk.

And he does.

He lays an envelope down on my desk, and because I'm

only looking at him and it out of the corner of my eye I almost imagine it's the one from Woods. Everything about it looks the same – the crisp paper, the letter *E* like a backwards number three.

But once I draw it off my desk I can see it's not. It's from Ben, and for a moment I'm so convinced it's going to be another letter littered with mistakes that it almost startles me when it's not. It's just one line, typed across the page – perfect down to the last detail.

I'm not *sorry that I'm this way*, it says, and oh it's enough. It makes a mockery of those last words Woods gave to me, because of course I know what he meant. He meant to suggest the most impersonal way of communicating, but this ...

It's not impersonal at all. It makes me turn away and face the window, so he can't see how full of feeling I am.

'I'd like you to take a letter, Benjamin,' I say, because if he can do it, I can too. He's given me a little out, a little way of doing this without coming apart and floating away on the breeze, and I grab it. I do. 'Do you think you could do that for me?'

'Yes, sir,' he says, and I hear rather than see him sit down, with his notepad in his hand. 'Whenever you're ready.'

Yes, I think. *Whenever I am.*

And then I just tell him, in a voice that wavers high and low:

'Dear Benjamin,

'You should know that I'm not sorry either. I'm not sorry that I want to do these things with you. I'm not sorry that I want you so much I can't think of anything but you. But most of all, I'm not sorry that I love you. I love you. I love you.'

I pause and listen to the low scratch of a pencil on paper as it carries all of my feelings to him, my one.

Before I finish, to the heavenly sound of him sighing with pleasure.

'Yours always, Eleanor.'

www.ingramcontent.com/pod-product-compliance
Ingram Content Group UK Ltd.
Pitfield, Milton Keynes, MK11 3LW, UK
UKHW022246180325
456436UK00001B/32